Stubborn Puckboy

Also by Eden Finley and Saxon James

Puckboys

Egotistical Puckboy
Irresponsible Puckboy
Shameless Puckboy
Foolish Puckboy
Clueless Puckboy
Bromantic Puckboy
Forbidden Puckboy
Possessive Puckboy
Stubborn Puckboy
Charming Puckboy

STUBBORN PUCKBOY

EDEN FINLEY & SAXON JAMES

canelo

First published in the United Kingdom in 2025 by Sadenverse Books

This edition published in the United Kingdom in 2026 by

Canelo, an imprint of
Canelo Digital Publishing Limited,
20 Vauxhall Bridge Road,
London SW1V 2SA
United Kingdom

A Penguin Random House Company
The authorised representative in the EEA is Dorling Kindersley Verlag GmbH.
Arnulfstr. 124, 80636 Munich, Germany

A CIP catalogue record for this book is available from the British Library.

ISBN 978 183598 527 4

Printed and bound in Great Britain by Clays Ltd, Elcograf S.p.A.

Look for more great books at
www.canelo.co | www.dk.com

FSC
www.fsc.org
MIX
Paper
FSC® C018179

PROLOGUE

COLBY

17 YEARS AGO

With my head in my hands, sweat dripping from my forehead, the stench of man musk mixed with gagworthy sweaty gear, and my entire hockey career draining the toilet, the last thing I need is Radimir Novicov's taunts.

"You, uh, how you say, suck."

I'll hand it to him though. He knows how to make me laugh.

I lift my head and come face-to-face with his towel-covered junk. If he only knew how much I suck and that, for the last six months, all I've thought about is sucking what's under that towel … Well, if he did know, my ass would be kicked six ways 'til Sunday.

Novicov and I were in the same draft class. Me, a top ten real prospect coming from the juniors, and him, a fourth-round choice from Russia, both picked by Anaheim.

We were sent to the AHL for more conditioning, and all I've done this season is prove that I did not deserve to be that tenth pick. Novicov is crushing it though.

I'd be jealous if he weren't all kinds of adorable. His hair is a mess from the shower, wisps of dark brown hair going in every direction. He has dark hooded eyes, thick eyebrows, and flat lips that aren't conventionally attractive, but they suit his face. His features make him look the part of angry Russian, but there's something about his dopey smile that speaks to me on a primal level.

I swear I sometimes see that same primal look in his eyes when he stares at me, but I'm not completely delusional about it.

I'm not out, obviously. No way am I going to fuck with my career that way. Not when the first out dudes in the NHL only came out last season. While it gave me hope that I could be an out player at some point, Caleb Sorensen and Ollie Strömberg are far from rookies. Soren is in his thirties and has kept quiet his whole career until now, and Strömberg is newer but still has three seasons under his belt.

I have to be smart about who knows and who doesn't, even if it's tempting to throw myself at my teammate. Maybe if he wasn't assigned as my roommate on the road and I got a few drinks in me, I'd try it. But being rejected and then having to share a room with the guy? Not going to happen.

Besides, he's never given any hint of swinging that way. Plus, with his Russian background, even if he did, I doubt he'd risk his life for a quick orgasm from me. If hockey doesn't work out for him, he has to go back to Russia, and everyone knows the political mess LGBTQ rights are there. Mainly, they have no rights.

I grew up in Massachusetts with a loving and open family, so for me, it's not a matter of hiding myself forever, but it's smarter to do it for now.

And no matter how cute I find Novicov, I'm not going to put my future at risk. At least, not when it comes to my sexuality. On the ice is another story. I'm screwing up royally, and the more I try to bring myself out of my funk, the more I choke.

Novicov, who's still standing in front of me, touches my shoulder. I'm sure it's supposed to be comforting, but it sends a jolt of lust right to my groin, and considering I've already stripped down to my base layers, I can't hide my reaction. I hold my breath and hope he doesn't look down, or if he does, he doesn't acknowledge it.

"I'm joking with you. Don't cry."

I shove his hand away. "I'm not crying." I might want to, but I also know I'm being dramatic. Slumps happen.

"Slumps happen," Novicov says as if reading my mind. "Even for top ten draft picks." This last part is heavily laced with condescension, and it's true, I probably shouldn't have been so gloaty about it because I'm paying for it now. But I also think Novicov doesn't know he's being condescending. His English is basic, so he doesn't always understand inflection.

"You're right. It's a slump." An entire season-long slump. We're inching closer to the end of the regular season, and I can't say I've lived up to any expectations set for me.

"Come drink with us."

"I can't."

He just turned twenty-one, so he can go out with the team. I'm still nineteen and look sixteen. There's no way I'm not getting carded, even if I am with a bunch of grown-ass adults.

"You did last week."

I snort. "Yeah, because we were in Canada. The legal drinking age is different."

He makes a "pfft" noise. "In Russia, it's ten."

"Is it really?"

"*Nyet.* Joking with you again."

I stand because if I sit for any longer, I'm going to be too tempted to stare at his crotch. I'm still trying to ignore my semi, pretend it doesn't exist, and hope he does too.

"You're messing with me."

Those dark brows furrow. "I make mess on you?"

I almost choke on my spit while I try not to picture what that would look like because fucking hell … that's not what I meant at all, but now I can't stop thinking about it. "Joking is the proper word, but you can also say you're messing with me."

"English does not make sense."

"Truth. But anyway, you go out. I'm going to shower and head back to our hotel room to wallow with the help of the minibar."

"Sounds fun. I'm in."

That annoying, delusional voice in the back of my head has me questioning, "You'd rather drink with me in a hotel room than go out?"

"One thing though. What is wallow?"

It doesn't matter what wallowing is because if Novicov is there, I won't be doing it.

-

"You cheat!" Novicov yells, and I laugh so hard I almost fall backward onto the dirty hotel room carpet. We've been playing quarters, and I'm really good at quarters. We don't have cups, so we're using a cap instead, so even though playing on the carpet makes it difficult, the wider goal evens the playing field. At least for me. Novicov is delightfully wasted and entertaining.

"There's no way to cheat in quarters. It's all talent."

"Give me your coin."

I swap out our quarters like that will make a difference.

Novicov takes his turn, and again, he bounces it way too hard, and it misses spectacularly. He throws up his hands. "I give up. Is this what it feels like to be you on the ice?"

This time, I really do fall backward, but not from laughing. "You're so mean. Hitting me where it really hurts."

"Wait, where hurt?" Without warning, Radimir Novicov is hovering above me, and I'm so lost in my fuzzy, tipsy brain that I take his lack of English comprehension and his genuine concern as something completely different.

He's not even touching me. Just kneeling above me, looking soft and relaxed, and it's instinct to reach for him. Our eyes lock, and his gaze sharpens from concern to hunger.

But that's when it happens. Before my fingertips even get the chance to brush against his chest, he grabs my wrist tight, and reality sets in.

"What are you doing?" he growls.

My heart races wildly as I try to come up with an excuse. He has lint on his shirt. My arm is what hurts, and I was showing him.

But we both know what I was really doing. I was making a move and screwing everything up. The only way I'm getting out of this without getting my ass kicked is if I make out like he's overreacting.

"Sorry, man. I didn't mean to ..." To what? Make him uncomfortable? I didn't even touch him. He didn't let it get to that. In a way, he *is* overreacting, and there's that stupid voice again saying his rejection is maybe too emphatic, but I finally tell that bitch to shut up because I know how dangerous this kind of situation can be.

Do I think Novicov would seriously assault me? I'd like to think we've become friends over the last six months and he wouldn't, but that's not a guarantee.

"I thought ..." Another unfinished sentence where I don't have the words, so I go for the good ol' cop-out of, "I was messing with you. Joking. Like you were in the locker room." I don't think he believes me, but he does release my arm.

"Joking?"

"Yep." Just ignore the hard-on in my pants. Thankfully, I'm no longer wearing my tight base layers.

"Okay." He stands. Then nods. His motions are jerky, his shoulders stiff.

"We good?" I ask, but my voice cracks.

"Yes, yes. All jokes. All fun. We're good."

And as much as I would love to believe him, I know it's not true. Especially when he asks for a new roommate on our next road trip, and he barely says two words to me for the rest of the season.

Then, as our regular season ends, Novicov gets the call. He's going to the big show, and my sorry ass will be ECHL-bound if I don't turn my game around.

If I keep playing the way I'm playing, I'm going to have to find a new career because there's no way I'm going to make it in professional hockey.

I could become a coach. Isn't there that old saying, "Those who can't do, teach"? That could be me.

I really hope it's not me.

CHAPTER ONE

NOVI

You'd think after spending seventeen years making a name for myself, I wouldn't be so nervous walking into practice first day back. These flutters, they're for rookies. Not for someone going for his one-thousandth NHL game this season.

I heard a rumor during last year's Stanley Cup game that I haven't been able to shake all summer. I've done my best to stay offline and ignore it, but even when I got weak and looked up hockey news, there wasn't anything there.

Probably a good thing.

I shove my gear bag in my cubby right as a text goes off. One glance at the screen, and I reluctantly open the message, knowing it's going to be peak Ezra.

> Happy "lose every game to Boston" season, bestie!

I refuse to smile. Or be amused. Ezra Palaszczuk decided we were best friends the moment we officially met off the ice. I'll never admit it out loud to anyone, but I've always been in awe of him—and borderline resentful. He gets to have everything I've ever wanted. So while being friends with Ezra is something I want, I'm also careful not to get too close. Being linked with his Queer Collective isn't something I can risk, but I didn't know how badly I needed that connection until I had it. Ignoring a large and important part of myself has worn on me.

The locker room is empty, so I switch on voice to text and reply.

"You are embarrassing yourself."

> Pala-SOOK: Nothing new there.

This time, my lips twitch, but I tuck my phone in my pocket without replying. Even with the messages as a distraction, I can't shake that lump building in my gut, and I remind myself that nothing is confirmed yet. And if the worst happens, *he's* the one who should be nervous. Not me. I've played with LA for seven years now. This is my home.

Colby Kessinger cannot take that from me.

Ah, I hope. He had me under his spell once, but I was young and reckless then. I'm much smarter and better prepared to handle him if it comes to that.

I stuff my hands into the pockets of my sweatpants and head up the hall to the video room. We're meeting our coaches this morning since Trent Beller retired last year, and there have been staffing changes in the hopes of a better season. I've won two Stanley Cups, but none since moving to LA, and at thirty-eight, I'm running out of chances to get my name on there again. I've given myself two more years of hockey before I hang up my skates and get to live the life I've kept secret for so long.

Out of the spotlight, I'll be able to finally have a relationship, and while giving up hockey isn't something that will be easy, knowing I will have that freedom helps.

Not many get to play as long as me, and I'm grateful to have this career and my life in the States. By the time I retire, I will have lived here as long as I lived in Russia, but I think I'll always miss my country. The nostalgia of home. The pretty buildings and familiar language. Novy God. Sometimes the sadness falls on me that I can never go back, but it doesn't last long. Russia, the people, my family, they're all things I love. The law is not. The government is a joke. But not a funny one.

Russia keeps going backward.

Most of my team is waiting, and I can already guess the topics of conversation. Vacations, babies, proposals, and weddings. These are things we do in the off-season.

More specifically, things *they* do.

My off-season was spent attending other people's weddings, fielding messages from Ezra, and visiting glory holes. What a life.

Still, after the months off, just walking in here feels like home. The mostly familiar faces, the same large white room crammed full of ergonomic recliner chairs, the LA logo on the back wall, and that familiar scent of too many body sprays in one place.

I will miss this one day.

Turkey gives me the two-finger wave thing that he does, and I slide into the back row with him. These English speakers kept butchering his surname Atatürk, so that's the nickname he's stuck with. If they'd tried that with me and called me Russia, it would get confusing, considering there are three other Russians on our team.

The media gives me enough nicknames like that as it is. Novi is what everyone calls me now, but Angry Russian was from early in my career and still pops up occasionally. It's hilarious. Only, I laugh on the inside so they don't see I have a big sense of humor.

I'm really a puppy.

"How are those knees, old boy?" Turkey asks.

"I have the knees of a twenty-year-old. You're the one who spent three weeks on IR last season."

"Hey, why you gotta bring that up?"

"Have to make sure you young plucks know your place."

"Think you mean young bucks."

Got him. "Huh. Do I?" I make a mental note to add a mark next to Turkey's name in my phone later. I don't know when my game of having them correct my English started, but it's always amused me how easily they think I mess everything up. My accent has morphed into a bastardized American one by this point, but they all still underestimate me.

I'm very smart.

"Welcome back," Coach Whelan says as he walks into the room. "I hope you're all ready for a big season and didn't overindulge during the time off." The look on his face makes it clear he knows most of the guys did. "Wouldn't want anyone throwing up from reconditioning."

Turkey leans in closer. "He's sadistic, I swear."

"*Da*. I like it."

"You would."

This is only Turkey's third season. He'll get used to it.

"We've got some new faces on board this year. Make sure to give a shout-out to Percy and Landers, who we snapped up from the East Coast. We've got the strongest team we've seen in years, and we're going all the way."

Percy, Landers. Yes. Good. Now, move on to the coaching staff and the reason we're here. The team lets out a cheer, but I'm too busy being distracted by the potential ghost from my past to give it my full enthusiasm. You'd think that close to two decades would be enough to rid his ridiculous face from my mind.

All chubby cheeks and puppy dog eyes. The way he'd get so frustrated when he ruined a play that I'd want to go and make him laugh to get rid of the concentration lines in his forehead.

It was hard to find someone I wasn't self-conscious around when I moved here, but there was something about Colby that made me feel like I could be myself. Always smiling. Always joking.

Until that very funny joking night where something happened that frightened the hell out of me. The moment Colby went to touch me filled my dreams for years afterward because of how deeply I wanted it. How, just moments before he reached, a stray thought had snuck into my mind.

What would it be like to kiss him?

To kiss a man. I still don't know.

Somehow, the seventeen years between then and now disappear, and I'm feeling that elated terror all over again. Soon, Coach will introduce the team. Soon, I'll know that he's not here. Rumors happen all the time in hockey. People change their minds easily. Maybe Westly Dalton had heard it wrong and it wasn't Colby coming here at all.

It's not safe for me with him around because after hiding who I am all these years, I'm sure he knows. I'm sure he remembers the way I looked at him, how tongue-tied I got after that moment, how I was too embarrassed to room with him and didn't trust myself to be strong.

I was so obvious.

Twenty-one-year-old Novi was an idiot.

And yet, there's a very small part of me that's worried after all this buildup, his name won't be called at all.

"Most of the support staff have stayed on this year, but with Beller's retirement, Ackerman has stepped into the head video coach role, with two new assistants joining us. Paul Nowak has come to us from New Jersey." There's a random *yew* as Nowak walks in and flicks a quick wave like he'd rather be anywhere but the center of attention. I'm too busy looking behind him though. "And from Penn State, Frozen Four–winning coach, Colby Kessinger."

Fuck.

My gut hollows like the morning after having too much to drink. But the man who walks in behind Nowak ... it takes me a second to recognize him. The chubby cheeks are gone, and in their place is a strong jawline. His shoulders and chest are broader, his black hair is longer, and those concentration lines in his forehead have become permanent, along with the happy creases by his eyes.

Colby Kessinger is no longer the young man who taunted my attraction. Now, he's much, much worse.

He says something that I miss because I'm too busy picking out all the changes. Have I changed as much as he has? Does he know I'm here? Will he even recognize me?

Is he going to tell everyone about me?

Or has he forgotten me and the touch and the way I was never myself with him again?

Coach takes over, running through some expectations for the year, and as he does, I watch Colby scan the room.

Nowak leans in to say something to him, and they both muffle their laughs.

I tell myself it's time to look away now, but my eyeballs aren't listening.

Seventeen years.

Almost half of my life has gone by since that one season we played together. Roomed together. Since he forced me to admit to myself that what I was feeling for men wasn't an accident or all in my head.

He wasn't the one who made me realize I'm gay, but he was the one who forced me to admit it to myself.

A flash of him lying under me crosses my mind. Black hair all ruffled, gray eyes fading from amusement to that intensity I felt in my chest.

My body seizes up the same way it did back then, when I'd snatched up his hand and panicked in a way I'd never panicked before. I didn't have the English words then for how freaked-out I was, but I do now, and so when Colby's gaze finally drifts closer and connects with mine, it hits me all at once.

Ya v glubokom der'me.

I'm in deep shit.

CHAPTER TWO

COLBY

Out of all the teams in the NHL, it had to be LA who headhunted me to join their coaching staff. Because of course. They've promised me big things, and sure, I'm starting at the bottom of the ladder, but my goal is to be a head coach of an NHL team one day. Starting out as an assistant video coach is paying my dues.

I almost turned it down. Not because I believe I should at least be head video coach or that winning the Frozen Four means I'm better than anyone else here, but because of one reason.

Him.

Seventeen years is a long time to go without talking to someone I once considered a friend, but it was one season we spent together. A million years ago. Novicov—Novi, now—probably doesn't even remember me.

Where his career took off, mine stalled. Flatlined really. I only made it one more season, bouncing between the AHL and ECHL before neither of them wanted me for a third. I played in Europe for a bit after that, but what started as a slump became a real slap in the face when I realized: I just wasn't good enough. My worst fear had come true. My professional hockey career was over.

The surprising part of it all was that I had no regrets. Disappointment, sure, but I thought my world would end if that happened, and it didn't.

And as much as I dreaded the thought of having to become a coach back when I was playing, it didn't take me long to fall in love with it. I started with Bantam, then after a few years of that, applied for a job at a prestigious hockey academy in Boston. Getting that position was the catalyst of my coaching career trajectory, which has only soared since then, moving up to NCAA, and then winning the Frozen Four my first year as head coach for Penn State. My coaching resume is impressive, but getting a chance to coach for an NHL team? It's almost as good as being out there on the ice.

Which is why I couldn't turn it down. Not for any reason. Especially not a homophobic ex-teammate I mistakenly thought might have been interested in me. I was nineteen years old and naive as hell.

I hope that he won't let one tiny mistake seventeen years ago ruin this opportunity for me. Since being pulled up in front of the team, I've refused to look directly at him. I can sense him though. His large, domineering presence takes up most of the room. It was the same back then. Wherever Novi was, my body knew.

Even though I tell myself to stay strong, to keep looking at everyone else but him, there's a moment where Coach Whelan draws everyone's attention to some motivational poster like he's taking a page out of Ted Lasso's book, and we can succeed if we all believe we can. And in that moment, I can't help myself. I take a peek.

Fuck my fucking life.

Not only is he as drop-dead gorgeous as he was back then, albeit now with a sprinkling of gray through his brown and now longer hair, but those whiskey-colored eyes are on me too.

If I had any hope of him not even remembering me, it's gone now. Especially when I fake confidence and throw him a half smile, but all he does is avert his gaze and pretend he was paying attention to Whelan the whole time.

I've seen him on TV countless times, watched him in press conferences, but there's something about being in his presence that hits me in the gut like a sucker punch. It's a weird mix between nostalgia, a stupid crush, and then topped with a healthy dose of fear.

He has the potential to ruin everything for me, so I have to do what I should have done seventeen years ago and talk it out with him.

Apologize. Though I remember trying to do that back then. He didn't let me get anywhere near him after that night. Not alone, at least.

I'm not going to hold it against him that he rejected me—that happens. A lot. Especially with straight guys. He needs to know it wasn't a big deal, and I'm not going to tell anyone, and that just because I'm an openly gay man now, that doesn't mean people will assume anything about him purely because we shared hotel rooms for one season way back when. No one will even make the connection if we don't tell them.

It's sad I assume he'd make that leap, but from what I've seen in his career—the way he refuses to wear Pride jerseys, the comments about it being against his beliefs—I'm assuming that's the kind of thing that runs through his head.

I want to yell at him that he's been in the States for almost eighteen years. It's time to let the brainwashing from his Russian upbringing go, but hey, who am I to talk about childhood trauma? I don't have any.

My parents are still together, and they're happy. It's gross, really. I can never blame any of my actions, faults, or regrets on them. It makes for boring therapy. I'm the reason I'm so fucked-up? Sounds like a scam. Then again, it's not like I've had it totally easy. Not when it comes to my sexuality.

Novi isn't the only friend I've lost because of my orientation. Working in an industry known for toxic masculinity means some colleagues have distanced themselves from me in the past, said some borderline homophobic things like, "I don't care if you're gay, but I'm not interested."

Thanks, Gary, like I'd ever want to have sex with your balding-ass self. Your forehead probably looks like your ballsack. Where do I sign up to get on that?

Now, I'm heading into inner rambling and ranting territory because I'm nervous. I'm nervous I'm going to try to talk to Novi, and he's going to ignore me or run straight to management to get me fired.

Maybe I should've made the effort to reach out before today, but I didn't want to be that guy. The one who assumes he's important enough to be remembered from almost two decades ago.

Novi's someone who has gone on to play for three different NHL teams, had countless other teammates, and is known as one of the great hockey players of our generation. I was sure he wasn't going to remember a guy he played with in his first year. My ego might have been inflated all those years ago because I let being a top ten draft pick go to my head, but I've learned humility since then.

Apparently, I was wrong though. Novi remembers me, and with one look, I know he wishes he didn't.

Whelan releases the team and tells them to go get ready to hit the ice for the first round of drills we have for them.

With it being training camp, we have not only veteran players here but prospects as well. It's my job to review all the tape from these practices and see if I can spot anyone with potential who can fill the spots of those who were traded or retired after last season.

I'm excited to get into it, but I won't be able to enjoy it if I'm worried about my future with this team. Which is why, when the room begins to empty and players come up to shake my hand and give a warm welcome to us new faces, I hope to stop Novi before he can walk out of here.

I have obviously underestimated his hatred for me, though, because he doesn't approach. He slips out behind everyone.

Other guys have done it too, so I'm trying not to take it as a complete snub from him, but … yeah, total snub. If he remembers me, the bare minimum he could do is say hi. Other than the disastrous moment that ended our friendship, we were fucking close, so this freeze-out, after seventeen years, seems like dramatic overkill. We're grown-ass adults now, damn it.

I shouldn't chase after him, but in the same way I shouldn't have reached for him that night, my body doesn't listen.

I make my escape politely, doing a big no-no, which is leaving with the team instead of after them—the talent always has right of way in these corridors—but I move quickly toward the locker room.

Novi is about to enter it when I call out, "Novicov!"

He freezes. His back tenses. I think he's going to ignore me and keep moving, but then he turns his head and glances back over his shoulder.

It's like he's contemplating whether or not he should come and talk to me or walk away and risk me yelling out again.

If it wasn't putting the final nail in my career's coffin, I'd yell out, "I'm sorry I hit on you seventeen years ago and made you feel uncomfortable, but there's no need to avoid me. I promise I will never try to touch you again."

Instead, I make up an excuse to get him to come to me. I take my phone from my pocket. "You dropped this on your way out."

His brow creases, and he puts his hand in his own pocket, realizing I'm lying.

This is the test. Will he accept my excuse as a cover for those around us and come talk to me? Or will he do the opposite and—

"Not mine." He holds up his phone and enters the locker room.

Opposite it is.

CHAPTER THREE

NOVI

I change into my practice gear with the rest of the team, then wait until they're all busy and distracted to duck back out into the now clear hall and find an empty corner where I'll see anyone coming before they're close enough to hear me.

Then I call my newest *friend*.

"Novi?" Ezra answers, sounding confused. "I'm not sure if you know this, but that button you hit, it was the *Call* button."

I know what the Call button is. I prefer to call people over texting, but I tried it once with Ezra and didn't get off the phone until two hours later. No one has time for that.

"We are best friends, so you have to help me."

He laughs. "Now, unclench your jaw and say it again. I don't know whether to swoon at you calling me your bestie or get turned on by the threatening tone in your voice."

In the background, I hear Ezra's partner, Anton Hayes's voice. "Stop hitting on Novi."

"Yes," I repeat. "Stop hitting on Novi."

"Maybe the two of *you* should be best friends," Ezra says.

"*Da*. Put him on."

"No, I don't wanna. Talk to Daddy Ezra. I'll help you out."

"*Ya ustal*."

"I speak some Russian too, you dick. And it doesn't matter which language you imply I'm exhausting in, you're still wrong. Now, spill. Why the call?"

"I'm …" Scared? Cowardly? Pissing in my pants? I quickly glance both ways down the hall before switching the whole conversation over to Russian. *"Your friend Westly Dalton was right. The college coach he knows? He's been introduced as part of our coaching staff."*

"I said I spoke some Russian. There's some crossover with Polish, which I also suck at but can mostly understand. Slow down."

I repeat myself.

"*Right. That is … cause for concern.*"

I sigh. His Russian is shit, but I get what he's trying to say, and of course Ezra is sarcastic in every language.

Seventeen years ago, I swore never to mention this part out loud to anyone. I was going to take this moment to my grave, and here I am, telling someone I only vaguely know. *"We were in the minors together. For a year."*

"Ohhh … what happened?"

"Nothing."

He huffs and says in English, "Novi, you're a terrible storyteller."

"I wanted something to, though. We were friends and roommates, and I was definitely attracted to him."

It's not often Ezra is serious, but this is at least something he gets. "*That must have been hard for you.*"

"I think he wanted me too. There was a night in our room where we were drinking and … nothing happened, but something did. I'm sure he tried to touch me, but I freaked out."

"Shit."

"And now he's here, and he knows my secret. How … how …" I can't even say it out loud.

"Your first step is to take a breath." Ezra switches back to English. "He's on the staff. He's not going to out you. It's specifically his job to make the team the best it can be, and that doesn't include ruining anyone's life."

"That's true."

"Could he talk to Whelan?" comes Anton's muffled voice.

The thought of talking to Coach has tension filling my body. "*Nyet*. I'm not talking to anyone. I haven't spent my career living in secret for it to all come out now. It can't." I'd thought getting my green card and moving my family from Russia would solve all of my problems, but I'd underestimated one thing. My eldest sister. She's a popular TV chef, and she doesn't want to leave her career or uproot her family. I can understand it, even if it makes me want to kick something. But people know her, and people know me, and if my sexuality gets out and she doesn't publicly denounce me—which is something she bullheadedly refuses to do—she could be in real danger.

I refuse to do that to her. We were close growing up, played ice hockey together as kids, and she came to every one of my games. I ate all her disastrous first cooking attempts, and when she got her license, she'd drive me to the rink at 4:00 a.m. so I could get some extra practice in.

"Maybe you need to talk to this guy, then," Ezra says. "Make sure he knows how important it is that whatever happened doesn't get out."

"Or …"

"Uh-oh. Sentences that start with *or* never end well."

I flatten my lips, glancing both ways again. "It was so long ago. Would he really remember?"

"Okay, that wasn't so bad … Truthfully, I couldn't pick half the guys I'd hooked up with out of a lineup, but I also never roomed with them for a year."

"Technically, it wasn't a full year. I asked to be reassigned right after that night. Told Coach there were cultural differences."

"Huh. Okay. So you had a moment, and then you ran away from him. Good chance he remembers something like that."

"He also tried to get me alone after the meeting."

"He knows. He remembers. You need to talk to him."

That's the last thing I want to do. Two years. That's all I need to get through before I can hide out from everyone. Where I can make sure people forget about Radimir Novicov. "I don't want to."

"Then … I don't know. Scowl at him a bunch. Give him the evil eye."

"I do not scowl."

"And I'm not a former fuckboy. This game is fun."

Unfortunately, Ezra has confirmed what I didn't want to think about. To get past this lump of nausea, I need to talk to Colby. No, Coach Kessinger. He's my coach now. Nothing more. Maybe if I can switch my mind to viewing him that way, it will make things easier.

Because while I might *need* to talk to him, I'm not going to do that.

I'm not going to be the fool who makes a bigger deal out of things than they are. Who hasn't been able to shake him from my mind all summer. Who doesn't want to find out anything about him or his partner or family or life.

He's my past. He can stay there.

"I need to go train," I say. "Some of us like winning."

"Or maybe we don't need to train to w—"

I show Ezra that I know exactly how to use my phone by hanging up on him.

-

I speed down the ice, Turkey on one side and Everly, a team hopeful, on the other. Coach Whelan is running drills specifically designed to push us right to the edge and see what we're capable of because he is, as Turkey says, sadistic.

The ache in my glutes is a welcome relief from the noise in my brain, and I keep my head down as I make a sharp stop and take off again.

I'm one of the fastest on the team, but I'm nowhere near my peak. Slowly, I can feel that things are getting harder, slower, and while I'm still one of the best in the league, I don't want to be one of those who goes long past his cutoff date.

I'm not going out on a shitty season or an injury. That's why forty will be it for me. I'm confident I'll make it, but I know my limits.

Coach's whistle is a sharp blast. "Alexei, Timbrook, and Ivers. Now."

I move off to the side and rest against the boards as I catch my breath. Sometimes I push too hard, and the rushing in my ears tells me this might be one of those times, but you don't get far without a little pain. Like the burning in my lungs.

"You're … possessed," Turkey pants. "How can I never beat you?"

"You eat too many cheeseburgers. They slow you down."

He hunches over, lips pulled back as he struggles like I am. "They're … my weakness."

Speaking of …

I accidentally glance across the ice as Col—Kessinger and Ackerman appear. They're both wearing sweatpants and an LA T-shirt, but one looks significantly better than the other. Ackerman points at where the other three are racing, and Kessinger makes a note on his tablet.

"Think Whelan's scared?" Turkey asks.

I pull my attention back to him, only for him to nod in the direction I was just looking.

"Rumor has it that Kessinger took Penn State from bottom of the table to champs in one season."

"That's a stupid rumor."

"I heard it from my girlfriend's cousin who plays there, and he's not stupid, so …"

I want Turkey to shut up about Kessinger already.

"They called him the play whisperer. Had an uncanny knack for knowing how the other team would react before they did."

"Sounds like witchcraft."

Turkey taps his stick against the ice, watching it for a moment. "Also heard he's gay." The sudden, intense eye contact catches me off guard. "That won't be an issue, will it?"

I send my glare—not scowl—Kessinger's way. It's only going to be the biggest issue of my life. "*Nyet*."

"I'm serious, Novi. Don't make me have to kick your ass. First, because I can't. Second, because my mom told me fighting was bad. But third, because I'll have to do it, and then all my family and probably Coach will get mad at me, but I'm not going to let you be a dick to someone for no reason."

"There's a reason." Kessinger is already making me lose my easygoing attitude that I'm so good at.

"If you don't want to wear the Pride jerseys or whatever, that's on you. But Kessinger can't help who he is."

"I never said he could."

"Then lay off."

That makes me laugh. Well, it amuses me enough to let out a "heh" sound. "You won't have a problem from me. I won't even talk to him."

Turkey sighs, and while I know he's disappointed in my answers, it's all I can give him. It feels good, though, in my chest, to know that he's ready to have the back of a man he's never met. If things get out about me, I have no fear that my team won't support me.

That's not my issue.

"Atatürk. Novicov."

My skates almost go out from under me. Kessinger has snuck up on us, and suddenly, I'm looking into those gray eyes that always feel like they're teasing me. Only this time, I know they are.

"You both played well last season," he says, like he can't tell my pulse is trying to hammer its way out of my neck.

"Thanks," Turkey says. "I know Owen Brown from Penn State. He has good things to say."

"Surprising since he once called me … what was it? Ah. A hack who couldn't make the big leagues, so now

I'm taking my bitterness out on a bunch of twenty-year-olds."

Turkey's eyes go wide, and I swear he loses color from his cheeks. "Umm … did I say Brown? No, it was, uh—"

Kessinger laughs, and I hate that it still sounds the same. "He was one of my favorites. I've learned over the years not to take things too personally."

He doesn't look at me, but it feels directed anyway.

Then he does look, and that's even worse. "Novicov, I need you for a minute."

Shit. Fuck. I don't think so. "Uh … no English."

Turkey rolls his eyes and skates off.

Kessinger drops the professional act and looks at me dead-on. "Ackerman wants you. Not me."

I go to walk off the ice when his arm flies out to stop me.

"But I'm next."

CHAPTER FOUR

COLBY

Radimir Novicov is a pain in my ass, and not in the fun way.

Somehow, he has successfully dodged me for three full days of training camp, even when I've tried to address him in a professional manner.

Saying "you're putting too much pressure on your old knees when you change directions on the ice" is totally one hundred percent professional … ish.

"I don't speak English, and I'm not fucking old" was a much more unprofessional response in my opinion.

I'm not going to let him get away with it today though. This is never going to work if we keep up this cat-and-mouse game—me chasing him, him blowing me off—and if I can't coach my players, how am I ever going to make it as an NHL coach?

Also, it's not going to be long before others notice, and then it'll be a bigger deal than it needs to be. Scandal is the last thing either Novi or I need. His amazingly long NHL career would be overshadowed if he went out on a scandal, and I still have twenty to thirty years at this. I can't start my career—at this level—by making waves.

I'm proud of what I've achieved, how far I've come, and I'm not going to let Novi interfere with my future goals and everything I want to keep working toward.

Novi doesn't have to like me. He can be a homophobe all he likes. I get it, bro. You're straight, you were always straight, and I crossed a line. But now we have to work together.

If I can get to him and explain all that, then maybe we can both take a deep breath and relax.

It's obvious he never learned how to do that. He's always been this tightly wound ball of tension. Even when he'd give me those goofy smiles when we were friends, they were always covering something deeper behind them. He wears his stoic expression like a mask, but I know that deep down, he's that twenty-one-year-old kid in a foreign country, scared out of his mind.

I've seen him lose the tough exterior before. I know he can do it. The hard part is getting him alone, away from prying eyes. I need to somehow catch him while he's in his comfort zone.

Which is how I come up with a brilliant—or not-so-brilliant—plan of taking his car keys from his bag in the locker room, unlocking his car, returning the keys, and then going back after my shift to slip into his back seat.

If our past won't get me fired, this possibly might. But I'm all out of ideas, and as much as I want to shake him in public and tell him to stop being so ridiculously … Novi, I can't.

While I wait for the players to shower and leave, I go back and forth, from telling myself this is the worst idea I've ever had to convincing myself it's what needs to be done.

I'm still arguing with myself when cars begin to pull out of the lot. It's now or never, and even though my fight-or-flight instinct is telling me to run and my heart feels like it might explode with how fast it's racing, I'm completely frozen.

I can't move now even if I wanted to.

And that's when Novi gets in his driver's seat.

I'm about to sit up, about to say something, warn him that I'm here, when he throws his head back against his headrest, looks up at the roof, and mutters something in Russian. It sounds like he's trying to console himself while having the tone of calling himself an idiot.

It almost makes me feel bad for him.

I need to let him know of my presence sooner rather than later, but when he starts the car and pulls out of his parking space, I worry I'll cause an accident if I do it while he's driving.

He's still talking to himself, and though I can't understand what he's saying, I distinctly hear Ezra Palaszczuk's name.

Perhaps he's ranting about gay people in hockey multiplying, and it's all Ezra's fault.

I want to be pissed off at him, but the anger isn't there. It's more pity than anything else.

When he stops at the boom gate and swipes his ID to get out of the lot, I finally make my appearance known.

I sit up and say, "Where are we going?"

He flips out like I knew he would, jumping a mile high and letting out a string of curses in both English and Russian. It's impressive how he can switch between the two and have it sound like he's speaking the one language.

"What are you doing in my car?"

Explain yourself. Don't get fired. Save your ass.

Instead, all I can do is blink at those burning whiskey-colored eyes. I can't remember the last time I had his full attention this close up.

One of Novi's teammates blasts his horn for Novi to move. I'm sure he isn't going to. I'll be surprised if he doesn't get out of the car, pull me out of his back seat, throw me to the ground, and run over me on his way out.

Me? Dramatic? Only when I'm under pressure.

"Drive," I say. "We need to talk."

"I don't speak—"

"If you say you don't speak English one more time, I'm going to scream at you."

Perhaps it's because Novi hasn't heard me ever scream or yell before that he listens and pulls out onto the road. Even on the ice, I was always calm and collected. I was the one throwing out chirps and riling the opposition, not even losing my cool when they'd try to fight me.

"This feels a lot like kidnapping," Novi says, and I laugh.

"Hey, you're driving, and I'm not holding a gun to your head. You keep running away from me, and all I want to do is clear the air."

"You want clean air? Is this going to be you trying to get me to join fight on global warming?"

I shake my head. "Still a smart-ass, I see."

"Yes. My ass is very smart."

"Will you let me apologize already?"

Novi's eyes are on the road, but in the rearview mirror, I see his brow furrow. "For what?"

"You can play like you don't remember what happened, but I think it's evident from your avoidance that you do. I was young and stupid, and I thought we had a moment. We didn't, and you don't want anything to do with me because I'm gay. But can we move past it? We have to work together, and I don't want to be walking around on eggshells with you. I know things won't go back to the way they were. We're not friends anymore, and I get it, okay? But you are going to have to face me eventually, and I'd prefer it if we didn't have this awkwardness when it happens. I'm sorry I wanted to kiss you and thought you might have wanted me to. Rule number one as a gay person: make sure the person you're making a move on is also gay. Or queer. Or bicurious." I throw up my hands. "Do you see why I had a hard time back then?"

I'm trying to lighten the mood after all that depressing talk, but Novi is his usual stoic self.

When he doesn't respond, I deflate. I should've known better than to try to negotiate with a bigot.

"You're allowed to hate me." I hate that my tone is so defeated. "But you still need to be professional. You can let me out here. I'll walk back to get my car."

He doesn't slow down. He doesn't stop. He does, however, lock the doors.

"Now who's kidnapping who?" I ask.

"Are you hungry?" Novi's eyes meet mine in the rear-view mirror again.

"Why?"

"I'm going to get food. You will come with me."

"By choice or by force?"

Novi does that lip-twitch thing that I learned a long time ago meant he was amused. "You're the one who got in my car."

"I'm sure that's what all the kidnappers say. 'Wasn't my fault. They voluntarily got into my car.'"

"Technically, you broke into my car."

"So now you're going to feed me and then take me out to the desert or the middle of nowhere and beat the crap out of me for even breathing in your direction. I'm terrible, right? How dare I find you attractive a billion years ago. You can't catch the gay, by the way."

"You talk so much shit."

"Better than not talking at all," I mumble like a scolded child.

Novi pulls into the parking lot for a steak house that I've heard the team talk about in passing. "You want to talk? Then have dinner with me."

My jaw ticks, and I ignore the way it sounds like he's asking me on a date when he's definitely not. "All right."

I'm still not convinced this isn't a last-meal type of situation, but on the off chance it isn't, I want him to say his piece. Even if it's only to tell me to never go near him again.

As we walk in together, I put my hands in my pockets. "Are you sure you want to be seen with me? Anyone from the team might be here."

"You are coach. I am player. Maybe we're talking strategy."

I am so confused, only made more confused by the fact that the minute we're seated and alone, Novi leans forward, forearms on the table, and stares directly into my eyes as he says, "I don't hate you. My issue with you was …" He averts his gaze. "The complete opposite of hating you."

Wait, what?

CHAPTER FIVE

NOVI

It is dangerous to say this in public, but my options were to drive us to a deserted underground parking lot or here, and for some reason, Americans get edgy in dark places.

At least Mastros is loud with the tables filling up, live music, and the staff more interested in personal conversations than taking orders while it's still so early in the afternoon. It gives us a shadow of privacy, but I still refuse to say certain things out loud.

"So you're ..." Colby shakes his head like a dog that's crashed headfirst into a wall. "Are you trying to tell me you're—"

"Do not say it." I pick up the menu, even though I always order the same thing. He looks like he has been slapped with a pancake, and if I have learned anything the last three days, it's that if I look at Colby Kessinger, it is hard to stop.

"I'm right though, aren't I?" He leans further over the white tablecloth between us, sucking the air from the room in the one movement. "That you're ... like me."

I tug at the worn corner of the menu. This clammy-palm feeling is not usual for me. At the very end of last season, I finally got the courage to talk to the Queer Collective group. The men in the league I have been envious of for years. There were no questions. No pushing. My presence was immediately understood, and I was able to come out to them, in my small way, without having to say words at all. No matter how well I understand English, Russian will always be my safety. My comfort. Which is why I always use it when I possibly can. And in situations like this, where my usual chill, joyful persona is overridden by nerves, it's needed more than ever.

Too bad Colby doesn't speak Russian.

"*Da*."

His whole face lights up. "I knew it. I *knew* it."

His explosion makes me glance around with wide eyes, but we're mostly ignored.

At least he takes the hint and drops his voice to an excited half whisper. "That whole season messed with my head. I swear I was picking up on something, and then that night ..." He's the one to look around this time, and when his attention falls back on me, his gray eyes are too shiny, and his smile is too big. "Tell me you were thinking the same things I was."

"*Nyet*."

"*Liar*," he breathes. "All this time, I thought you wanted to kill me. But you wanted to—"

"Steak and fries. What are you getting?"

"Steak and fries, huh?" He pumps his eyebrows. "Is that what you Russians call it?"

"You are still annoying."

He picks up his own menu. "Funny. I remember us being friends."

"Of course. I am delightful."

He shows off too many teeth when he laughs. "I know you used to be. The last few days, you've been like a ghost."

This happy sort of feeling bubbles in my gut. "I am like that too. Very talented at all things."

His laugh continues for another few seconds before it slowly slides off his face. "Is this why you've been avoiding me?"

"I thought you knew that night. Why I really freaked out and ran away. I've been worried you might say something. About me. It's not something I talk about."

"But ..." His forehead creases deepen. "Why? There's a lot of support in the league for ..." Something clicks behind his eyes. "You weren't bullshitting with your reasons for not wearing the Pride jerseys, were you?"

"You thought I was shitting bulls?"

It takes him a second, but he cuts himself off from correcting me. Damn. I almost got to add him to my game. "Smart-ass. But yeah. Pretty much everyone thinks it's a homophobic excuse."

I know they do. I do not want to let down the young fans who look up to me, but I also can't carry all that weight either. I want to be someone worth idolizing, but it's not possible for me. I can handle people thinking I'm an asshole if it keeps my family safe.

"My sister is still there."

"In Russia?"

"*Da*. I thought she would come here with the rest of my family, but she is stubborn like a fox."

"An ox." Boom. There it is. It's automatic the way he corrects me, and I'm hit with a spark of glee that I got him as well. I will add his name to my list later. "So, your family is in America?"

"Canada. It was easier for them to immigrate there than the States."

"Why didn't she move with them?"

"She has a whole life there. It was not fair of me to ask, but after seventeen years here, I would like a whole life as well."

For the first time since we sat down, there is sympathy lurking in his eyes. "That sucks."

"It does. But I am a millionaire NHL star, Stanley Cup winner, and a very fun person to be around. I can't complain."

"Glad you're still so humble."

"Why humble? These are all facts. Am I supposed to say I am not a Stanley Cup winner? Twice."

"Most people avoid talking about all their accomplishments."

"I am not most people."

"I know …" He lowers his menu back close to the table. "I really liked that about you."

The soft tone takes me back. Back too far than I usually let myself go. Back to the AHL and hotel rooms, soft snoring, and hushed conversations once the lights were off. Colby's vulnerable words.

I never fit in much in high school. I dunno. The team was always fine, but I never really felt like I was in the inner circle, you know? Like they were them and I was me. I can already feel it happening here too …

We did not talk about it again, and not too long after that was our moment and me being too scared to be around him anymore. The guilt that I couldn't be there for his worry always tried to pull me back to him, but I was strong. Now, meeting Colby Kessinger's eyes and watching him watch me, I'm not feeling so strong. Men are my weakness, so I don't bother looking.

That was my first mistake with him.

I am sure I see it. That same curiosity I have always felt for him reflected back at me. The same curiosity that made me fall over myself to get away that first time.

"Ready to order?" The waiter appears out of nowhere.

I jump, and my eyes shoot back to the menu as my mind goes blank. "I … I, uh …"

"Sorry, he doesn't speak English." Colby smirks at me. "He'll take the steak and fries. I'll grab the burger."

"Thanks." The waiter grabs the menus and leaves again.

"Funny."

Colby folds his arms over his side of the table. "Gotta keep up with you and your witty retorts."

I copy him by crossing my arms. It was something I learned early on. Copy people and they feel more comfortable, and now that Colby knows about me, I want to make sure we're in a comfortable, friendly place. "You cannot tell anyone about me."

"I wouldn't."

"I'm serious. My sister—"

He reaches across to place his hand on my arm, and I jerk away from him like I've been burned. In my defense, it felt like I had been. His hand is too warm, too rough, too … I swallow and cut off the thoughts.

I watch as Colby tucks both hands under his arms and lowers his voice. "Sorry. I just want you to know that I get it. I know."

"Okay."

"I wish you'd said something back then." He isn't looking at me. Or smiling. His face wasn't made to be serious; it looks unnatural on him. "I was scared and lost too, you know."

"I'm … sorry."

"That sounded like it hurt."

I clear my throat. "I was wrong. This is something I can admit."

"Wow. Seventeen years later, and I finally have my answers."

My forehead gets heavy with my frown. "But you said you knew."

"No, I said I thought. After *what happened*, I convinced myself that I read it all wrong and that you hated me."

"But I was so obvious." My voice squeaks higher.

"Obvious?" His eyes almost shoot out. "What do you mean?"

"I …" I quickly glance around again, then lean closer. "I was always tripping over my words. Being silly idiot. My face is very expressive, it gives everything away."

Unlike how blank his face goes now. "Novi, I'm not being dramatic when I say this, but other than that goofy smile I'd get sometimes, your face never changes. You were impossible to read. And when we were friends, there was something called a language barrier that always made you trip over your words. How was I supposed to know it wasn't the Russian-to-English translation you were tripping over?"

I don't know which part to laugh at first. Yes, my English was basic, but that's not what made my brain so blank around him. My mouth forms and forgets too many things to say back until it lands on, "*Goofy*?"

"Super goofy. It's okay, I think your face was in shock over doing something it had never done before."

Never *done* before? Does he remember me at all? "I smile always."

"Maybe on the inside. That doesn't count."

"Of course it counts."

His eyes slide up to meet mine again, full of challenge and something else. "Maybe. But I like the goofy version anyway."

I turn away, arms pulled in tight to my chest. He doesn't know what he's talking about.

"Are you really sulking?"

"I am ignoring your taunts."

"It looks a lot like sulking to me."

That earns him a sharp look. "I thought I was impossible to read."

"I'm not a kid anymore."

For some reason, those words trigger something in me. Something that makes my gaze drop to the way his LA polo looks tight over his chest. These tables are very much too small, and this restaurant is very much too hot.

Colby lifts an arm to run his hand back through his dark, messy hair, and when I pull my eyes back upward, he purposely flexes his bicep.

I look away. "You are fucked."

"Just giving you what you want."

"What I want is peace. Something I will not be given with you here."

"Why?"

I tap my blunt, chewed-off nails against the table. "I will always be worried about it getting out."

"I said—"

"You won't tell. *Da.* But it is accident sometimes."

"Look … all I want is for you to stop making my job difficult. I'm here to help you. You're here to play.

I want my first season in the NHL to start right. More than anything, this is my career. My future. I can't mess with that."

His future. The thing I love so much is almost my past, and it's the complete opposite for him. Who would have picked this back when we knew each other?

"I will play nice," I promise him.

"Thank you."

"And you will keep my secret."

"Always."

"Then we are okay."

"Yeah." He stares across the table, frozen in place for a moment. "Wow. I did not see this coming when I broke into your car."

"Scare me like that again, and I *will* drive you to an abandoned parking lot."

"Ah … come again?"

When I smile, I make sure to do it on the outside this time. "Just a promise."

"Damn, Novi." Colby looks over his shoulder. "I said your *goofy* smile, not evil villain smile. I think you made that kid cry. What is that?"

I flip him off. "There is no crying."

"I was talking about my *inner* child. You just killed him."

"Stop talking to me."

"Nah, I know now that you liked it when I talked. So I'm going to keep doing that. For you. All for you."

I very much hate that he's right.

CHAPTER SIX

COLBY

I wish Novi hadn't said anything. I love that he did, that he felt comfortable enough to tell me, and I'm relieved he's not a homophobic dickweed, but now I replay our moment in my head every time I see him.

And as one of his coaches, I see him a lot. Not only in person but on a screen.

I have to analyze the way his body moves, and even though he's covered with all that padding, I know what he looks like underneath all of it.

He might no longer be the fresh-faced rookie I knew, and he might have had almost two decades of strain on his body, but he's still as solid as ever under that jersey. I know because I'm staring at his naked abs. Right now. And the trickle of water that slips between them.

It's not like I'm purposefully looking. I'm making my way through the locker room, which is noisy with conversation and heavy with body spray, trying to get to the team trainer's office, and he's in my direct line of sight. Fresh out of the shower. Wrapped in only a towel. It's my feet's fault for slowing.

The view takes me right back to being beside Novi as his teammate. All those showers together. Well, not *together* together, but in the same vicinity. Dressing down after a game, suiting up to go home, we'd been in ten different states of undress every single day. It took all my strength not to watch him the whole time like a creep.

I force myself to keep moving past him before I can repeat old patterns. I'm not allowed to think about Radimir Novicov in that way. I shouldn't have done it back then, and the stakes are even higher now.

Everyone knows he's going to retire when his contract is over at the end of next season. If I can keep my thoughts under control until then and Novi wants to come out and have a real relationship, maybe that's when I can think about asking him on a date. Until then, I have to be professional. One hundred percent hands-off.

Where am I going again? Why am I in the players' locker room? I can't remember.

"Turkey," Jeremy, our head trainer, calls from the door to the treatment room. "You're up."

Ah. Yes. Trainer. Talkies. All of the professionalism.

Jeremy sees me coming and gives me an up-nod. "You need to see me?"

"For a moment, if I can."

Turkey follows me into the room, whips off his towel, and throws himself on the massage table face down. "I swear my ass is on fire."

Do not look at the gorgeous man's hockey butt. Do not look.

"You might need to see the team doctor for a Z-Pak about that," Jeremy snarks.

Turkey doesn't even lift his head, only throws up his middle finger. "My sciatica is acting up."

"Oh. That I can help you with." Jeremy grabs some massage oil and gets to work on Turkey's lower back, but I tell myself to look at the roof and not the naked ass.

I haven't had sex since moving to LA, Novi is in my head, and I'm a gay man with a bare ass right in front of me. Life is not playing fair.

Having been in locker rooms for most of my life, I know how to keep boundaries in place, but when Jeremy starts massaging Turkey's glutes, I again forget why I'm even here. I'm thankful that it's Turkey and not Novi on that table, or I might be in real danger of crossing professional lines.

"Coach Kessinger?" Jeremy says, and I snap out of my "do not look" mantra.

My gaze snaps from the ceiling to his. "Sorry, I can come back after the team has cleared out."

"You can talk freely," Turkey says. He lifts up on his elbows and holds up his headphones. "I won't be able to hear if you say how everyone else sucks while I'm the best."

Jeremy switches from his hands to working his elbow down Turkey's lower back.

"Ah, fuck," Turkey grunts.

Yeah, I can't do this. "A-all good. I-I I'll come back." I turn on my heel to walk out the door, only to run right into more naked skin. This time with my body and not my eyes. My face connects with a hard nose, and whether it's his familiar scent or the Russian curse that comes out of his mouth, I know it's him without having seen him yet.

My eyes are too busy scrunched together against the pain from headbutting Novi.

Of course it had to be Novi.

"No wonder you didn't make it out of AHL. You move with your eyes closed."

If I weren't so mortified over tripping over my feet, my words, and making my coworkers uncomfortable with my inappropriate thoughts, I'd laugh at Novi's perfect deadpan delivery.

I've missed it.

Even though my insides scream at me to flee the room, I hold strong and shake off the awkwardness as much as I can.

"I actually came in here to talk about you," I say to Novi.

Even though the scrunch in his forehead lets me know exactly how much he distrusts me, I keep in my eye roll.

"You refuse to listen to me when I say your knees are old and you're pushing them too hard."

"My knees are not old. You're old."

Behind us, Jeremy and Turkey snicker.

"I'm younger than you," I point out.

"Same draft class. Same age."

"So you're admitting you are old, then?"

Novi grumbles under his breath.

"All I'm doing is trying to make sure you get through the next two seasons without an injury that could leave you retiring early."

"Why would you put that in the universe?" Novi looks up at the ceiling and around the room. "He didn't mean it. No injury. No retirement."

"I see you've only gotten more superstitious since we played together."

"Wait," Turkey says. "You two used to play together?"

Still being horny, still being in Novi's general vicinity, instead of picturing us on the ice together, my mind immediately goes to that night in our hotel room. Him hovering over the top of me.

"You didn't tell me that," Turkey says to Novi.

That is to be expected, considering Novi's concerns over his and his family's safety, but it still hurts that he hasn't even acknowledged that we know each other.

I force a small smile. "It was one season a billion years ago. He didn't even remember me until I reminded him. I don't hold it against him. As well as old knees, he also has an old brain."

"You have old face," Novi grumbles some more.

"Were you needing some physiotherapy, or do you want to come review your game tape with me so I can show you what I'm talking about?"

Novi glances between Jeremy and me. "I was only looking for massage. I don't need physiotherapy."

I internally sigh. Big macho man will risk his remaining two years in the league to avoid admitting weakness.

"Then meet me in the video room." I gesture for him to leave and then turn back to Jeremy once Novi's outside the treatment room. "Can you keep a spot open for him to come to you after I've spoken to him about his knees?"

"Will do." He goes back to working on Turkey while I catch up with Novi.

"I'm not injured," he says like a petulant child.

"I'm not saying you are." I walk with my hands in my pockets as we leave the locker room and head into the hall outside so I'm not even tempted to reach for him. To reassure him, stop him from continuing so we can face each other to talk about his future in hockey. I won't do any of it.

Hands in pockets. Eyes straight ahead.

"Then what is your problem with my knees?"

"I'll show you."

We reach the video room, and I hold the door open for him.

We're the only ones in here, which, normally, I'd be fine with because it would give me that chance to work one-on-one with my players. But with Novi, one-on-one is dangerous.

"Sit," I say, and Novi sits in the closest recliner chair.

We have state-of-the-art technology here, so when I pull up some shots of Novi on the iPad, I can send it to the large screen on the far wall. I refuse to sit, and I hold back from even standing near him.

"Here." I circle a still shot with the stylus pen where Novi's knees are too far inward while he's changing direction.

"I see nothing wrong."

Stubborn son of a bitch.

"This"—I circle it again—"is what people do when they're overcompensating for the pressure on their knees. It's a reflex brought on by your hips to try to protect yourself, but in the long run, all it's going to make you do is tear something. A ligament, a tendon, your meniscus."

"I've always done that. Hasn't been a problem."

"That's what I thought it could be too. So when I noticed it, I went back to old footage of you." I pull up some other stills I saved from my very professional research of looking up old game tape of a man I used to jerk off over.

If being gay hadn't already reserved my spot, this is what would send me to hell.

"Look. No pigeon knees, and this was only a couple of seasons ago. See how your thighs and knees are completely parallel to each other? And, in fact, if you can almost see the slow progression from this point to"—I flick through more images I've lined up—"now."

Novi's finally quiet. It's slowly sinking in. He's coming around.

"I don't see a difference." He really is stubborn. "But hypothetically, how would someone fix that?"

CHAPTER SEVEN

NOVI

It's possible I'm overdoing it. *Coach Kessinger* immediately worked with Jeremy to come up with a training plan that would strengthen my knees, and I have been working at it like a man possessed. Not that I will admit to anyone that I'm having trouble.

I will not let my career end on a low, not after having made hockey my entire life. I'm ready to fight if I need to.

Besides, the more I am working out, the less I am seeing of Kessinger. He has to know that I am avoiding him by now, and he's letting me do it. I hate it as much as I love it because I am no longer tense about him telling my secret. Instead, the tension is something more primal.

Something that reminds me of how close I was to touching a man all those years ago.

The two years left on my contract felt like such a short time when I walked into training camp on that first day, but now they feel like they'll never end. I don't wish my career away, but I'm almost forty, and for the first time in my life, I'm really craving sex. Not in a horny way, but in a way where I'm with someone. Where I can touch freely. Kiss. Maybe hold him afterward instead of sticking my dick through a hole while a stranger on the other side blows me.

That used to feel good. Used to take the edge off. But every time over the summer that I gave in and used a glory hole, all I walked away with was frustration and something that almost felt like shame.

I sink lower against the wall in the training room, legs straining under the pressure of my squat. I've been holding it for longer than I'm supposed to, but the burn is taking over everything else, and I like the way it's all I can focus on.

A bead of sweat rolls from my hairline and down my face before I finally push back to my feet.

"You're in early again," Turkey says as he walks over. He's texting rapidly, gear bag hanging from his shoulder and LA hat on crooked.

"Training." I grab a band and stretch it across my chest.

"You got preseason jitters?"

I don't think I have ever had jitters. Even in my rookie year, I was calm as a bug. Still, it's easier to lie. "*Da.* Nerves. Many nerves." Nearly all of them belonging to Coach Kessinger.

Turkey dumps his bag and tosses his phone on top.

"Why are you here early?" I ask since he's usually one of the last people to arrive.

"Jitters." He grabs a band to stretch next to me. The silence in the room is the heavy kind though.

Turkey slants a quick look my way. "So, you and Kessinger—"

My gut twists painfully at that short sentence.

"—used to play together?"

My thoughts are too conflicted to answer, so I grunt in response. He can interpret that however he wants to.

"Is that why you've been so weird?"

"What do you mean?"

"The way you run out of a room when he walks in. How you refuse to see him about game tape. I thought you were doing some *not wanting to catch the gay* thing, but … I dunno, he seemed friendly with you."

"He is friendly with everyone."

"Right." Turkey grabs the band in both hands, then stretches it across his chest. "So what's the reason?"

"What do you mean?"

"I told you not to be a dick to him for no reason, and you said there's a reason. I thought it was you being homophobic, but …"

I'm not used to the way this heavy weight sinks through me. Not used to the sweat I've worked up cooling so rapidly on my skin. No one, ever, has gotten close to the truth, so I've never had to face this moment before. "I … *ya ne uveren* … and then … *eto potomu chto*." *I'm not sure … It's because.*

A laugh breaks through my panic.

"Come on, Novi, you can tell him." Kessinger is grinning at me from the doorway, and it doesn't do anything to make my body feel alive again. His gray eyes slide from me to Turkey. "Look at him wanting to protect my reputation. I was a cocky shit with none of the skill to back it up. I never let Novi forget that I was a top ten draft pick, and look which one of us made it."

Cocky … yes. Slowly, my brain comes back online. "Was very irritating."

"At least you don't have to hear about that anymore," Kessinger says.

Maybe, but that never bothered me. He *was* a top ten pick. It was that he thought that was all he had to do to make it and then choked when it wasn't enough. I felt bad for him and knew he could do better, but he didn't give himself the humility to learn how.

"Now I can taunt you about how I'm a Frozen Four–winning coach instead."

I squint at his teasing. "Tell me. Is Frozen Four ranked higher than Stanley Cup?"

"Don't worry, I plan on adding ol' Lord Stanley to my list of accolades. Watch out, Novicov. You haven't won yet."

"And when I'm in Hall of Fame, you can finally admit defeat."

"Has to happen first." He brings his hands together. "But to get there, we have work to do. I want to run you through some footage from training yesterday."

"This is a waste of my time."

"Yeah, yeah. Humor me." He leaves, expecting me to trail after him like a good little player.

Considering I now vow to only see him as a coach, I do. At a distance. So he knows this is reluctant and that I might not always do as he says. The second I walk into the room, he quickly closes the door and turns to me. His gray eyes hit mine, and I immediately realize I've been played.

His voice is too familiar. "Are you okay?"

"This is not about hockey?"

Kessinger gives me a flat look, and it's hard to remind myself he's my coach when the professional line dims between us. "I know your conversation with Ätaturk was getting uncomfortable, but I didn't expect you to panic like that."

"I was not panicked."

"Uh-huh."

This time, I give him the flat look. "I don't panic."

"Okay, so you weren't panicked, I didn't save you, and I won't say you're welcome. I'm also not surprised about how you've managed to keep your business under wraps for so long when that's how you get whenever someone comes even vaguely close to figuring you out."

"No one gets close to figuring me out."

"Then—" Something clicks for him. "I've seen you brush off questions about the LGBTQ community for years in press conferences, and I thought you did it so easily because you really didn't care. But it's because it was all unfounded speculation, isn't it? No one knew anything. Whereas back there—"

I drag my sneaker over the highly polished floor. "He was close to truth. It caught me by surprise. Surprise. *Not* panic."

"Right. Well, we'll have to make sure it doesn't happen again."

I reluctantly look back up at him. "We?"

"I know we haven't been friends in a long time, but it doesn't change that I cared about you at one point. If your sexuality getting out will get you or your family into trouble, of course I'll be on your side to make sure that doesn't happen."

My mouth inches open as I search his eyes. He said that so easily. That he cared about me. I want to question him more, find out if he cared the way I cared or if it was all friendship with flares of horny moments. Or … moment. One moment. That one moment that ruined everything between us. Maybe that's why I've been so on edge about whether or not he was working here. Colby Kessinger was the first and last man I let myself care about.

While I am confident about many things, talking about whatever there was between us is not one of those things. So I don't make him talk more. Just mutter, "Thank you."

"I've got your back." Then, before I can react, he reaches out and squeezes my upper arm.

A bolt of lust spears through it, and my whole body locks together. The warmth from his hand burns. Bare skin on bare skin. Lingering contact that raises a longing in my gut so powerful I can't even speak.

Kessinger's expression tightens, and slowly, he peels his hand away. "Sorry," he croaks.

It's hard to work out if I'm shaking or if it's the adrenaline making it seem that way. Somehow, with that one touch, we're standing closer than the comfortable distance from a moment ago.

My teammates and I touch all the time, but the difference is that I don't desperately want to fuck any of them. And I haven't wanted to fuck any of them for almost twenty years.

Kessinger manages an awkward laugh, and the way it brings cute lines beside his mouth has fluttery wings in my gut. "I wasn't thinking," he says. "I promise I won't do that again. Now, footage—"

He goes to turn away, but before he can get far, something completely uncontrollable comes over me. My hand lifts, and my fingertips skim his collarbone.

Only the very start, at the base of his throat, the prominent curve that sinks beneath the collar of his shirt.

His skin there is so soft, and I'm mesmerized as his chest expands on a sudden, deep inhale.

"Novi …"

My eyes snap to his as my hand drops. There's so much questioning in the way he looks at me, the way those forehead creases deepen as his eyebrows arch. I'm still too caught up in the way he felt to have any answers for either of us.

"I think the footage can wait," he says. "Coach Whelan will want you on the ice soon."

I know his words are supposed to make sense, but my brain has gone very stupid. "Coach."

That small, crooked smile again. "On the ice. Yes."

"Yes."

His smile twitches wider. "*Da*."

"*Da*."

This time, he full-on laughs, and it breaks through my misty brain. "You really need to stop looking at me like that."

I blink back to reality, and what happened hits like an anvil to the head. My heart rate takes off worse than when I'm on a double shift, chasing an opponent down the ice. "*Blyad*. You have food on face. Very messy. Embarrassing for you," I choke out before almost wrenching the door from the hinges and storming from the room.

It's only once I reach my locker that I realize it looks like I was running away from him. Radimir Novicov doesn't run from anyone.

Not even messy, sexy, annoying men who I wish had stayed in my past.

CHAPTER EIGHT

COLBY

Novi is messing with my head, and I wish I could say that I hate it, but I really, really don't. When accepting the job in LA, my biggest worry was Novi trying to ruin things for me because he hates me so much. This … I wasn't expecting this.

It's thrown me, and I need to work out how to handle it all. Distancing myself from him as much as possible is the smart thing to do, and I wasn't lying when I said I'd have his back no matter what because his family's safety is the most important thing here. Not my physical reactions to his touch or his mere presence.

I can go out and hook up to take off that edge, and Novi can … Huh. If he's been so adamant about keeping everything about his sexuality a secret for so long, does that mean he doesn't hook up? That he never has?

Surely he's done … some stuff. Anonymously.

Damn it, why does that thought turn me on so much? Oh, right. It's Novi. Anything to do with that man has my body raring to go at a moment's notice.

Stupid old crushes and that saying about them dying hard.

Why did he have to be nice and come out to me? He should've silently tortured me like he did back then. I'd be none the wiser and all the less hornier for it.

By some miracle, I make it through the rest of training camp without another close pass with Novi, and I'm in a good headspace to get my job done and do my part to help lead the team to victory this season.

The first preseason game is against Anaheim, and even though they're only thirty miles away, I wish it were a home game. Lugging the video equipment is my least favorite part of this job so far, but as the assistant video coach, I am paying my dues.

I've been promised big things by LA management, but I still have to prove that I'm worthy of working my way up that ladder. If I want to be head coach by the time I'm forty, I only have four years to show them why I deserve it.

At Penn State, being a video coach was part of the head coach job. Some NHL teams still only have the one, and I don't know how they do it. We're a small team of three, with Nowak being a general assistant coach, meaning if they need him on the ice to help with training, he's their guy. I'm more of a specialized kind of coach, focusing on the tasks I need to do to get the experience required of a head coach.

Head coaches aren't out there on the ice every day leading practices. They're on the sidelines analyzing everything. How everyone looks. How the opposition looks. It's their job to come up with the plays that will hopefully get around the opponents and score goals. And the skills of having been a video coach is imperative to doing that.

We're the invisible right-hand man of the head coach. We put in the long hours, cutting tape together, sending the players their ice time to review their own plays, and then combining everything in a cohesive way for game tape meetings. Which there are a lot of. There was a lot back when I was playing in the AHL, but with technology advancements, more cameras than ever on the ice, and the quick pace in which the game is played, I have no idea how some of these teams still only have one guy.

Especially when on top of all that, we're picking apart both teams and how they're playing. We have to look for strengths and weaknesses on both sides so we can pair up the right players to give us a chance at scoring. That all rests on our shoulders.

I'm pushing my trolley of hard cases filled with equipment into Anaheim's arena when someone calls from behind me.

"Hey, wait up."

It's a voice I don't recognize, and when I turn, I'm faced with the six-foot wall of Anaheim's best defenseman, Oskar Voyjik. He's in casual sweats, gear bag over his shoulder, and he approaches confidently, like we're already friends.

Does he think I work here and is about to ask me for a pumpkin spiced latte?

What comes out of his mouth is much more surreal. "You're Colby Kessinger, right?"

"Y-you know who I am?"

"My husband made it a point to show me the articles on you since joining the LA team."

With Oskar Voyjik's reputation, I'm mildly concerned he's about to ask me for a threesome.

"Okay?"

"I thought I'd introduce myself, offer to go out for drinks after the game."

Definitely looking for a threesome.

"Thanks, but ..." How do I say there's only one hockey player I'd consider risking my career for, and it ain't him.

"Us queer dudes in the NHL need to stick together," he says, and I'm back to that surreal blinking thing again.

"Uh, I'm not a player."

"You don't need to be. We're expanding. Before, our Queer Collective was a couple of dudes who happened to like other dudes, and we needed that support system in an industry that was otherwise ... uninviting. But now, we've got players, support staff, we've got the Bahs, a referee, and hey, even a team owner. You're welcome to join us anytime you want, and according to Ezra, I'm not allowed to take no for an answer."

"E-Ezra Palaszczuk?" I'm about to ask how he knows about me, but hockey is actually a pretty small community. I know Ezra is best friends with Westly Dalton, who used to play for Boston but is now a head coach at another D1 school. We've crossed paths a few times over the last couple of years, so it's not a big leap.

We're all part of one big murder map with six degrees of separation.

"So what you're telling me is after I'm done with cutting all the game tape from tonight, I'm going to go out with you for drinks."

"Lane will be there too."

"Are you sure you'll be out when I'm done? I'm sometimes stuck in that room until midnight." I'm lucky a West Coast team wanted me. The poor souls on the other side of the country have to stay up and watch the West Coast games of upcoming opponents to pull tape for training sessions. At least I get to watch East Coast games before any of the games start here.

"Lane might be very, very old, but I'm not. I'll still be awake." He glances around where he's standing. "Damn it. I forgot he wasn't with me. It's only fun to tease him if he can hear me."

Seeing as I'm new to LA and I don't have many friends, going out with Oskar and his husband doesn't sound like the worst idea.

"Give me your number, and I'll text you when I'm done." I hand over my phone, and he punches it in.

"Done. Okay, I'm gonna head home for my downtime before I have to come back tonight. I might even tell Lane how old he is to his face."

I snort. "Sounds like a good plan."

"See ya round."

Yeah. I guess he will.

Their Queer Collective thing or whatever they're calling it is an amazing idea and would help Novi so much … if he could bring himself to take that step. But that's up to him to decide when he's ready.

Until then, I'll take advantage of the free friendship on offer and hope it's not an offer for something more.

-

As I walk into the packed bar and spot Oskar and his husband, or who I assume is his husband, in a booth making out, I almost turn and walk back onto the street again.

I keep running the offer to catch up through my mind, switching between them doing a nice thing and wanting to bone me.

If it were two random guys who weren't involved in the NHL, I'd be all for it, but with my inappropriate feelings toward Novi, I can't be throwing extra fuel on my career. As it is, Novi has the power to set the whole thing aflame.

Still, I give Oskar and Lane the benefit of the doubt and hope that if they are looking for a threesome that they're cool enough guys to still want to be friends when I turn them down.

Considering I haven't been laid in forever, I should get a medal for not even contemplating it.

As if sensing my presence, they pull apart as I approach their booth.

"Hey, you came," Oskar says. "Lane, this is Colby, Colby, my old ball and chain."

Lane reaches across the table to shake my hand as I slide into the booth, but his head is turned toward Oskar. "Go play with your teammates while the grown-ups talk."

He doesn't hesitate to abandon me here with his husband, but that's when I notice the rest of Anaheim's team and the number of people dressed in Anaheim colors.

"Did you bring me into enemy territory?" I gasp.

"Don't worry. Everyone will move on soon. Actually, you probably got here in time to see the show."

I cock my head. "The show?"

"Yup. All the husbands turn into pumpkins at midnight, and then one by one, you see the rest of them either find someone to go home with or disappear as a group to another bar."

"Lifestyles of the rich and kind of famous, huh?"

Lane chuckles. "Don't let Oskar hear you say he's only kind of famous."

"You know what I mean though. Unless someone is a superfan, they're not going to recognize Oskar on the street."

"I do. But hockey players' egos are fragile. You should know. You were one."

It's always so weird hearing that I *was* a hockey player. Or I *played* hockey. I still play hockey. Just not at this level. But I guess that doesn't count.

So instead of correcting him and boasting about my very cool and not at all dorky queer beer league I was involved in back in Pennsylvania, I say, "True. You're right. Big egos."

That's one thing that is different between me back then and now. My ego? Not so huge anymore. I stopped feeding that hungry bitch years ago.

"How did you know I used to play?"

"I'm the PR manager for King Sports. I have multiple sources."

"But why check up on me?"

Lane smiles. "We need to vet anyone joining our inner circle."

What in the hell have I walked into?

"But why? At first, I thought Oskar and you were wanting a threesome with me, but now I'm worried you want me to join some kind of cult."

Lane stares at me for a moment, completely expressionless. Maybe I still have time to flee. But then, as if my words finally process in his brain, he bursts into complete laughter.

I didn't think it was that funny, but okay.

I sit and wait for him to calm down. "Are you done yet?"

"I am … I am."

He's not. He takes a deep breath and continues my humiliation. Not that I'm actually humiliated. I'm relieved that I'm wrong. But I don't see me living this down anytime soon.

As if proving me right, when Oskar comes back, Lane's barely composed himself, and then it starts all over again when he tries to explain but can't even get words out.

Oskar turns to me. "Did you give him drugs? Or, what ..." His gaze ping-pongs between his husband and me. "What is happening?"

"He's laughing because I asked if you two were in a cult."

Lane shakes his head. "That's not ..." He takes a deep breath. "That's not the part I'm laughing at. He also thought ... he thought ..."

Ah. "It had crossed my mind that you'd asked me here for a threesome, and he lost it before I could tell him—"

Now Oskar joins in with Lane before I can defend my assumption.

"It's not my fault. I've seen the tape."

That sobers both of them.

"What tape?" Lane asks, his face now serious.

It's scary how quickly he went from laughing manically to looking just plain manic.

"The infamous one of Oskar in the alleyway. What tape did you think I meant?"

They look at each other and then back at me, both looking relieved. Ooh, someone has a sex taaaape.

"No, no, that's the one we thought you meant," Lane says.

I don't believe him.

"As much as you are a very pretty man," Oskar says, "Lane doesn't let me do those kinds of things anymore."

Lane pinches his side. "You mean you love me so much you couldn't even fathom doing that kind of thing anymore."

Oskar snaps his fingers. "Right. That. That's what I meant."

"Good," I say. "Because I didn't want to make it awkward by having to turn you down anyway."

Oskar makes an offended *pfft* sound. "Excuse me?"

"Ignore him," Lane says. "He's dramatic when he's rejected for perfectly valid reasons."

"How do you know his reasons are valid?" Oskar asks.

"Because I'm married to you. That's why."

I'll hand it to them, they've successfully broken the ice with me and made me feel comfortable around them relatively quickly. It's not that I'm bad at making friends. I just haven't had time to yet.

So as we sit in the booth in the slowly emptying bar and talk bullshit, it's not until I start yawning that I realize it's coming up to three thirty in the morning. And then I notice the bar is practically empty.

Hours have flown by, and it feels really fucking good to be welcomed to a new city this way.

But maybe not as good as catching someone's eye as they enter the bar.

Not any someone.

My someone.

My dream man from a billion years ago.

Novi's here.

CHAPTER NINE

NOVI

Oskar's mouth gapes open and closed as his gaze pings between me and Kessinger. The three of them together this late does look very suspicious, but because of my many conversations with Lane, I know it's not what it looks like. I'd opted to meet Oskar now because there are fewer eyes to see us, and even if I am not an actual Queer Collective member, I could not break Ezra's heart by refusing. It looks like they found a way to pass the time while they waited for me.

"Ah …" Oskar has progressed to noise now. Interesting. "Look. It's Radimir Novicov. What a, umm, coincidence."

"I know who I am."

"At three thirty in the morning, it's totally likely we'd run into each other by complete accident at the same bar in Anaheim." Oskar's had way too much alcohol.

"I'll get us drinks," I say.

When I get back to the table and hand them out, Oskar scoops his up and takes a large swig.

Then sprays it across the table.

"The fuck is that? Are you trying to poison me?"

"If I was trying to poison you, you'd be dead already."

Kessinger takes a sip, and a relieved laugh falls from his lips. "It's water."

I take the seat across from Lane, which unfortunately puts me right next to Kessinger. Kessinger and his lemon tart scent. His too-broad shoulders. The searching gaze on the side of my face.

"So …" Lane studies me before glancing at Kessinger. "Neither of you look surprised to see each other."

"Impossible. I am very surprised."

"It's not a threesome thing," Kessinger hurries to say.

Oskar throws his hands up. "Why does everyone always make that assumption?"

Lane smirks. "I'll give you a second to find that answer on your own."

"It was *one* time."

"One time *on camera*."

Oskar takes another swig of his water like it's hard liquor. "It's not my fault that everyone wants to bone me."

"It's not." Lane crooks a finger under Oskar's chin and turns him so they're facing each other. Then he kisses Oskar softly and says in a hushed voice, "I love you."

My eyes immediately shoot away from them. The bar is nearly empty, with one drunk patron at the bar and two older men and one older lady, swaying and singing too loudly together on the dance floor. I study them until I'm sure it's safe to look again without having to face everything I've never had.

"I know it's not a threesome thing," I say like nothing after that ever happened. "And Coach Kessinger knows about me."

"Really?" Oskar's eyebrows meet his hairline.

"*Coach* Kessinger?" The man himself swings around to look at me. "What is that?"

"It's who you are." I can still feel his confusion as Lane takes over.

"I get the feeling there's backstory we're missing here."

"Not much," I say. "We played AHL together, were roommates, then he tried to make a move one night, and I panicked. Very standard stuff."

"Standard? None of my teammates ever tried to make a move on me—well, other than Aleks," Oskar says. "And I'm a thousand times hotter than you, Novi."

"Disagree," Kessinger immediately says, and my gaze shoots to him. He's already grinning my favorite smile. "What? You're not going to get all humble on me now, are you?"

Maybe not humble, but my face is heating. "You called me goofy."

"That's what does it for me."

Someone kicks my foot under the table. "Colby's pretty hot too, isn't he?" Oskar prods.

"His face is not symmetrical," I say, hating that somehow that only makes him hotter.

"Good season opener?" Lane asks, desperately trying to change the conversation. He reached out to me after the Stanley Cup game last year, where I met most of the Queer Collective to offer his PR expertise. We've had a lot of conversations about why I won't come out, and he's been unofficially keeping an eye out for any rumors about me.

If I wasn't close to the end of my career and my agent wasn't so good to me, I would have considered signing to King Sports for him alone.

"It was good," I answer. "Beating you guys by one goal was a sweet victory."

"Beating us by one goal when we had all our rookies out there isn't a great sign for the season."

"Don't worry," Kessinger says. "I have enough game tape from the rest of you that you'll be begging to be beat by one goal next time we're up against each other."

"I'll remind you of this conversation when we play a real game."

Preseason might not count for standing, but it is a good way to get into the headspace you'll carry through the whole season. Players can choose not to take these games seriously, but I always do. Whether it's a fun match or preseason or playoffs, I play every game to win.

"Your knees were looking good," Kessinger says, and I force myself to look at him again. No matter how much I don't want to be doing that, he gets my attention back far too easily.

"Not *old?*"

"I didn't say that." He props his head on his hand. "Still old. But much straighter."

"I have been exercising."

"Constantly."

"Isn't that a good thing?"

His gaze drifts slightly. "You haven't changed, have you? You used to train like that when we played together. Always have to be the best."

"If you're not trying to be the best, why bother playing? Mr. Number Ten."

"I dunno, some people play to have fun, Novi. Some people are happy for this to be their career; they don't have to be the best at it."

And that's why teams lose games.

He laughs. "You're thinking about how stupid those people are, aren't you?"

"*Da*. So much for me being hard to read."

"Your condescension comes through the loudest."

"We're going to head out," Oskar says suddenly. "If Ez asks, yes, I tried to convince you to officially join the QC. Told you it could be all hush-hush if needed and that there's no being added to the group chat until you're a member." He surprises me by looking at Kessinger. "You too. If Ezra's going to get a member in every team, he's going to have to be a lot less picky about who qualifies. The teams are made up of more than the people who end up on the ice."

"That's very astute of you," Lane says, standing and holding his hand out for his husband as he looks our way. "We're practically neighbors, so let's not wait until after a game and it's close to sunrise to catch up again."

It's not until they're halfway across the bar that it hits me that them leaving has left Kessinger and me alone. The realization sinks in slow and heavy until I'm sure he's aware of it too.

"Are you in a hurry to run off?" he asks.

"Yes."

The muffled chortle drags my attention back to him. "Can you *not* be in a hurry to run off?"

I shift, turning to face him, and my knee ends up resting against his. "Are you saying you want to hang out with me?"

"There's no one here to freak you out. And if I have to wait until four in the morning in a dive bar to get your attention …" He shrugs. "I'll take what I can get."

"Why do you want to hang out with me?"

"We're old friends."

The challenging way he says that has the corner of my lips tugging upward. "And not because you think I'm more attractive than Oskar Voyjik?"

Kessinger fake gasps, hand over heart. "That almost sounds like you're accusing me of flirting. I would never."

"Never?" I give him a doubtful look.

"Fine. Never where someone might overhear us and jump to conclusions. Unlike now."

Hearing that sets off something jittery inside me. Flirting is completely foreign to me, but knowing that someone wants to do it feels ... nice. More than nice, actually. "What if I don't flirt back?"

"I dare you not to."

"Now who is the one that needs to be humbled?"

"Still you. Always you." He turns fully, breaking the contact of our knees as he tucks his leg onto the booth between us. "Is my face really that unsymmetrical?"

"Very." I can't look at him as I add, "Makes it interesting."

"I'll take being interesting over boring any day." He leans in. "So when did you start last-naming me?"

"What?"

"*Coach Kessinger*? Come on, half the team doesn't even call me that."

Of course he'd pick up on it. "You are coach."

"Colby. You call me Colby. Otherwise I'll have to start calling you Radimir."

"Radimir is a great name."

"It is. But now you're Novi, and I've always been Colby. Why change it?"

I can skirt around the issue all night, or I can tell him the truth. My usual tactics to avoid conversations won't work. He won't give up if I switch the conversation to Russian before pretending to be tired. He'll probably follow me home and keep questioning me through my front door. Colby's always been an open guy, and our friendship bordered on something special before the night we ruined it all.

"It keeps you separate in my head," I say. "Kessinger is my coach. He's a professional. Colby is the man I used to jerk off over."

He chokes on air, and as his surprise melts away, something more intense fills his eyes. "Used to?"

"Used to." As much as I've wanted to touch myself over him since he came back into my life, I have refused.

"Can I … ask you something?"

"*Da*. I might not answer you though."

He's gorgeous when he smiles. The bow in his lips, his hard, scruffy jaw, and the cute lines that appear by his mouth. "You've been closeted this whole time … have you ever had a secret boyfriend?"

I let out a harsh breath. "*Nyet*."

"NDAs exist. What about … hooking up?"

"I do not trust NDAs. It doesn't silence people forever, and if your threat is not strong enough, people will still talk. I will not risk that."

"Then …" He chews on the corner of his bottom lip. "What do you do for sex?"

"I just told you."

"Jerk off?" His gray eyes are bright as they search mine. "Nah … there's no way that's all …" He inches closer. "You've got toys, don't you?"

"A few."

"Does that mean … have you really never been with … anyone?"

Most of the time, I don't let people get this far into questioning me. It's no one's business who I have sex with or if I do at all, but with *Colby*, I think I want him to know. "Yes and no."

"How can it be both?"

"I've never been with someone the way I want to. But I have found a system that works for me. Or … *worked* for me."

"What was it?"

"I sometimes visit glory holes."

"Huh." Colby rubs his rough jaw. "That's kind of hot. I've never done it."

"Lucky you."

"So why isn't it working anymore?"

Because roughly five months ago, Westly Dalton reminded me that Colby Kessinger exists. "What about you?" I ask, ignoring the question. "Do you have a boyfriend?"

"You mean you haven't stalked me on social media?"

I tried, but his accounts are locked up and private. "*Nyet.*"

"Damn. I stalked you the second I was offered this job. Why do you want to know if I have a boyfriend?"

"We've established you don't use glory holes, so I'm working backward with the same questions you asked me."

"I asked if you had boyfriends—past tense. Not now."

"How do you know I don't have one now?"

This time when he leans closer, his leg presses up against my thigh, and that minor contact instantly has my body overheating. "Because I see the way you look at me, Novi. It's the exact same way I look at you."

CHAPTER TEN

COLBY

I hold my breath. It's late—or early, depending on how I look at it—I'm tipsy, and my skin is buzzing. I'm practically shaking with need. All because Novi is looking at me and undressing me with his whiskey-colored gaze.

Encouraging it is dangerous because I don't want to cross lines we can't uncross. He has his limits, and I should have mine. But I don't. Not when it comes to him.

Not when I thought that stupid crush from almost twenty years ago was misplaced. It turns out it wasn't, and he wanted me as much as I wanted him.

Still want him, evidently.

It's either my body wanting to fulfill the fantasy of him, or maybe I had real feelings for the guy, and being in his orbit again has made them resurface. All that's running through my mind at the moment is this is our chance, and my brain won't let go of that. Even if I know it's better for both of us if we don't follow through on this.

Novi sips his water, staring at me over the rim of his glass, and then he places the drink back on the table and pushes it away from him. "Spending time with you is dangerous." His Russian accent sounds thicker as he rasps the words, and his voice travels down my spine and spikes lust in my gut.

"I could say the same about you."

Novi's contemplating it. Us. Hooking up. He glances around the bar like he's committing every person in here to memory in case he needs to track them down and kill them afterward. I wouldn't put it past him.

If it all came out that Novi was sent here as a Russian spy and actually moonlights as an assassin, I'd believe it. Though, it would be impossible to pull it off with his schedule. Maybe his kills take place in the off-season.

"Whatever you're thinking," he says, "it's not a good idea."

I huff because my wild train of thought derailed somewhere around hooking up with Novi. "Actually, if you knew what I was thinking, you'd assume there was something wrong with me."

"I don't kink shame."

This time, it's more than a huff. I have to hold back laughter. "Nothing like that. I was curious if you gave in to temptation and kissed me right here if you'd have to kill everyone in this bar after the fact. Which then made me worry that your angry Russian reputation isn't only a rumor. That maybe you were sent here as a spy."

Novi can't fool me though. He might have those sexy, hard features, the stone-cold face of an assassin, but he can't hide his true self from me. Not when he gives me that goofy smile of his that looks more menacing than like happiness.

"I am big Russian spy. When I'm not on ice, I use my skates as weapon."

"Checks out."

His eyes shine the way they used to. When he wasn't being so serious and dropped his guard.

"It's fun to joke, but you're forgetting I know you."

"Do you? You knew twenty-one-year-old Novi, not grown-up Novi."

I want to keep flirting and tell him how much I've noticed that he's now all grown up and sexy as hell, but I fear if we keep entertaining this and lines do get crossed that we will regret it in the morning.

So I'm going to be the bigger person and leave before it goes too far, but not without one more snarky observation.

I lean in close to him. "You're still the same old Novi. You act tough and joke about being a delightful ray of sunshine, but the truth is, you're not joking at all. Deep down, you're a gentle sweetheart who wants to be loved for who he is."

He sucks in a shuddery breath, and for a moment, I get lost in his eyes and almost forget that I promised myself I would leave. The only problem is he's blocking me in, and I need him to move first.

But no matter how many times my brain tells my mouth to say the words, my lips don't obey. They're too busy thinking about what it would be like to kiss Radimir Novicov.

Novi leans in, and my gut swoops. He's not really … going to kiss me here … is he?

His tongue darts out, licking his bottom lip, and my heart rate kicks up a notch. He is. He really is going to—

Behind the bar, a tray of glasses smashes to the ground, and it's as if the sound of it breaks Novi's spell.

He pulls back, I slump and run a hand over my hair, and then we go back to our respective sides of the booth seat, leaving a huge gap between us.

"I should go," I say. It's late.

Novi nods. Just the once. And then he doesn't move.

"Kind of stuck in here," I point out.

He glances at the table, the seat, and then at me. "Right. Yes. Stuck." Yet, he still doesn't move.

We can't start this loop again, so I shove him playfully. "Come on, Novi. I'm tired. Let me out already."

He slowly stands, and his hesitance to let me go is palpable. There's a pull between us, like an invisible string tying us to one another, but I know if I give in to it and let it happen, that string will wrap around us, and we'll have a noose hanging around both our necks.

It's 4:00 a.m., I'm tired, I'm weak, and it would be so easy to go home with Novi if he asked, but I can already tell by the stubborn look on his face that he's not going to ask. And I'm not going to push.

"I've already sent you game tape from tonight for you to look at. Let me know if you have any questions about it."

"Will do … Coach."

And the spell is broken. I'm back to being Coach Kessinger again.

-

From: Radimir Novicov
To: Colby Kessinger
Re: Watch those knees

Why you send video of my perfectly straight knees?

Sent via voice to text

From: Colby Kessinger
To: Radimir Novicov
Re: Watch those knees

Oh, sorry, you're right. They are straight. About as straight as I've ever been. I'm just warning you. You have two seasons left. Don't blow them by blowing out a knee.

Coach Kessinger

This is what our professional relationship has come down to, and even this straddles the line between a coach-and-player relationship. Nothing is explicit, but they're not exactly formal emails either.

It's all through the team's official emails too, and even though team management wouldn't have a reason to look through our interactions, they still have the ability to, so I have to remind myself to behave. It's probably the only thing holding me back from saying something like he has to take care of his knees because the minute he retires from hockey, I plan to put them to good use.

Ever since that night in the bar, we've successfully avoided being alone together. In fact, the only time we've been in the same room has been during game tape meetings where Ackerman, head video coach, has had me breaking down tape of our upcoming oppositions, so I haven't even had to address him.

I've wanted to, of course. I've wanted to ask him to stay behind, wanted to ask him how he's doing, but we both know we got too close to doing something we'd regret. It's like we've had a silent agreement to stay away from each other.

It sucks, but it's for the best.

And now, going into the regular season, both of our schedules are going to keep us busy.

When I arrive at the arena for tonight's home game, I dump my laptop bag in our office and head for the main desk, where Ackerman is already making sure all our equipment is working. Because we pack it up and take most of it with us on the road with the team, we have to do a check before every game. It's a painstaking task, and I'm happy when someone else has to do it.

"How we looking?" I ask him.

"All good, but our electrical tape is running low. Can you go to the storage closet near the main office and get a new roll?"

"No problem. I'll be right back."

With our office being deep in the bowels of the arena, I have to pass by the locker rooms and players' entry to get to the storage closet for the entire franchise's office supplies. It's mostly a room full of boxes with printing paper and shelves of replacement staplers for whenever they go missing. Which is a lot.

When I started here, I was warned about the faulty internal lock that hasn't been fixed in over a year, so I make sure the door stays ajar once I'm inside.

The electrical tape we need to stick our cables to the floor so no one trips on them is kept on the back row of shelves, so I make my way through the cramped space, not even registering the footsteps behind me or the door clicking closed until it's too late.

I turn around, and there's Novi, his usual happy scowl on his face that I can't even appreciate right now.

"What did you do?" I rush back toward the door, but he blocks me with his wide body.

"You have been avoiding me."

That snaps me out of my claustrophobic panic. "What?"

"You run away every time I walk into a room."

"I do? I thought we were both keeping our distance. Because …" *Because I desperately wanted to kiss you when I knew I shouldn't.*

"Because I am too irresistible. Got it." Such a Novi thing to say.

"So irresistible. I'm a sucker for a dumbass."

"My ass is not dumb."

"Are you sure about that?" I push past him, hating the ripple of want shooting down my side as our bodies brush against one another. I want to stop and rub myself against him like a cat, but we have a more pressing matter than the uncontrollable hard-ons I get around Novi.

I try the handle, knowing it's futile. Novi's happy scowl drops the happy part.

"Congratulations. You locked us in here."

CHAPTER ELEVEN

NOVI

Normally, my English is impeccable, so it takes me a minute to realize I am stuck on one word. "Locked?"

Kessinger groans, dropping his back against the door. "The door is busted. Can you call someone to come and let us out?"

"No." I pat my pockets, knowing full well that Palasook annoyed me, so I buried my phone—and him—deep in my gear bag. "Where is your phone?"

"On my desk."

"Well, we are out of the shit luck."

"Do you mean shit out of luck?"

I struggle to keep my amusement down. That is second tally for him. "Someone will come looking soon. We are supposed to be on the ice in fifteen minutes."

"And you really think they're going to be looking for you in a storage closet?"

"There are stranger things."

Kessinger smiles suddenly, and I forgot how easily that crooked smile captivates me. "You should be used to being in the closet."

"Very snug in here."

"Snug? Feels claustrophobic to me. If we'd hooked up, I would have been forced back in here. No, thank you."

I lean my shoulder against the door next to him. "You say that like it was an option."

"We both know if I'd kissed you, it would have happened."

Those simple words make my brain a mess. Kessinger has very kissable lips, and I've wondered so many times before today what they might feel like. "And we both know," I murmur, "if it had happened, it would have been worth hiding back in the closet for."

"Why are you such an asshole?" he asks in a strangled voice.

"I am stating facts."

"Facts, huh?" His challenging stare meets mine. "Super confident of you to assume you'll be good in bed when you've never actually done it before."

"I have nice dick." It amuses me the way his eyes widen.

Then he buries his face in his hands with a laugh. "You can't say that, Novi."

"Why not, Kessinger?"

"Quit it with the last name, first of all. And second, you can't because … because …"

I catch on. "Because it turns you on?"

He waves a finger between us. "You really saying you get nothing out of standing this close to me?"

I could lie, but the hunger in my gut when I look at him says otherwise. I've never had someone I can flirt with like this, both because I've never trusted anyone enough and I've never been so attracted to someone that I want to. I've thought a lot about it lately. I'd be lying if I said I hadn't found teammates attractive in the past, even ones I roomed with, but the difference is that those attractions could die quickly because I never sensed anything back from them.

With Colby, I could feel it. Maybe subconsciously, but it was like my body knew what my brain didn't.

And now that my body and my brain know both of the same things, every day is a struggle to keep myself from seeking him out. I get high from these small moments together.

"I am a master at self-control," I say.

"You might need to teach me some of that because avoiding you only goes so far."

Feeling evil, I can't help taunting him. "Remember that time when half the team came down with stomach flu?"

Colby's eyes narrow.

"I picture you hugging toilet, and it's enough to cool me off."

"Still not fair that you somehow escaped that," he says.

"My stomach is pure vodka."

"You were only twenty."

"I have had it in a bottle since I was small baby."

It takes him a second. "It's truly terrifying how easily you bullshit like that."

"I don't get to do a lot that makes me happy, so I have to make do with teasing. People make it too easy."

Some of the tension between us lessens. "I'm sorry. That's stupid."

"It is."

"I wish … I wish I could help."

There is one way he could help. One way I've been thinking about over and over. The burning I feel to touch him, to spend the night wrapped around him, is not like anything I've experienced. To get that, just once, would be enough to tide me over forever.

Or ruin me forever.

Waiting until my career is over really should be that easy. I have done it for half of my life already. What's two more years? Unfortunately, Colby Kessinger has given meaning to time, and a day might as well be a year. A year might as well be infinite. How do I wait when the urge to touch him in this moment is already too strong?

"Maybe I quit," I say. "Maybe I move to mountains and drag you with me."

His lips tick up. "This is one of those moments you're supposed to smile, or it sounds like a threat."

"Who says it's not?"

Our eyes catch, and he gives me one of our endless moments.

"Stop looking at me like that," he warns.

"I can't."

"You control your face better than anyone I know."

"*Ty zastavlyaesh' menya poteryat' kontrol'*." *You make me lose control*. My voice is so husky I barely recognize it.

"Novi ..."

With a mouth dry like the desert, I lift my hand. It shakes as it creeps closer to his face, desperate to feel his jaw under my fingertips. Does it feel as hard as it looks? Is his skin scratchy? Smooth? Will my touch do anything to him?

He's completely frozen, and his gaze searches my face as I concentrate on that one small stretch of skin I'm an inch away from. Getting closer. Heart erratically aware of the intentional way I'm about to touch him.

Then I'm falling.

Literally.

I scramble for footing as light blasts over us, and I go ass over. I collide with Colby on the way down, both of us a scrambling mess of limbs until my shoulder and hip land hard.

Our legs are tangled together, and it takes me a moment of panic to get away and push to my feet.

Colby's still sprawled on the hallway floor, gaze in shock and hair a mess, while Ackerman gapes.

"Sorry. I wasn't expecting you to be leaning against the door. And … Novi?"

I turn on my heel and stalk away. My whole face is flushed, and the speed my heart is running at has reached unhealthy levels. There is no way I could stand around and answer questions about why I was in that room after the sudden way I was pressed up against Kessinger. I felt leg and muscle and chest, and maybe too many other things that my brain isn't processing.

That was very, very stupid.

And I'm worried it won't be the last time.

-

Landers, one of my new linemates, sets a round of drinks down on the table. "Your slapshot tonight was something else," he says to me.

It was an easy win against Chicago, in large part because all the tension I have no outlet for had nowhere to go, so Chicago took the brunt of it. I've considered resorting to old habits to get some of this sexual tension out, but a glory hole makes me feel *more* frustrated. It's not only the orgasm that I want.

A message comes through as my team starts talking about the game, and I pull my phone out, expecting to see it's from Ezra.

Whoever it is, I don't have their number saved in my phone.

With a quick glance around the table, I open the message with the screen in close.

It's a video. I tap it to play and watch footage from tonight's game, where Bauer crushes me up against the boards. His forearm presses across my chest, and … the way he keeps shoving me almost looks like he's thrusting against me.

I read the message that came with it, and the pieces click into place.

Should I be jealous?

There's only one person this could be. Normally I hate typing in English and do everything I can to avoid it, but there are too many people here to talk out loud. There is a large difference between speaking a language, reading a language, and then writing in a language. English barely makes sense half of the time when it is spoken, so when it comes to spelling, it is a mess.

Bauer nd I r very close.

Your knees were worse tonight. Is he the reason?

Da. He would not stop pownding me.

Unknown: You call that a pounding? He needs work.

"Look at that smile."

I glance up to find Turkey, Landers, and Everly all watching me. The happiness immediately drops from my face. "What are you talking about?"

"You were smiling," Landers pushes. "I know because it's the first time I've ever seen it."

"Lies. I smile plenty."

"I legitimately thought you were plotting my murder the first few times we trained together."

"I might be plotting your murder now." I force a broad smile, but the three of them recoil. "*What*?"

They eye me with concern.

"That was *happy*!"

"Novi, my man," Turkey says, slinging his arm over my shoulder. "I don't know what *that* was, but happy wasn't even close."

I shrug him off, and it takes a second to work out he's trying to peek at my phone. "Don't snoop."

"We want to know who she is. This is a big moment. I've been on your team for three years, and I've never seen you interested in anyone."

Because I have never been interested in anyone. It did cross my mind a few times to pretend to be dating someone. To find a beard. Besides not wanting to drag someone else into my mess, it also would mean more attention, and I'm very happy only being talked about on the ice.

Some of my other teammates have whole internet sites dedicated to them. Have fan accounts that track their every life moment, post rumors and conspiracy theories. The few I've seen made in my name are very boring.

"It was news article about how I am the best on the team and everyone else is terrible." Their eye rolls amuse me. "It had lots of good points and evidence. I was smiling at how LA is absolutely nothing without me and the rest of you suck."

Turkey's lips flatten disapprovingly. "Figures you'd get all lovesick over work. Bet you jerk off over the thought of pucks and your skates. Do you do it in your full uniform too?"

"*Nyet.*"

They laugh.

"I do it in yours."

Turkey scoops an ice cube out of his drink, and I only narrowly avoid it hitting me as he flings it my way.

"And that is why you did not score tonight. Horrible aim. Maybe you should jerk off over pucks as well."

"The fact I never know when you're joking is a real problem."

This time, my grin is a real one. "Problem for you." I shoot my drink as another text comes through. "Ah. That is another article about my supreme skill. Excuse me as I read more about how I am the best in the universe."

A barrage of ice hits my back as I walk away.

I will miss their love when I retire.

CHAPTER TWELVE

COLBY

"It's your first long road trip with the team," Ackerman says as we check over the video gear we're packing up. "Are you sure you can handle it?"

Ever since he caught Novi and me in that locked closet, he's been somewhat overprotective of me. He thinks Novi followed me in there to make me uncomfortable or say something homophobic, and no matter how many times I tell him nothing like that happened, he's still looking out for me.

I love my new boss for wanting to defend and stand up for me, but he has it all wrong, and I wish he'd trust my word. But I get it. If that is what was actually happening, I wouldn't want to say anything because if they have to choose between a veteran player and a new assistant coach, the franchise will always pick the player.

I wrap a cable around my hand so it can fit in its spot in the hard case. "I've got this."

Ten days on the road with the team. With Novi. Totally got this and in no way have been fantasizing about finding myself in Novi's room in the middle of the night.

I can't be sure if it's pure will, stubbornness, or fate that has kept us from hooking up, but we can't keep going the way we are. Every time I see him, my body lights up, and I get tunnel vision.

I should probably take Ackerman up on his offer for him to go on the road while I work the cutting room in LA because I don't know how much longer I can hold myself back. If how Novi acted in the storage closet is any indication, I'd say he's as close to breaking as I am.

I've contemplated suggesting we should get it out of our systems, but I'm not that naive. Sure, there's a chance we could hook up, get rid of all that building sexual frustration, and then remain friends, but the smarter part of my brain is telling me that if I get the chance to have Novi in my bed, I'll never want to let him out of it.

"If anything happens on the road, I hope that you'll tell me about it."

Ackerman snaps me out of yet another fantasy about someone I shouldn't even be thinking about, and because I'm so lost in my head over Novi, at first, I think he's saying I should tell him if Novi and I hook up. It takes a moment for me to remember Ackerman is worried about Novi for a whole other reason.

"Seriously," I say. "Novi and I are fine. I appreciate you looking out for me, but like I told you, he saw me slip into the storage room. We used to play in the AHL together, and he followed me to say hi. That was all it was."

"When I walked in, he was blocking the doorway," Ackerman says.

And I wasn't complaining. "He was standing in the doorway because he thought he would be smart enough to unbreak the lock. Hockey players, am I right? If it was that simple, we would've done it by now."

Ackerman finally releases his pursed lips to show a small smile. "True. And okay, if you're telling me everything is fine between you two and he wasn't harassing you, I'll leave it alone."

"Thank you."

"But if he did ever—"

"I'd come right to you," I promise.

Even though I don't anticipate having those kinds of issues with Novi. No, if I were ever having to go to my boss to talk about a situation with Novi, it would be that my teenagery crush on him from a billion years ago has made me do something stupid like put my career on the line for a quick orgasm.

I don't want Radimir Novicov to be my downfall, but at this point, it might be too late to stop it.

-

By the time I get all the footage from tonight's game cut and emailed to the individual players, Ackerman, and the rest of the coaching staff, it's late. Whether it's because I'm in a foreign environment and still sinking into my role, or I have a small case of ADND: Attention Deficit Novi Disorder, I'm finally able to drag my ass back to the hotel.

Luckily, we have a back-to-back, so I don't have to pack up the equipment and can walk out those arena doors with nothing more than my own personal laptop.

The arena is empty. Long gone are the players, fans, and really, anyone outside of cleaning staff, and because of that, I'll be able to order a ride without much of a wait, but first, I need to figure out what hotel I'm staying at. It's difficult when on the road to remember each and every hotel on the itinerary. If I hadn't spent hours watching Dallas footage and trying to find weaknesses in their exceptional playing tonight, I'd probably forget which city I'm even in, and we're not even halfway into this road trip.

I pull up the email the PR department sent out with all the information on it and then order a ride share. There's one a few minutes away, so while I wait, I open my messages, hoping there'll be one from Novi but knowing there won't be.

It's silly of me to even check, but ever since he cornered me to ask why I've been avoiding him, I've second-guessed my decision to keep my distance. At the same time, it's not like he has reached out to me. I'm assuming he got spooked with how close we were to being caught—not that we were doing anything—and he doesn't want to risk being seen with me. Then again, I also assumed he didn't want me to reach out last time, and then he cornered me because he thought I was ignoring him.

Why does he have to be so stubbornly confusing?

I don't want to be the instigator. I don't want him to feel any pressure from my side. But if I don't message him, he might think I'm avoiding him or that he's done something wrong.

By the time my car pulls up, I'm ready to bang my head against a wall.

I don't like this. I'm all jumbled up inside, being torn between my wants and my career goals while always worrying about Novi's mental health and his overall safety.

From what Novi has told me, his sister isn't willing to denounce him if he comes out because she doesn't agree with the Russian government's views on homosexuality, but that means she's forcing Novi to stay in the closet. She might not be scared about the repercussions, but he is.

I can't put all the blame on his sister though. Novi's determined to wait until he retires after next season, as if fading from the spotlight will give him a sense of privacy. But what if it doesn't? What if he gets offered a job as a sportscaster—though with his rough English and always messing up phrases, that probably won't happen, but my point is, what if he falls into another job where he can't be himself?

There're so many questions that should have me running for the hills, but all I want is for him to be settled.

It's as if I can feel every knot of unease in his gut. There's no question he wants me, like there should be no question for him that the feeling is mutual. But he also knows he should refrain. I know it too.

So as much as I'm tempted to text him and ask where he's at, I don't. And I'm not going to.

I'm not.

When I get to the hotel, I force my phone into my pocket and continue to tell myself that I'm not going to text Novi.

The elevator doors open, and I hit my floor. Still not going to text him.

I fish out my keycard and swipe it so I can select the 9 button, all the while refusing to give in to the urge to take out my phone.

But texting isn't my only way of contacting him. And it seems he has the same idea.

Because when the elevator opens on the ninth floor and I turn toward my room, I find Radimir Novicov walking toward me.

I cock my head. "Not out with the team?"

He pauses in front of me, a mere few feet away. So close but still not where I want him—right against me.

"*Nyet.* They went drinking."

I nod in understanding. "And you're too old to do that and play hockey tomorrow. Got it."

"Bullshit. I could still drink you over table."

Goddamn the images that wrong phrasing conjures up.

Novi stares at me expectantly, and for a moment, I begin to suspect he mixes up English phrases on purpose. For entertainment.

I wouldn't put it past him.

"Where are you off to?" I ask him, cautiously moving closer.

"Bed."

"But not because you're old."

"I am young and beautiful. Very energetic. Lots of stamina."

And this is why I can't interact with him. If he doesn't know what he's saying, he's adorable. If he knows exactly what he's doing, he's sadistic.

I pat his chest and then curse my hand for doing so. Then I curse my brain for picturing the hard muscles underneath his shirt. "Sure thing. Not old. Can drink me over a table."

"Isn't the saying—"

My eyes widen, and he stops himself.

That son of a bitch does know he's fucking up his words on purpose.

"I mean, uh, I'm saying, I challenge you," Novi says.

"Challenge me? To what?"

His lips curve upward. "To a drinking game. We'll see who's wearing for worse tomorrow."

I'm pretty sure he means worse for wear, but I'm not going to play that game anymore. "And what drinking game do you propose?"

"Quarters."

The way the word falls from his lips has a shiver of anticipation run down my spine. "Are you sure you want to go there again? Remember what happened last time? You got so drunk you forgot who you were for a second."

Novi steps closer to me, and I breathe in the strong scent of musk coming from his clothes. Or maybe it's his aftershave. Either way, he smells intoxicating. So intoxicating that when he stares me in the eyes, I get lightheaded.

Then he says something that has the power to bring me to my knees. "That's what I'm counting on."

CHAPTER THIRTEEN

NOVI

I lead Colby into my room, trying to pretend like this is a casual hangout between friends. I know why I want him here though, and I'm certain he knows why he's here too.

My mouth is dry as I close the door to the darkened room and then fumble for the light switch. The brighter it is in here, the easier it is to face my decision.

"So, quarters?"

I glance over at his teasing tone.

"Should we crown me the winner now, or …"

"It has been very long time since we played. I might beat you."

Colby's chuckle is husky and masculine. "Got any cups?"

I hold his gaze and lift the hat from my head before dropping it at our feet. I'm almost too nervous to speak. "This is how we play." My hand plunges into my pocket, and I grab one of the quarters there. "Who goes first?"

"You. I'm a gentleman like that."

Colby sits, and I grab the bottle of vodka stashed in my bag before lowering myself opposite him. Memories of that night flood back to me. His sweet, round cheeks. The cocky glint to his eyes. How he laughed so freely.

Neither of us is laughing now.

Colby's watching me with the type of curious hunger I feel in my bones. It's about the only thing overtaking my nerves because as much as I want this, I'm scared it won't happen. Or it won't be good. Or I'll forget what I'm supposed to be doing.

He wets his lips, and it takes everything not to kiss him on them right now.

Since that night with him, I have practiced quarters like a man possessed. If someone could play, we'd play, and now, I am quarters king.

Which is why I know, when I take my shot and the coin veers off to the left, that it was on purpose.

Colby gives me that crooked grin as I take a swig from the bottle. "Have you gotten *worse*?"

"I never get worse."

He grabs the quarter, lines it up confidently, and then pauses. Colby's eyes flick to mine for a fraction of a second, right before he takes the shot.

And he misses.

"Ooops?" His fingers brush the back of my hand as he takes the bottle from me. "I'm rusty."

"Rusty. *Da*." I watch the way his throat arches back as he takes a sip and then follows it up with a muffled cough. "That's fucking nasty."

"American vodka is not strong enough, so my sister sends me the good stuff. My uncle makes it."

"I better not miss any more shots, or I'll end up passed out on the floor."

We will stop before then. Much, much before then. All I need is enough of the alcohol to switch off that worried voice in my head. I am a confident, easygoing person, but this is a big thing. A weight I have carried since that night I looked into his eyes and knew my life would always be different. That I would never get to have the free-spirited future I always saw for myself. It has been all secrets, holding back and ignoring my needs above everything else.

I am tired of it all.

Surely I deserve this one moment of weakness.

My next quarter flings off to the right. "Ooops," I copy him. Then I take the bottle, trapping his hand under mine as I lean forward and lift the drink to my lips.

Colby's eyes darken as I watch them and take a long sip. The harsh liquid slides down my throat, warming me from the inside out.

"Your turn."

He gets this one in.

I miss.

And miss.

And miss.

The edge in my personality finally starts to soften.

"You're going to get drunk," he warns.

"There you go underestimating me again."

His laugh is cute, and his eyes crinkle as he buries a hand into that messy black hair. "I don't think I've underestimated you a day in your life."

I lean in closer, wanting those lips and ready to take them.

Instead, Colby flops backward onto the floor. "Don't look at me like that, Novi. You have no idea what you're doing to me."

I only hesitate for a second before I lean over him. "I know."

"Novi …"

I rest one hand by his head, waiting for a sign, anything to say I can move closer. My heartbeat is loud in my ears, and I want this like I have never wanted anything.

The first time I got the courage to visit a glory hole, I was terrified. When it was over, I stood in that stall for way too long, trying to work out what the hell I had done. It was not at all the euphoric high I thought it would be.

I'm not scared now.

Not with Colby.

"You're drunk," he whispers. "You don't know what you're doing."

With a heated look, I reach into my pocket and pull out another three quarters. I take aim for my hat and bounce all three perfectly into it.

Colby's mouth is hanging open. "You …"

He looks back up at me, and when his gray eyes meet mine, I decide they might be my favorite color I have ever seen. Colby's hands bunch in my shirt, and I don't know who moves first.

I dive on his mouth as he arches toward me, and no matter how ready I am, nothing can prepare me for his skin touching mine. I hover for a moment, tasting his lips, feeling the way they mold to mine, the want we exchange with every firm touch …

And then I lose it.

I flatten Colby to the floor, bringing our bodies together, and all that hard muscle under me does more than vodka ever could. His lips part against my tongue, and I forget to be self-conscious, forget I have never done this before. I kiss Colby in a way that feels like the most natural thing I have experienced.

When my fingers twist in his hair, it is as easy as a slap shot.

When our hard cocks rut together, it is as instinctive as slamming a player into the boards.

And when our tongues meet, when he feeds me his hunger and I give him mine back, it's that out-of-body high I felt the first time I hoisted the Stanley Cup.

Kissing Colby might be better than hockey.

The warm blast of his mouth, the strong feel of his tongue, the rough scrape of his stubble against my skin. I'm swimming in an oxygen-deprived bliss.

Seventeen years, I've waited for this. Seventeen long fucking years.

Colby's hands close over my hips and guide me, rocking down against him. I've completely lost control and given myself over to him because this is all too good to think it through. To worry about what comes next.

My free hand finds the bottom of his shirt, and I reach up under it, hand splayed over abs, skin, the light hair that brushes my palm.

I grunt into his mouth, and suddenly, it's wrenched from me as Colby shoves my shirt up over my head. I'm quick to follow him, desperate to feel his bare chest pressed against me, maybe feel if his heart is racing as quickly as mine.

As our mouths come together again, Colby flips us, pressing my back to the carpet and slotting between my legs. His hips are a slow, sensual roll against mine, teasing my cock to full hardness but not getting me where I want to be.

Until he reaches for my fly. He pauses our kiss, just for a second, and I arch up toward his hand. Encouraging more. Begging to move faster.

My zipper slides down, and with one rough hand, he tugs my pants and underwear to my thighs. He goes to reach for his own, but I stubbornly take over. I might not have experienced this before, but I'm a man who knows what he wants, and my nerves have long gone.

My hands brush the hard ridges of his cock as I undo his pants and pull him out. The silky skin is slippery with precum and hot to the touch. He's as achingly hard as I am, and as I stroke my hand over it, Colby's breathing gives a hitch.

His forehead meets mine, and he's panting like I am, breath tickling my wet lips.

"Years …" he says, a hitch in his voice. "I've pictured that night going like this for years."

"Me too," I admit, voice hoarse. "So show me the rest of your fantasy."

Colby spits into his hand and brings our cocks back together. Then he wraps us tight in his grip.

He's confident with touching me, driving my body wild with want, and it reminds me of younger him. Cocky beyond annoying on the ice. Only this time, he has the skill to back it up.

My vision bursts with stars as I tug his mouth back to mine. The kiss is aggressively needy. Our bodies are twisted together, all hard edges and muscle touching everywhere we can physically touch. The way he confidently moves against me, with firm strokes and frantic thrusts, turns me on more than I ever thought it could be possible.

I've never dared imagine this in so much detail. Never thought to picture how his sweat would feel against mine. Never pictured the way our balls would brush or his glutes would flex under my grip. Never imagined his leg hair coarse against my thighs, or the deep breathing, or bruising kisses.

I tighten my hold on his ass, tipping up into his fist, faster and harder with each thrust. My other hand finds his hair, fingers twisted through the strands, keeping him in place as I kiss him like it might be the last time.

It cannot be the last time.

I never knew how much I needed this.

Colby's hips shudder, and his teeth graze my bottom lip. "Close, Novi. So close."

My balls are so tight they're almost painful. "*Da.* I'm ready."

I suck on his tongue as I fuck his fist, chasing something I've never experienced.

An orgasm is one thing. Sex, touching, kissing, indulging in a man's body … I've never been this horny before.

My orgasm builds, burning deep in my gut, cock thickening with pleasure, before it all crashes into me. I moan as I come, filling his fist with my release, and he's not far behind. His whole body jerks as Colby's cum spurts onto my abs. It's euphoric and surreal, lasting long enough for me to remember every smile he's ever given me. Every look. Every pillow he'd throw at me from across the room to get me to stop snoring. And as our past friendship flashes before my eyes, he finally collapses against me.

Hair is plastered to the sweat on my neck, our lungs are greedily gulping down air, and my lips feel bruised. Tender, like he's kissed them raw.

"Holy … shit …" he gasps.

You'd think between Russian and English, I'd be able to find words for what happened, but I'm empty.

He pulls back. "Novi? Are you okay?"

"I am everything. The best sex you have ever had, *da*?"

"*Da.*" He brushes his lips with mine. "Well worth the wait."

CHAPTER FOURTEEN

COLBY

That … was … Nope. There are no words. Actually, there are too many words.

Mistake.

The best orgasm of my life.

Wrong.

Way overdue.

Risky.

Not enough.

And now, as I lie on top of him, reality sinking in, I can't bring myself to pull away. I swear it's ninety percent because I don't want to let him go and ten percent because of how awkward this next part is going to be.

Navigating his regret, my guilt over not being strong enough to stop it … it's going to be horrible. I just hope he doesn't resent me for it.

"I'm so good at sex you can't even move," he taunts.

"I can. I don't want to."

Novi's large arm wraps around my back tighter, and then his lips land on my shoulder. "Then don't."

That's good in theory, but as much as I'd love to live here now, the hotel floor is not sanitary or comfortable.

"I probably should." Slowly, I pull myself up and climb off him.

Novi's stomach muscles contract as he sits up, our mixed cum dripping down his abs, and it's only another reminder of why this was wrong but totally inevitable. He's so hot I can barely stand it, and when he's covered with my release? I'm about to tackle him back to the ground while I still can.

Instead of doing that, I fix my pants, run my hand through my sweaty hair, and then find my shirt crumpled on the ground.

"What are you doing?" Novi asks.

"Getting dressed so I can go back to my room and pretend this never happened." Because it's what I have to do.

But Novi's frown has me pausing.

"You're not staying?"

"I didn't think that was an option."

Novi stands, picking his own shirt off the ground and wiping himself down with it. "You regret hooking up." He does up his pants.

It doesn't matter how hot it was, how much I want to do it again, and that it might have been the most intense sexual experience of my life. If it got out …

"You don't?" I ask.

The shake of his head is subtle. "No regrets." When he holds out his hand for me to take, I can't resist. And when he pulls me to him and crushes me against his wide chest, I don't resist then either.

"My only regret is not being able to do this again," I mumble into his neck.

"Why not?"

I pull back from him. "You know why. You still need to keep a low profile. I need to prove to team management that I can be their next head coach. Or the one after that.

Sleeping with a player my first year on the job? By fucking you, I fucked myself … without lube."

Novi winces, and I close the gap between us again.

"That's not to say I didn't love what just happened. I've thought about it for so long, and I knew taking this position and being around you again would be difficult, but I thought it would be because you hated me. This is … this whole thing between us is … unexpected. And overwhelming. And—"

In the blink of an eye, Novi's lips are back on mine.

It's amazing how a simple kiss can make all the bad thoughts go away. How easy it is to forget about the fight I had to make it to the NHL. Sure, I'm not playing in it, but I gave up that dream years ago. I'm where I'm supposed to be, in the role I'm supposed to be in, and because of a boy I met when I was a teenager, I'm putting it all on the line.

I lean into it and push my tongue inside his mouth, swallowing his hitched exhale as he holds me tighter. He lets me take the lead, his lips pliant under mine, but when we pull apart, it's him who initiates it. I would kiss him all night if I could.

"Our situation …" he croaks. "Not ideal."

"Definitely not ideal." I'm out of breath, and my voice is wispy.

"But I don't want to pretend like nothing happened. I don't want to forget. You're the first man I …"

"First man you what?" I ask, my throat suddenly tight.

"First man I've been with … in this way. Without a wall between us. Without that anonym … aninamy … that word I can't say."

"Anonymity?"

"That one. I've never seen faces. No kissing."

When I'd thought about the lengths he's gone to so he can keep his identity a secret, the anti-Pride drama, the glory holes … I didn't stop to consider—

"That was your first kiss? Tonight? Like, ever?"

He casts his eyes down. "*Da*. In case you were wondering why it was so bad you regretted it immediately."

That is the last thing I was wondering. "It's not because it was bad."

His gaze flicks to mine. "You saying I am bad at kissing?"

I laugh, but it's not really humorous. "Not at all. I love the way you kiss." To prove that, I kiss him again. Yes, proving a point and not doing it only because I want to. Have to. But this time, I make sure to let him lead and let him kiss me how he wants to kiss me.

He pushes me toward the bed, my shirt discarded to the floor once again, and he lands on top of me as I fall backward onto the mattress.

I never would have guessed he'd never kissed someone before. He's not in a rush, not slobbering all over me. It's as if he's savoring every second he can. Tasting me. Exploring my mouth.

And to think I'm the only man he's ever kissed? The only one he trusted enough or wanted enough? Maybe losing my job might be worth holding that title.

I don't think I've had a proper make-out session since I was a teenager, but I'm not going to stop him. He should get to have this.

I run my fingers down his back, his muscles contracting under my touch. He's so strong, so big.

His mouth breaks away, and then he lays his head next to mine while muttering, "You're going to be the death of me."

"Literally? Like if Russia finds out what you're doing?"

Novi rolls off me and onto his side so he's facing my direction. "Technically, Russia decriminalized same-sex relationships decades ago, so no, they won't kill me. But they have laws about gay propaganda and not exposing children to it. If I come out and then go home to Russia, I could be arrested. If my sister doesn't denounce me as her brother, she can be arrested."

My heart hurts for every queer person who happens to be born in his country.

"I said you will be the death of me because I can't help myself when I'm around you."

"I could say the same about you. You might be the end of my career, but that didn't stop me tonight."

"This is why you regret it?"

When I really think about it, I can't regret what we did. I'd fantasized about it way too long and way too hard to turn it down. I do regret not being able to hold out two measly years, but I don't regret him.

"There's only one thing about tonight I regret," I say. "And that's not knowing you'd never kissed someone before. If I had known, I would've made it special."

"It was special."

"How was it special? It was quick and lustful. It might have been passionate, but it was more about sex than the kiss."

"It was special because it was with you."

Damn, if that's not the most perfect thing he could've said.

-

I set my alarm for 4:00 a.m. so I could get back to my room without anyone seeing me sneak out of Novi's.

Even though I was adamant we couldn't hook up again, I'm not entirely sure I said that out loud. If the way he pulls me back to him and kisses me when I try to slip out of bed is any indication, I either didn't voice it, or he's ignoring it. Or maybe he thinks because I haven't left yet that this still counts as the one hookup.

Either way, I have to go, and I will.

In a minute.

Any minute now.

Damn it. I force myself to push him away from me.

"If we keep this up, I'll be stuck in here until the team is all on the ice."

"I don't see problem with that."

"Ackerman will ask why I'm not in the video room doing my job."

"Mm, quit your job."

He's joking, but there's a real possibility I might have to if we're really going to do this. Maybe there's a hockey academy I can coach at in LA.

I shake that thought free because contemplating quitting my dream job, all because Novi wants me, is a terrible idea. "I wish there was a way to postpone it, at least. I should've asked the team to come back with an offer in two years."

Though I wasn't to know that in getting my dream job, I'd get my dream man as well.

Not to say I actually have Novi. One closeted forbidden hookup doesn't scream epic romance, but it's obvious we both want more. Maybe not a relationship, but more sex.

The question is, how much are we willing to risk to make it happen?

"But then you would not have been my coach, and this would not have happened." He's thinking the same thing I am.

As much as I love the thought of not having to deal with the stress that comes along with being attracted to someone I'm not allowed to date, I can't say that I really do wish this job had been delayed.

"Last night was amazing, but I have to go before anyone can see me sneaking out." I lean in and kiss him with a closed mouth because if our tongues get involved, I know I won't drag myself out of this bed.

Novi falls back on his pillow and sighs. "I know."

"Go out there tonight and kick some ass."

"Will do."

And when he does hit the ice later on in the evening, and I'm in my hidey-hole with a million different camera feeds on my screen, I watch as Novi has the best game he's had in a long while. Possibly the last few years.

Does … this mean if I make every guy on the team come his brains out, we'll have a winning season?

I'm going to make sure Novi knows the magic on the ice tonight came from my dick.

Best coach ever award goes to me.

CHAPTER FIFTEEN

NOVI

I hope Colby is watching. It's his job to, so he will be, but I hope he's really *watching* watching. After my amazing follow-up game in Dallas, I decided I'm going on a streak. Since that game, I've kicked Utah's ass, and now we're in Colorado, and I'm planning to annihilate them. All for Colby.

I am showing off for him, and that has breathed new life into my game. Tonight is one of the funnest games I have played in a long time. My skates have wings, my hits don't miss, and I sank one motherfucker of a goal.

Unfortunately, Colorado is also having a solid night. We're two for two, and while an easy win is always good for the team, I love the intensity. The chase for the W. Having an opponent worthy of a fight is one of my favorite things about the game. Every team has good and bad nights. Easy and hard-fought wins.

Easton Kikishkin is out to prove himself without his big brother on the ice to protect him anymore, and he's had one hell of a preseason. There was much speculation that the Kiki brothers' magic was over and that it would affect the middle Kiki brother this season, but Easton is as stubborn as me.

He's put those rumors to bed.

Played hard.

It is unlucky for him that I am better.

We pull up for a face-off.

"You watch," I tell him. "I will win the puck, and we'll score off it."

"Good luck."

"I don't need your luck." I set up in position. "I am just going to do it."

Easton's eyes narrow as he leans forward and touches his stick to the ice, but he redirects his focus a millisecond too late. That's how fast things move in this game. How easily a split-second mistake can cost you the win.

The puck is released, and I swipe it out behind me to Timbrook. He shoots it across to Turkey, who passes back to Landers, who I'm prepared for as I shoot along the side. Landers hits it into the boards behind Colorado's goal, and it loops around to me.

Easton's on me, and I get the puck out right before he flattens me so hard I almost lose my skates. Timbrook recovers, passes to Turkey, who passes it right back.

I'm covered in sweat, glutes burning, almost done with my shift, but I've caught the scent of the win. I'm not leaving this ice until we're ahead.

Colorado gathers around their goal, and my team makes fast passes between them. Quick as I can, I duck behind the Colorado goal, and Turkey is ready for me.

As soon as Lander's pass hits his blade, he flicks the puck off the ice and sends it my way.

The puck shoots hard and fast toward me, and before Flores can turn, I clip it in midair and redirect the shot into the top right-hand corner.

The lamp lights up, and I roar with adrenaline and then point Easton's way. "How you like that, sweetheart?"

He mouths something angrily back, but I'm impossible to ruffle. I hit the bench, and the next line takes over, glee flooding through me that Colby would have seen that.

I think when I get back to the locker room, I will text him that the goal was dedicated to him. He will not be able to forget it with how highlight reels will cover it for at least the next few days.

-

My hat is pulled down over my still-damp hair as the journalists run through their questions for the post-game presser. All I can concentrate on is that this is the same hat that led to having sex with Colby Kessinger, and my lips keep tugging upward at the memory.

"Novicov."

I glance toward the woman who's started her question.

"You looked like you were enjoying yourself out there. What was the difference tonight?"

I dip my head toward the mic. "I enjoy myself always." If I have one rule for these moments, it's that I will never give people anything they can use against me. My sound bites are bland and sometimes taunting but always at surface level. I do not want to be memorable or to have people looking at me for anything beyond how I play. So I play well, and then I play with them and their questions.

She pushes for more. "Yes, but you're not known as the angry Russian for nothing. You almost broke the internet when you laughed at Easton Kikishkin."

"I was amused."

"What about?"

"He told joke." It's harder than usual tonight to disguise that I'm messing with them.

"What was the joke?" someone else asks.

"His playing."

A chuckle goes around the room, and I know they'll use that. The next question is for Coach, and I think I'm free from attention, but apparently, Colby is right when he says I'm hard to read because they're not letting this curiosity drop.

"There's speculation that you've started a friendship with Connor Kikishkin. How do you think he'll react to you taunting his little brother?"

This question takes me off guard, and a shadow of the familiar panic at being found out creeps up. I knew that crossing the line and being seen with the Queer Collective members was risky, but I am being careful about a public friendship. The only time they could have seen me with Connor is during the Stanley Cup final in his rich boyfriend's suite, so as much as my brain immediately wants to assume I've been found out, I remind myself that they know nothing. That being seen with him one time isn't going to out me.

"He will be pissed." I shrug. "Hopefully."

"Lucky he's not playing anymore, huh? He's got a protective streak when it comes to his brothers."

"Connor Kikishkin is like a little bug. I am too big to worry about bugs."

"But you're friends?" someone else pushes.

I remind myself not to panic. This is fine. Standard stuff. Connor is not out, and no one knows Ezra Palaszczuk has claimed me as his bestie. So I resort to old tricks. "I do not understand this *friends*."

"Friends, as in you talk and hang out."

"Hang what out?"

"Hang out as in socialize."

Someone else jumps in. "Do you hang out with his brother too? It's no secret you don't agree with his sexuality."

Then another. "How did this friendship start?"

And another. "How do you feel about the news Connor Kikishkin is retiring?"

The questioning is coming faster than I'm used to, and I can't figure out a way to twist their questions. So angry Russian, it is. "I shoot goal of the season, and you want to trade petty gossip? No surprise print media is dead."

"We're asking what our audience wants to know."

"All your audience wants to know is that Radimir Novicov kicked ass tonight and made show of Kiki brothers."

A smarmy-looking man in the front row jumps in. "Do you think you unfairly targeted Easton Kikishkin on the ice?"

"I target everyone on ice."

"You seemed to have a real aggressive streak when it came to him though."

"First you say I am having fun, then you say I am aggressive." I throw my hands up. "This does not make sense."

"Maybe you were having fun *being* aggressive toward him."

"I was having fun *winning*. I like to win. I like to play hard and prove I am the best. Which I am. Even though they are not in my league, I have much respect for Kiki brothers. I can enjoy rough play on the ice and then be friends off it."

"So you *are* friends with Connor Kikishkin?" someone in the back pushes. "And you respect Easton, even though he's openly gay?"

My throat closes over at the word. "I … uh … I …"

"Let me guess, you don't speak English?" another voice pipes up, and the room fills with laughter.

My face burns.

Heart beats faster.

This is the point I'm supposed to deny friendships and turn us back to hockey, but I can't make my mouth move.

And then Coach takes the chance away from me.

"Are you sports journalists or gossip columnists? If that's the hockey talk finished, we're done here." He stands and nods at me to do the same. There's a disconnected sort of lightness to my limbs as I push my chair out and trail after him, out of the press room and into the hall.

He pauses as soon as the door closes behind us and sets his hand on my shoulder. "You okay?"

"*Da.*"

"Don't worry about those jackals," he says. "They only want a story."

"*Da.*"

"Novi …" He studies my face. "Why'd you let them ruffle you like that?"

"I am not ruffled." The feeling in my chest is very ruffled. "I do not like talking to stupid people."

"You and me both, but you're usually a lot better at it than that."

I don't answer.

"You let them get to you. Now, I don't know why, but do I need to?"

Does he? After six years of playing for Whelan, I trust him completely. I could tell him. Let him know I'm gay and it can't get out. He'd support me and make sure it happened.

Our PR team aggressively going after rumors would only open more questions though, and it's easier to ignore my heart and who I am when absolutely no one knows about it. The last thing I want is for Coach to treat me with kiddie gloves.

"Okay," he eventually relents. "I'll chalk it up to a long night and exhaustion. But if you're ever asked that question again—about whether you respect a gay man—the answer is *yes*, Novi. Easton is an incredible player and so many other things than his sexuality. No matter what your beliefs, the answer is goddamn *yes*."

He stalks off, shaking his head, and I know he's disappointed in me. Which might not be so bad if I wasn't so disappointed in myself.

I get back to the visitor locker room, where most people are in their suits already, and try to avoid eye contact with anyone. Turkey is oblivious, though, and can't read my mood because he comes over and grabs both my shoulders from behind, giving me a shake. "Ready to go celebrate?"

"*Nyet*."

"*Nyet*? Fuck *nyet*. We're going. And we won't take *nyet* or no or fuck off or Russian death glares for an answer."

"I do not death glare."

He snorts. "You're doing it right now."

With a huff, I glance around the locker room to make sure no one is listening. "The press conference was not fun."

"What?" He drops onto the bench beside me. "But we won, and you played like a beast. What the hell did they have to come at you for?"

"Easton Kikishkin."

"But we smashed him. I don't . . ." Turkey trails off, and I know he's gotten it.

"I do not need lecture," I say before he can start.

"No lecture."

"You lecture me with your eyes."

"Oh good, you're rubbing off on me."

Instead of getting changed into my suit, I sit down next to him. I am tired.

"All I'm saying," Turkey says lightly, "is you've been here for . . . seventeen years? Eighteen? A hundred?"

I give him a *stop talking or die* look.

He does not listen. "Your time in Russia and your time here are pretty much split by this point. You have a lot of great things you're holding on to from your days in the old country, and I get why you love it and feel that allegiance to Russia, but . . . do you really have to hold on to the bad things from there too? People are just people." His tone takes on a begging note. "Come on, Novi, you know that."

I do know that. It's the part that makes me want to scream.

"What would you do if I was queer?" he pushes. "Cut things off? Hate me? After everything we've been through together?"

I hunch over and set my elbows on my knees, staring at my hands clasped between them. "People willfully misunderstand me."

"Didn't answer my question though." His tone tightens. "So I guess that's my answer."

My brain is screaming at me to reassure him. It would be easy. Simple. *We'll still be friends if he's gay*—admitting that doesn't hint at anything about me, except maybe clear my name of being a homophobic asshole. Even though I know all that, my mouth refuses to work.

Turkey stands up before I can get a word out. "You know what, Novi? I'm definitely straight, but maybe I'm the one who should cut things off. All this time, I thought people were wrong about you. That there was more to the story, or maybe you needed time or someone to help you understand. I had your back with that shit, man, but I guess I was making excuses for your terrible behavior." He glances back at me. "My sister's trans, by the way, dickhead. Her, Coach Kessinger, Easton Kikishkin, and everyone like them exist. And they deserve to do that with respect. Go whine about being misunderstood somewhere else."

And as casually as he says that, he walks away. All I can do is stare after him with hollow eyes, wondering at what point any of this actually gets easier.

CHAPTER SIXTEEN

COLBY

Whether it's because I'm a former hockey player and understand superstition, or maybe I'm using that as an excuse, either way, while Novi's on the precipice of a hot streak, I have been going straight from the arena to my hotel room and staying there. I don't want to be responsible for killing his possible streak. Even if I'm the one who totally created it to begin with.

Novi hasn't come to me either, and I'm deluding myself that he either listened to me when I said it was too risky for us to do it again, or he is also a believer that having sex again could undo the good luck having sex gave us to begin with. We're all about superstition, us hockey players.

Yup. All superstition and not at all insecurities over the real reason we might be staying away from each other.

Tonight, though, after that shitstorm of a press conference, I yearn to go to him and make sure he's okay.

The problem with that is the team is out who-knows-where celebrating their win, and if he is in his room, he's ignoring my knocks. And texts and calls.

I didn't catch the whole press conference as I was cutting tape, but I saw the aftermath of it when I looked at my phone.

Reporters sensationalizing what really happened. Novi says he respects the Kikishkins, but because he flat out refused to say he was friends with Connor, they assumed it was because Connor's brother is gay, and therefore, Novi is up to his old homophobic behavior again.

The comment section on all of them is a mix between hating on him and support for him standing strong against the woke agenda.

As a gay man, I should be flattered so many people want to stick up for me, but when they're only getting half the story, they don't have a full picture of who Novi really is. That, combined with the blatantly homophobic comments, and there's a gnawing ache in my gut that I haven't felt in years.

I wish I could say that coming out would be better for him, but I'm not the one who has to make that decision, and who's to say that it actually will be any better?

The potential comments run through my mind as if they're happening in real time: "*I guess it's true what they say: those who protest too hard are hiding something.*" Or "*He is still homophobic because he has spent his whole life hating himself.*"

It's so frustrating that the simple refusal to admit he has friends in queer circles has set off a slew of media drama.

What should have been one of Novi's best games is now being reduced to gossip fodder.

I can't stand around his room all night. Particularly in the open hallway.

When the elevator dings behind me, I quickly turn on my heel and pretend to be typing away on my phone as I head for … nowhere in particular because my room is not on this floor.

"Kessingerrrrr," a loud, sadly not-Russian, hockey player calls out.

I turn to find Turkey, drunk off his face, woman under his arm, and wearing a wide smile. "Atatürk."

"You should've come out and celebrated with us."

"I should have. Thing is, though, no one told me where you were going to be."

"You didn't see us in the bar downstairs when you came in?"

Technically, I did, but there was one person I noticed was not there, so I didn't stop. "Oh. Right. I thought that was pre-drinking drinks. Did … any of them move on? Go elsewhere?"

"No, but they might now. The enemy came looking for Novicov. Probably because of his refusal to be friends with them." He taps my shoulder. "But don't worry. I already told Novi I have your back."

Okay, he really is drunk because he's not making any sense. "What are you talking about?"

"The Kinishpkins. They came in looking for him."

"Easton?"

Turkey sways on his feet. "And Connor. And a dude who looked a lot like that young owner dude from Colorado. Oh shit, do you think they're here to try to sign Novi? Wait, that wouldn't make sense. I heard the owner is as gay as … well, you. You two should date. And then—"

I turn to his date as he continues to ramble things like happily ever afters to give the world hope, and I say, "Maybe you should get him to bed."

"Right," he says. "Bed. That's where I was going. This road trip was long. Thank fuck it's almost over."

Yeah. Thank fuck. It should be easier to avoid Novi's irresistible charm if I'm not sleeping in the same building as him.

"Have a good night." I head for the elevator, still unsure of where to go to find Novi, but with Easton and Connor being in the bar looking for him, maybe they're still there, and they can help me. I wouldn't feel comfortable asking anyone else.

I rush downstairs in the hope they haven't left, but when I get down to the bar, I can't see the brothers anywhere. I also have another look for Novi, but I still can't find that adorably grumpy face. I'm starting to worry.

Then, as I get to the front of the bar, close to the street, I see Connor Kikishkin. He has his phone to his ear, and I can't see his brother or Parker Duchene, but I practically trip over my feet trying to get out to him.

I tap his shoulder, and he jumps, but when he says into the phone, "Ooh, wait," and spins to face me, I try not to be offended by his obvious disappointment. He slumps. "It's not him."

"Novi?"

His eyes narrow for a second. "Hey, you're that new video coach … Kessinger, right?"

"Yeah. Are you looking for Novi too?"

He taps the phone he's holding. "I'm on the phone with Ezra Palaszscuk. Novi randomly called him, saying something about going swimming. Sounded drunk."

"Going swimming? In Denver? In November?"

Shit.

"We'll find him," Connor says. "We don't know how, but—" He sighs. "Of course you do. Drop me the pin." He ends the call.

"What's happening? Drop you the pin for what?" I ask.

"Word of advice. Don't leave your device alone with Ezra. He'll infect it with stalker apps."

"But in good news, we know where Novi is?"

Connor's phone dings, and he looks at the screen. "Hopefully just his phone." He turns the screen toward me to show the location. Its last known whereabouts is inside the Denver Country Club … in one of the water traps on the golf course.

"Let's go."

Connor grabs my arm. "We have to wait for East and Parker to get back."

"From where?"

"No … where?" he says, his voice innocently going up at the end like he's asking a question.

I put my hands on my hips. "Who is Parker Duchene trying to poach from us?"

"I have no idea. I'm retired. They don't talk shop around me anymore."

"I feel like that's a lie, but I would also like plausible deniability if anyone asks about wheelings and dealings of trades and whatnot, so I'm gonna go ahead and get started on walking toward the golf course."

Connor doesn't let me get far. "Wait up. I'll drive you. I'll tell Parker and East to call me when they're done with—"

I cover my hands and sing, "Lalalalala."

Connor laughs and then unlocks a car in the mall parking lot that's next to the hotel. "Get in."

Once we're on the road, I ask, "How did you know Novi was missing?"

"He didn't show up to meet with us at our agreed spot, and after Parker told me what happened in the press conference, I figured he's feeling pretty shitty right about now. So we came to check on him."

"That's what I was trying to do, but he's not answering my texts."

"It's probably difficult if his phone is in the drink."

I purse my lips. "I hope you know that he—"

"He *what*?" Connor sends me a curious look.

"He's not a homophobe."

"I know that. How do you know that?"

"How do *you*?" There's a long moment's pause. "You *know* about him?"

"I think you're talking about the thing I'm talking about. Scary Russia and being on the down-low."

He definitely knows. "Yeah, we're talking about the same thing. I didn't want you to assume the press conference was about you."

"Him hiding himself from the world has nothing to do with me or my brothers. I know that."

"Good. I think he's really struggling with it all."

"Why?"

I glance over at him. "What do you mean, why? Because of Russia, because he was raised to think it was—"

"Not why is he struggling. Why now? What's changed? He's been closeted for seventeen years in the NHL. He only has this season and the next one left. So … why now?"

I wish the answer to that is me, but I'm not that egotistical. It had to have been a long time coming. "Maybe he's so close to the end now, he's getting impatient."

"Or maybe having you back in his life has made him realize he's wasted half of his life pretending to be someone he's not."

Isn't that a depressing thought. Though is he saying he knows about us? About the past, and—

As if reading my mind, he says, "He, uh, told me. About how you played in the AHL together. I figure you've gone on to become an out and proud coach, just starting out in the NHL, and he has spent his last seventeen years hiding. You becoming part of the LA franchise has probably been a wake-up call he wasn't ready to have. You took your path, he took his, yet here you are years later in the same place."

I don't want to be his source of turmoil. I want to be something he can look forward to. Retirement is scary for these guys. Most of them retire in their early thirties, which means they have a whole-ass adult life to lead afterward, and it can be daunting. Budgeting, staying relevant, keeping those revenue streams coming. Novi might be older, but financially, he's going to be fine. It's the other side of him that will have to start over. The side he's never let himself show. Rarely let himself feel.

And I fear that things like those articles tonight are only going to hold him back from getting what he wants: the freedom to be confident in who he is.

CHAPTER SEVENTEEN

NOVI

My toe keeps catching on uneven grass and making me stumble. Someone needs to maintain this stupid golf course better.

I stagger to the side and catch myself before I face-plant onto the green. Actually, crawling feels easier. Crawling over stupid, nobbly, tuffy grass.

It is not often I get drunk, but I suspect tonight I might be close. Either that, or Colorado is suddenly having constant earthquakes.

And making my gut all twisty.

I groan as my hip starts to vibrate. What fresh hell is this?

I reach for it, my other arm buckling beneath me, and my chest hits the ground hard. I'm still spitting out grass and dirt when my hand closes over my phone, and I pull it out. The bright screen is a blast on my eyeballs after all this shaking.

It takes me a minute to blink into focus.

Elena.

A feral noise builds in my throat as I answer.

"What do you want?"

"Considering I have ten missed calls from you, I was going to ask you the same question." The Russian wraps around me

like a warm hug. Speaking it with Ezra is not the same, mainly because his is a mix of broken Polish and Russian.

"I am going swimming," I tell her, rolling onto my back. The stars blur and twist over themselves in the sky, and I can't make any of them stay still.

"You called me … to tell me you're going swimming?"

"Yes. I am depressed."

"And drunk. Don't you play tonight? Or did that already happen?"

"I did. I won."

She laughs. *"You? Or your team?"*

"I suppose they helped. But they hate me, so fuck them."

"Radimir." There's an edge to the way she says my name. *"What happened?"*

"They all assume I'm a homophobe. Me. I piss rainbows, but no one knows, so they say all these nasty things about me."

"Sounds like a medical condition you should get checked out."

"Fuck off."

Elena doesn't rise to my tantrum. *"You know how easily you can fix that? Tell people."*

"I can't."

"No one's going to arrest me. I'm safe."

"You don't know that!" This is the same thing I've been trying to convince myself of all night. I've typed out lots of social media posts that ranged from *I have struggled for so long and now it's time to live my truth* to *I'm gay bitchesssss dick dick diiiiick* and deleted them all. Every time I tried to post, I pictured the police showing up at my sister's door. I pictured her being arrested or fined, or calls to boycott her show, or it being shut down. Her entire life upheaved, all because I wanted to have sex.

"I do, actually. Hardly anyone has been arrested with these anti-propaganda laws."

"There was a doctor yesterday. And this is only what they actually report. I have been following the news."

"Why would anyone care what my brother in another country is doing?"

"You are a pseudo-celebrity and the perfect person to make an example of."

There's a long silence. *"I don't want you to be miserable because of me."*

"And I don't want my nieces or nephews to become a target because of me."

I am a selfish man. Sulking about not being able to have a boyfriend, or keep my friends, or speak up and be a role model for younger LGBTQ kids. Some people in the league do not want all that responsibility, but I do. I want to wear the jerseys, I want to use rainbow tape, I want to marry a man and plaster my husband all over social media. I want to be the *You Can Play* spokesperson. I want other people to see me the way I see Ezra Palaszczuk.

Fearless.

Instead, stupid Radimir Novicov is drunk on a golf course who the hell knows where. I will not be surprised if I pass out and miss the team plane tomorrow.

My whole head swims. *"Come to the States,"* I beg. *"Or Canada. Just come. I will pay for everything. Our parents love it in Canada."*

"Yeah," she agrees. *"They said."*

"I'll buy you a nice place, and we will get the kids into the best school and—"

"Uproot them from everything they know? Separate them from their friends? From Ivan's family?"

"Then denounce me. I will come out, and you'll tell everyone you hate me, that I'm misguided, and everything will be okay."

Her sniff is the first thing to let me know she's crying. *"I can't do that."*

"It will be lies. I'll know it."

"You're my brother!"

"And I am miserable." There was a very brief time when it looked like Russia was heading in a positive direction for queer rights. I'd hoped, waited, assumed it was only a matter of time before I could come out and everything would be okay. I almost did it at one point. But slowly, things are going backward, and I've had to watch as the country I love so much works to criminalize my existence again.

I'm lost. There are too many choices to make, and I'm paralyzed that I won't make the right ones.

It shouldn't be this hard.

"Just come out," she whispers. *"You handle your life, and I'll handle mine."*

"It doesn't work that way!"

She might think the possibility of anything happening is slim, but it's still there. Even a slight chance is too much of a chance, and if something *did* happen because of me, I'd never forgive myself. Things have already gotten worse—there's no way to tell that it won't get worse again.

"You're so stubborn," she pushes. *"Stop trying to put it all on me."*

"You're forcing me to."

"I'm not forcing you to do anything."

She doesn't get it. She hasn't lived outside of Russia before, so she has no clue what it's like in the rest of the world. She's happy and safe there, for now, but what happens when she's not?

Elena has always believed things work out happily and that the world is good, but the world is fucked-up for a lot of reasons, and what I have to deal with is only one of them.

Before she can say anything else, I sit up and throw my phone, hard, fast, as far as I can.

Then I hear the telltale *ploink* of water.

Oh no.

I stagger to my feet and trip over myself as I head closer to confirm with my eyes what my ears heard.

Did I … throw my phone … into a lake?

I stare at the body of water for a long, long time.

Well.

This is a perfect night. Everyone thinks I'm a bigot, I've lost a friend, I'm fighting with my sister, and now my phone has taken a swim. There's no way in hell I'm finding it now.

Which means no money, no way to order a car, no way for directions back to the hotel.

This is perfect.

Tonight is perfect.

On top of all that, I really might throw up. Apparently, I drank *a lot*.

I flop back down on the grass. Screw it. I will sleep here. They can kick me out in the morning after they've ordered me a lift, and I can grab my wallet once I'm back at the hotel. Until then, I might as well sleep off this gut-twisting, head-spinning daze.

I tuck my hands behind my head and close my eyes, trying to ignore the way it makes me even dizzier. My head is so messed up I swear I hear my name.

"Novi!"

Actually, that *was* my name. I peek one eye open, but there's no one here.

Wonderful.

I am being haunted.

"Novi!"

That was *definitely* my name.

I open both eyes this time, and to my left, I swear I see a long shadow.

"If you have come to murder me, you have picked the perfect night for it."

"He's over here!"

I know that voice, and a moment later, I see the face it belongs to. Connor Kikishkin.

"Of course I would hallucinate you."

"I'm honored."

Colby jogs up beside him. "You asshole. We thought you'd drowned."

I look between them both. "I am not hallucinating?"

"Nope." Connor reaches for me to help me sit up.

"Thanks, *friend*."

He laughs. "That interview got you, huh?"

I shake him off. "They did not got me. They got shit."

"And how many bottles of vodka did you need to drink to get to this state?" Colby asks, setting his hands on his hips. On those sexy, sexy hips. Sexy … hips …

"Dude, you're drooling." Connor hooks his arm around me and hauls me to my feet. "There we go. Let's get you to the car."

"My phone is back there."

"In the water?" Colby sighs. "Hold on."

He pulls his own phone out, like he's rubbing in the loss of mine, but a second later, he points to the water. "It's there."

Under the water, there's a soft blue glow.

I lurch toward it, but they both pull me back.

"No way are you going in like that," Colby says as he empties his pockets and passes things off to Connor. "Give me a second."

Then I watch him stride purposely into the lake. The water reaches his knees before he leans down right beside the light and pulls my phone free. He's half-drenched when he climbs back out again, and as Colby passes over the phone, I grin at him.

"You really do like me."

"Yeah, yeah. Find someone who'll rescue your phone from a puddle of water or whatever."

"True hero."

He taps my screen. "I have no idea if it's fucked or not, but you should probably turn it off and cross your fingers in the morning."

I do as he says. It's supposed to be waterproof, but worst case, I have to buy a new phone. I don't mention how easy that would be after he went swimming for me.

"Are you okay?" he asks like he can't stop himself.

"I am drunk. Everything is wonderful."

"I think that usually means the opposite. What happened?"

"*Moya sestra zanuda.*"

"No clue what you said," Connor points out.

"My sister. She is being annoying."

"That's why you're upset?" Connor asks. He's still helping me stay upright. "You should try having two brothers like Lachie and East. For years, I thought it was their life missions to give me a heart attack."

I would kill for a sibling who understands me the way Easton would. "She is what made my phone go swimming."

"And before that?"

Before that … the memory of Turkey walking away from me hits, and I hate it just as much the second time around. I'm too embarrassed by how spineless I was to tell them about that though. When people think of Radimir Novicov, they think of an excellent player who is kind and fun to be around.

Not someone who can't even support their friends.

"I was sad," I finally say.

"Sad about what?" Colby asks.

"Sad that I am such a good player and everyone else is not."

Connor grunts. "I'm so tempted to drop him."

I wheeze. "You are weak since quitting."

"I'm still holding your dumb ass up."

"Barely. I am holding myself."

He steps suddenly away from me, and the ground falls out from under my legs. For the second time in one night, I eat grass. "Ouch?" Nothing hurts though. The vodka made sure of that.

Connor crouches beside me. "Are we ready to play nice now?"

"I am always playing nice."

"It scares me that you really believe that." Connor helps me get my arm back around his shoulders.

Then, a thought hits me. "Why are you here?"

The look he gives me is pitying. "Because no matter what everyone thinks, we're friends, Novi. Friends show up when they're needed."

Unlike me with Atatürk. "I do not deserve friends."

"I used to think the same." Connor drags me to my feet, and Colby steps in on my other side. "But my people didn't give up on me, and we're not giving up on you."

I glance over at Colby. "Are you giving up on me?"

That gorgeous crooked smile lights up his face. "It's been seventeen years, Novi. Clearly, I don't have it in me. And neither do you."

It's nice Colby thinks that. Because I'm not so sure.

CHAPTER EIGHTEEN

COLBY

I knew Novi was going to take the online comments badly, but this is a whole other level. By the time we get Novi in Connor's car, drive back to the hotel, and then help the practically passed-out big guy upstairs to his room to sleep it off, Connor's phone is nonstop ringing.

We both heave Novi onto his bed, where he gets comfortable. But instead of wriggling up the bed, he pulls a pillow down to him and then proceeds to roll over and snore.

Meanwhile, Connor and I are breathing heavily, and his phone is still going.

"You can answer … that … now." I feel like I've carried a couch up three flights of stairs.

"Can't." He pants. "Talk."

I break into laughter. "Shouldn't you be fitter than this? At least I have an excuse. I'm rarely on the ice anymore. Plus, you're, like, ten years younger than me."

"Novi's a heavy fucker."

Novi slurs something in Russian.

"Who's calling so much?" I ask.

He takes out his phone. "Ugh. Both of them."

"Your brothers?"

"Worse. My brother and my boyfriend."

He taps his screen and holds his phone to his ear, but I'm still tripping over his words. He did say … boyfriend, didn't he? And his boyfriend, not East's? Did I hear wrong?

"Come up to room 1402. We have a … situation."

"You can go if you need to," I tell him.

He waves me off but keeps talking into the phone. "Do you need a key or … That's handy. Thank Turkey for me. Now I don't have to go get you."

Turkey? He went to bed ages ago. He's back downstairs?

I've just about had all the drunk hockey players I can handle tonight.

Connor ends his call and stares at Novi's sleeping form. "He looks so peaceful and cute."

"Now that he's not putting his full body weight on you and rambling about his phone going swimming, you mean?"

"Exactly. He's not scowling at me or telling me I was terrible at hockey. I think this is the most agreeable Novi I've ever met. Hey, Novi, am I the best hockey player there ever was?"

"*Nyet*. Still shit."

Connor leans closer to Novi. "I take back the agreeable thing. Is he sleep talking, or do you think he's still awake?"

"Why? You going to draw a penis on his face like we're twelve?"

Connor's face lights up. "That is a great idea."

I shake my head. "It's really not."

"What do we do with him?" Connor asks.

"Let him sleep it off and wake him in time for the plane tomorrow?"

There's a knock at the door, and Connor goes to open it.

"What's the situation?" Parker Duchene, my future husband, according to Turkey, asks.

And I really do hate to break poor Turkey's gay dreams of us, but by the look of it, Parker Duchene is a taken man.

By Connor Kikishkin. One of his players and the person currently kissing the fuck out of him.

Connor's early retirement makes a whole lot more sense now.

"What happened to Novi?" Easton asks.

Connor pulls away from Parker. "The backlash from tonight's press conference happened."

"Actually, it was probably that a giant bottle of vodka happened," I say.

"Because of the presser."

"I'm … confused," Easton says.

"Why?" I ask.

"Because he's been known as the homophobic Russian his whole career. Why is it getting to him now?"

Connor looks at me, and I hang my head. Connor can think it has everything to do with me, but I don't think it's that. Me and him hooking up is probably a factor, but I doubt it's the main reason.

"I think he's tired. He doesn't want to fight it anymore. But he says he's worried his sister might get arrested if he comes out and she supports him. She loves Russia too much to leave, but she loves Novi too much to denounce him."

Easton rubs his chin. "Huh."

"What's that supposed to mean?" Connor asks.

"It's interesting to me that siblings can be unsupportively supportive in any language. You'd be the same. If someone asked you to denounce me, you wouldn't."

"I'll denounce you right now," Connor snarks.

East grins. "No you wouldn't. You big protective brother, you. Who's a good boy protecting me like a guard dog?"

Families, man. Hooray for being an only child, I guess?

"Either way," I cut in. "Let's leave Novi to sleep it off, and I'll deal with him tomorrow."

They murmur their agreements and head for the door, but before they can leave, Connor turns to me.

"You mind if you keep this a secret?" He waves a finger between him and Parker.

"Of course."

"I figure you'd understand." He glances back at Novi's sleeping form. "And after tonight, I'm guessing you understand more than anyone."

That even if Novi could come out, I still couldn't be the one beside him publicly because of who I am to the team? Yeah. I understand how upsetting that is.

-

Despite my rational side telling me that Novi is a grown-up and I don't need to stay in his room, I don't want him to wake up alone. I also don't want to make him more confused or add to his stress by sleeping in the same bed as him.

And that's how I've ended up sleeping on the uncomfortable day lounge in the corner of the hotel room. I'd contemplated the floor, but I've already had sex on dirty hotel floors once this trip. I wasn't going to bathe in the remnants of all the people who've had sex in this room too.

I don't sleep well, if at all, but it doesn't have anything to do with how uncomfortable the chair is.

My heart yearns while it also breaks for him, and all I want to do is be able to fix everything for him, but I can't. There's nothing I can do but show him he has support.

The other thing keeping me awake is wondering if I'm making things worse by being in his hotel room. Being around him. Being friends. I can't stop being his coach, but if he needs me to step back, I will. I'll stop fixating on him. Stop emailing him other than the footage he needs to review.

But what if … what if he needs me to be a constant in his life? What if I give him something he has deserved to have his whole adulthood? Will that make him feel better or worse about his situation?

Novi groans in his sleep and stirs.

When I look at my phone, I realize it somehow became morning, so I guess I did get some sleep throughout the night. Today is going to be rough for me though.

Not as rough as what Novi has coming his way, but hopefully, coffee will fix both of us. I pick up the hotel phone and order room service, making sure Novi gets a good, hearty breakfast that will either cure his hangover or make him puke. Either one will make him feel better.

He has seemingly gone back to sleep, and I don't want to disturb him, so I go back to the tiny sun lounge I don't fit on and then check the cesspool that is the internet.

With any luck, the presser drama will be over already. News like this doesn't tend to stay around long in hockey circles. NHL players might like to think they're famous, but the truth is, while a lot of people might know their names, they're rarely recognized out there in public. They're not Hollywood A-listers, so their gossip tends to die down quickly.

While there are a few new articles like the ones last night, there's really only one that stands out. Mainly because my face is all over it. And Connor's. And sandwiched between us in a photo that someone obviously took on their phone because it's all grainy is a very drunk Novi.

It was taken in the hotel lobby, but I don't even remember seeing someone with their phone out to take photos of us. Then again, all I was focused on at that point was not dying under Novi's weight.

I'm terrified of what the article says, let alone the comments, and as much as I wish I could not read it and pretend it doesn't exist, I need to know what it says.

"Kikishkin and Novicov Friends After All?"

Okay, that's not too bad. And hey, maybe this is a good thing because it shows—Ope. My thoughts are getting ahead of myself.

When the entire article is about how the queer population are still good people, even to those who hate them, I feel sick. Not only because it's the same rhetoric as last night, but it's also bullshit. I've been in queer circles a long time to know that you can be under the LGBTQIA rainbow and still think one or more of those letters don't belong there. I hate people like that, and they're also most likely the ones to say that Novi is a coward for not standing up to his homeland and coming out already.

Anyone can be a judgmental asshole, and the internet gives them free rein to do it.

Room service arrives, and either the smell or the noise wakes Novi. The hotel worker leaves, and as soon as the door closes behind her, Novi sits up with a scrunched brow and a confused look on his grumpy face.

He seriously looks like one of those memes where a kid is trying to look grumpy, but he's so damn adorable you can't help but say, "Aww."

"Why you still here?"

I hold my heart. "Thank you, Colby, for looking after me last night. Thank you, Colby, for risking hypothermia and fishing my phone out of a lake. Thank you, Colby, for ordering my hungover ass breakfast."

Novi doesn't react because he's Novi, but he does stand and walk over to the table where the food is. "I need vodka."

"As one of your coaches, should I be worried about your drinking?"

"Hair of dog. Best hangover cure ever." Novi's accent is thick this morning. He must be really hungover.

"Sorry. No vodka. You drank it all last night."

"Drank all of it? In this hotel?"

"In the entire United States."

He rubs his jaw. "Including Hawaii and Alaska?"

"Yes."

"Why you lying to me?"

Because I'm worried about you.

I don't say that though. Instead, I lift the cloche off the plate of food and move it closer to him. "You should eat up. We'll have to have our stuff packed for the team bus soon."

He takes the plate and goes back to bed to eat, but as he sits, he eyes me hard. "Why did you stay?"

It's a fair question. Why did I stay? I shouldn't have, but I did.

Novi might be the man I once had a crush on a long time ago, but now, all he is is a risk to my career. A risk I have to be sure I'm willing to take.

If it was a promise of something more, of something other than sex, it might be worth going back into the closet for a while. But he can't promise me that, and I can't promise that if we did start dating that we would last. And then if we didn't, we'd still have to work together, see each other.

Would it be better to step back now and deal with the cravings my body has for him on my own, or do I risk an uncomfortable future at my job to see if grown-up me is still as gone for Novi as teenager me was?

"Colby?" he prompts, breaking me out of my inner ramblings.

I don't want to lie, but I can only tell him a version of the truth. "I wanted you to know that you have my support in whatever you decide to do in regards to the news articles about last night's press conference."

He throws his head back. "So you stayed to babysit me. Is that why you slept on couch?"

"We need professional distance."

"I've never had a coach sleep in my room before."

"That's good. I'm the first one to cross that power imbalance line. Fun for me."

"You know what I mean. To me, you're not my coach. You're Colby first. Kessinger. My best friend in AHL."

I'm trying really hard not to cross the room and dump all his food off the bed so I can tackle him and kiss that delectable mouth the way I did only a few nights ago.

Time is a bitch. A few nights without him have felt as long as the seventeen years I did actually live without him.

Novi forces a full American accent as he says, "Yes, Novi, you're my best friend too."

The sad thing is? I think that's true. Back then and now.

I always thought the best friend feeling I had with Novi was about wanting to jump his bones, but I've had best friends in the past who I've fucked, and once it was over, I no longer felt drawn to them—as a friend or as more.

Since getting off with Novi, all I've wanted is more.

So as much as I think I'm being strong, I'm really not. I'm on the verge of breaking, of throwing everything I've worked for out the window, and for what? A man who can't even acknowledge me in public?

How did this get so messy so damn quickly?

CHAPTER NINETEEN

NOVI

One of the things I love most about my kitchen is how calming it is. Like a cave. Polished cement floors, black cabinetry, and a ten-foot-long milky bench top with deep brown vein running all through it.

Plus, it is always stocked with food.

I hunch over my counter, shoveling chicken and rice into my mouth and pointedly ignoring my constantly ringing phone. Maybe I should have left it in that lake. Every time there is a pause in the buzzing, my whole house presses down on me in comforting silence.

The vibrating goes off again, and Pala-SOOK lights up the screen.

He is not giving up.

I drain my water glass, and when it is still not done, I finally answer.

"*Da.*"

"Bestieeee!"

"This was a mistake."

Ezra's husky laugh answers me. "Why am I reading an article about how you're besties with big Kiki?"

"You jealous?"

"Of course I'm jealous. I'm outraged. I claimed you."

My low chuckle is loud in this room. "I was friends with Connor first."

"With shitty decisions like that, you're lucky you have me."

"So this call has nothing to do with all those drunk photos of me online?"

Ezra makes a strange sound. "What a man does with the other end of a bottle of vodka is his business."

"If it is anything other than drinking it, I don't want it to be my business either."

"Did you want to talk about it though? I feel like that's probably something a best friend should offer."

"Which part?"

"The part where you drunkenly rambled about being stupid and going swimming?"

Nope, I do not want to talk about that. "*Nyet.*"

"Okay, so let's discuss the part where you confessed your undying love for me and Anton had to defend my innocence?"

"Never happened."

"You were all, '*Ezra, you're so sexy and the best hockey player ever. Gretzky, who?*'"

"That does not sound like me at all."

"Sorry." He drops his voice, all deep and angry. "Gretzky, who?"

"That definitely did not sound like me."

From the background, I catch Anton's voice. "Actually, that one did."

"You always need your husband there for backup?"

"It's more that I'm here for your sanity than his," Anton replies.

"If it will make you get off the phone, we can talk about me getting drunk." As much as I really don't want to go there, there's a small part of me that does. I have been keeping it out of mind as best as I can, but even without focusing on it, there's this lurking feeling of wrongness.

"We already were," Ezra says.

"The *real* reason."

Ezra drops his playfulness. "Your coach did you dirty. He should have ended that press conference about six questions earlier."

"I should not have gotten all twisted up."

"They pushed you into it. Those assholes were baiting you to get something homophobic."

It's not like they had to try hard. "Maybe I am homophobic."

He grunts. "Closeted doesn't equal homophobic. You—"

"I had sex with Colby."

Ezra stutters to a stop. There is a long silence before he replies again. "How was it?"

"Incredible. We kissed. I have not kissed a man before."

Ezra breaks into laughter. "Before we became friends, I never would have thought Radimir Novicov was a gossip. Listen to you."

I smile at my empty bowl. "He was very good kisser."

"You wanna do it again?"

"Repeatedly."

"Then go for it."

This is one of the many things I admire Ezra for. Everything is easy for him. Would I have been the same way if I wasn't so worried about my family? If I wasn't raised with the idea that straight was the only way to be and everything else was wrong? "I am very confident on the ice, but for this, I have no idea. What if he doesn't want to do it again?"

"From what big Kiki said when I called him to tell him to back off my bestie, I don't think you need to worry."

"Now look at who is gossiping."

"Yeah, but people expect it from me." Ezra has a point.

Though I don't know why people don't expect it from me when I am always having cute gossip huddles with my teammates. I can't hold back my next question. "What did Connor say?"

"That your coach was all heart-eyed for you."

"He said that?"

"Well ... no. What he actually said was that he thought he was picking up on a vibe between you two, and since I'm an amazing best friend, I told him he doesn't know what he's talking about. But if there was enough of a vibe that Connor-I'm-so-straight-Kikishkin could pick up on it, you don't have to worry about Kessinger."

Somehow, that terrifies and excites me. I hate knowing we are so obvious but love that maybe he's thinking of me the same way I'm thinking of him.

"What should I do?"

"Taunt him until he shoves you up against a wall and takes you there and then?"

I'm concerned by how easily that came to him. "That is not a thing that would ever work."

"Ah, yeah, never," Anton mutters somewhere in the background.

"Do I text him?"

Ezra makes a noise of disgust. "Seems sort of basic and normal to me, but be boring if that's what you want."

"Colby will like it."

"Urgh, he's boring *too*? Where have all the fun people gone?"

"I am very fun. I went swimming last night."

"No, you tried to go swimming. Your phone is the one who made it. I was about to give up calling in case it was broken."

"You give up?"

"Only when Anton promises sex."

From how they both talk, the need for it does not lessen. If I reach out to Colby, that might be a mistake because then if I get it again, will it help? Or will I keep wanting more? We could keep things quiet. Private. But is that something he would even want?

"I need to message him. We will talk later."

"Before you hang up," Ezra rushes out, anticipating me. "Love you." He is mocking, but he won't let me go unless I say it back.

Little pest. "*Ya tozhe tebya lyublyu.*" *Love you too.*

We end the call, and I agonize over what the hell I'm supposed to text Colby. It might be boring to Ezra, but my nerves are running high. It's like I'm on skates for the first time when I hit the speech-to-text button. "What are you doing?"

That doesn't give anything away, and if he's busy, I can leave it at that.

He doesn't keep me waiting.

About to pick up lunch.

That doesn't tell me anything. Technically, he is busy, but is he only picking it up, or is he eating it with someone, or … or … I scrub my hands through my hair and pace to one side of my kitchen and back again. I activate and deactivate the speech button a few times but still have nothing to say.

You hungry?

I glance over at my empty bowl, think of my fridge stocked full of meals, then hit the button again. "I'm starving."

Burritos are on their way.

My nerves soar. This is promising. We can talk when he gets here and work some things out. At least face-to-face, Colby will not be able to resist my boyish charms.

The whole house is spotless, so I have nothing to do to release some of the restlessness taking over me. After signing multimillion-dollar contracts for close to twenty years, I can afford a big house and people to look after it for me while I'm gone. This might be the first time I hate that they do their jobs so well.

I glance over at the little pink bunny sitting on my mantle that my niece Mishka sent me for Novy God and am hit with guilt again. My sister and her family have only visited me a handful of times, and I used to go back there every off-season but haven't made the trip the last two years. Mishka calls me her *Zaychik*—her bunny—and by following this path to Colby, owning who I am, I have to come to terms with the fact I will never be able to go home again.

Probably ever.

Most people cannot understand why I love Russia so much, but they do not understand growing up there. The sense of community in the town I lived in. There's a small part of me that doesn't blame Elena for not wanting to leave, but it's being quickly drowned out by the part of me that wants to shake her.

All she has to do is denounce me, goddamn it.

My phone buzzes with another text.

> Are you going to send me your address or am I expected to guess?

My face floods with heat as I quickly reply. I have been waiting here for nothing. It takes way too long for my front gate to alert me to a visitor, and when the gate slides open, I head to the door and wait for Colby.

He pulls up in his black E-PACE, and when he climbs out, I forget to be guilty. I forget to worry about consequences.

His black hair is slicked back from his face, sweet lines settled on his forehead, sunglasses blocking his eyes from my view, but not that goddamn crooked smile. He cradles our burritos in one big hand as he hits the lock button on his keys with the other.

"This is showy," he says, nodding toward the house.

"It was well below budget," I reply. Then I kick myself because I sound stupid.

Colby breaks into laughter. "I don't think you're supposed to say that about a place that most people will never afford in their lifetimes." His feet slow as he reaches me, hovering right in my space. "You said you were starving?"

I clear my throat. "Ravenous."

"Let's go inside and get you fed."

CHAPTER TWENTY

COLBY

Me: I should keep my distance from Novi and only see him in a professional manner.

Also me: Want me to bring food to your house all because you messaged me the equivalent of a booty call text?

What am I doing, Novi? That's what you wanted to know? *I'm driving myself crazy thinking about you. Wanting you. Trying to convince myself that I can't have you.*

Yet, here I am, unable to stay away. It's as if I don't even want my job anymore.

"You are quiet," Novi says as we eat our burritos.

"Can't talk. Eating." I shove a big bite in my mouth to prove my point.

"Good, then. Because I have a lot to say."

I want to tell him that he doesn't have to do this. He doesn't need to explain why inviting myself over to his house is only asking for trouble. I know but did it anyway. But because I had to go and shove so much food in my mouth at once, I haven't completely chewed and swallowed it all, and Novi beats me to talking.

"I … I want something with you."

A chunk of meat gets stuck in my throat, and I cough. I bang on my chest until I'm able to swallow it down.

I wasn't expecting him to say that, and I don't think he was expecting my reaction to it. He frowns. It's not his usual grumpy face he pulls when he's trying to look mad. It's a questioning look—one asking if he fucked up by putting that out there. I don't want him to be insecure about doing that, but what the hell are we able to do?

"Can I clarify here because, you know, language barrier. Y-you want something with me? Or you want to do something with me. Like go somewhere. Do something."

"My English is not that bad anymore. I want … to … date you."

I try to hold in my frustration because he's putting himself out there, and it probably took a lot of guts to say that to me. "And what does that look like to you?"

"Okay, my English is bad. I don't know what you're saying."

"If this was happening two years from now, I would jump at the chance to date you, but … we can't."

"Is it because I'm not out?"

He had to have been doing a lot of thinking about this to come right out and say it, and I hate being the one to dull his excitement. It's not possible though. As much as we want to be together, there are too many reasons why it wouldn't work. "No, of course not. That's not an issue with me, and if we were to do this, I would understand that while you're still playing hockey, it would have to be a secret. I would be going back into the closet. And I would be okay to do that for you. But … it would mean putting my career on the line for it. If anyone found out a coach was dating a player … the power imbalance, it would—"

"What if I only ever top you? No power imbalance."

As much as that makes my dick hard and my ass plead for it, I can't help laughing. "Sure, let's go to team management with that when they try to fire me."

"Team management? We can't tell team management."

"That's my point. We wouldn't be able to tell anyone. The Collective would be safe, but anyone outside of that can't know, or it puts both of us at risk. I'm risking my career, and you're risking having the one secret you've kept for so long being revealed before you're ready. Sure, we could be careful. We could sneak around. But if I'm seen coming or going from here or someone on the team catches me going into your hotel room on the road, it's all over. It only takes one person to see something or to suspect, and everything we've both worked so hard for could go down the toilet."

"So you are saying you don't want me." Novi presses his lips together.

"You have no idea how much I want you, but I'm not willing to risk it all on a maybe. I know having sex with you again will only make me want more, and then I'll become addicted, and then eventually, something will have to give. The more I want you and the more chances I take to see you, the higher the risk. I'm not sure if I'm willing to put my entire future on the line." He's being honest, so I have to be. I'm so torn it hurts. "Are you?"

Novi hangs his head. "Ezra was right. Maybe I should have answered door naked so you could not resist."

He says that like I'm able to resist him as he is.

"Ezra gave you advice about me?"

"He is very wise. He got someone as hot as Anton to love him, even with his annoying personality."

"Unlike your sunshiny disposition that everyone loves so much."

"Exactly. Ezra is lucky I was not out when Anton was free."

"Still as delusional as always."

"I'm not delusional about you," he says, and his confidence about that is both warranted and a little sad. For me. Because I'm trying to be good here, and all he's doing is tormenting me into doing something stupid.

"You're not, and it's true I want to date you too. I want to see if this thing that I felt for you a million years ago could actually be something. But I *need* you to be levelheaded about this."

"I am always levelheaded."

"Uh-huh. Here's where I don't mention the other night on the ice when you were tripped, and instead of taking the power play, you instigated a fight and got two minutes yourself?"

"He pissed me off. I was going to score."

Despite the serious conversation, at least he's still able to make me smile. Even if he's being infuriatingly shortsighted.

"Being in a secret relationship won't be easy, and we both have to be okay with the consequences if it gets out. If you can agree to that, then I will let you take me on a date. Of course, it will have to be either here or at my place, and we'd need to make sure no one could see us hanging out at the arena. Or on the road."

"We could say we're friends."

"Last time you admitted to being friends with someone in queer circles, you threw your phone in a lake."

"I was teaching it how to swim."

"I want you to really think about us and decide if I'm a risk worth taking."

I've pretty much already made up my mind. If I do screw up my first year as an NHL coach by dating a player, maybe I'll be able to go back to college hockey. There are other paths I could take if I had to. I don't want to, but my life won't be over if my screwup gets out.

If Novi's secret is revealed before he's ready or before his sister decides to either denounce him or leave Russia, I can't say the same for him. He would never forgive himself if he brought harm upon his family.

"Okay," he says and stands from the table. "I will think about it." He balls his wrapper up and throws it in the trash can all the way in the kitchen.

I hate that he doesn't miss, but I also hate how hot I find that.

I take my last bite and don't bother trying to do the same with my wrapper. I carry it over to the trash like a grown-up.

But when I turn back with the intention to get my stuff and leave, Novi's right there in front of me. Almost chest to chest.

"I have thought about it."

"That wasn't long enough."

"Yes it was, because the answer is simple. I want you. I want you now. And if I have to face the reality I've been hiding from for the last seventeen years to have you, then I will. Because I didn't let this happen once before, and I'm not going to make that same mistake again."

How the hell am I supposed to stay strong when he says stuff like that? The answer is I don't.

"Fuck, Novi." I move first, but with his hockey reflexes, he's ready for me when I slam against him.

We're not gentle as our mouths come together, and it takes all my willpower not to rip his clothes off. Literally.

I do not care if I destroy his brand-name sweats or if I do bodily damage while I do so.

My body isn't as conflicted as my head. Not when it comes to Novi.

I used to think about what this would be like. Kissing Novi, having his hard body against mine. I've fantasized about it more than I should admit. But none of those fantasies could live up to the real thing.

He gropes at my clothes, and I do the same as he leads me toward his bedroom blindly. We only pull apart to lose our shirts and then come back together until it's time to ditch the pants.

We make our way through his house, banging into walls, tripping over our pants legs, but it doesn't faze either of us.

We can't get enough.

Novi's mouth is even more confident than the last time we did this, his tongue brushing against mine so passionately I might never want to stop kissing him.

His chest, so wide for a forward, is hard under my hands, but not as hard as his cock trying to escape his boxer briefs.

He moans into my mouth, and it's like I can't breathe. Every rational and logical part of my brain is screaming at me to slow down, but if I do that, then there's a good chance I'll come to my senses and tell Novi he needs more time before making this decision.

Full and logical thought process? Who needs that when you can have hot and heavy man-on-man action that results in orgasms?

Smart decisions going on all around here.

Novi pulls my hips against his, pressing our hard cocks together behind our underwear. He grinds against me as his fingertips dip into my waistband, and he grasps my ass cheek, squeezing hard.

He breaks his lips from mine but continues to rut against me. "I want to fuck you."

I huff a laugh. "If I had known that, I wouldn't have brought over burritos for lunch." I step away from him but take his hand and pull him over the threshold to his bedroom.

It's large but very gray, like the rest of his place, and his super king bed looks tiny in it. Seeing how big it is, though, and knowing how lonely Novi must have been for all these years, never sharing this with anyone else except in some seedy hookup situation where they never even saw each other … suddenly, my rush to get it over with before I can change my mind changes to wanting to give him everything he deserves when it comes to sex.

He's ready for real intimacy, and even though it might break my heart, ruin my career, and fuck me over in the long run, I'm going to give it to him. Freely. Because going through what he has … I wouldn't wish that kind of loneliness on anyone.

"Okay," I turn to him.

He already looks blissed-out, and we haven't even come yet.

I hook my fingers into the sides of his underwear and pull them down his legs. "These can go."

I straighten back up and do the same with mine. Standing before him naked isn't a big deal. We used to do this weekly, though maybe not this close to each other.

"Tell me what you want me to do," he says. Maybe it's nerves, or he had plans to top me and now he can't, so he's unsure of what else there is to do, but it's okay because he doesn't need to know.

"Do you have lube?"

He rubs the back of his head. "Uh, no."

"That's okay. Spit will work. Get on the bed."

When he passes me and I get a view of his amazing ass, I have to bite my knuckles. I have visions of the future, where there might be a day where I get to pull those cheeks apart and dive right in, but Novi deserves better than to rush this.

He gets to have new experiences, and knowing I'm the only one that's kissed him is a high in itself. Knowing I'd be the only one to ever be inside him?

I shiver in anticipation even though that's not on the table today. It might never be on the table, but that won't stop me from thinking about it.

Novi lies on his back, his head propped up on two pillows with an arm bent underneath it.

On full display, he's without a doubt the hottest man I have ever been with.

His chest is hairy with grays smattered in the dark curls. His abs are cut, and his cock is long, thin, and dripping precum onto his happy trail.

My mouth waters, and when I glance up and meet his stare, he's giving me a Novi smirk. It's the one where he's actually amused, but he looks like he wants to murder. "I know. I am fine specimen of man."

If I wasn't so fucking horny, I'd have the energy to dispute him.

Instead, I relent and drop my knees to the end of the bed. "You really are."

He reaches for me, but instead of going to him and embracing him, I bend over and bring my mouth to within an inch of his cock.

I don't take my eyes off him as I lick the bead of precum off his skin and then give his happy trail a soft kiss.

His hard length twitches and hits me in the chin. It would be funny if I didn't want him in my mouth so badly.

I close my lips over the tip and then work my mouth down his shaft. Novi's breathing is stilted, and I have to remind myself that I can't let him blow in my mouth. He's had blowjobs before. This is only a way to drive him crazy so that when his slick cock is buried between my thighs, it won't take him long to cover me in his hot, sticky cum.

I use extra saliva and make sure his dick is nice and wet and then release his cock with a soft pop.

When I glance up at him again, his pupils are blown, and he whines.

"Why'd you stop?"

"Because I want you to be looking at me when you come." I climb up the bed and grab Novi's shoulder to pull him toward me.

He follows my lead and rolls on his side, and when he does that, I reach between us and guide his cock between my thighs while trying my hardest to press them together tightly.

Novi understands what I'm doing and wraps his arm around my body and supports my upper back as he thrusts forward, sliding his cock in and out the tight gap between my legs.

Each move he makes, my own dick gets friction along his abs and hip.

We hold on to each other tightly, but he does as I asked. He doesn't take his gaze off me once.

"I want to see it," I say. "I want to see your face when you fall over the edge."

Novi moans and closes his eyes. His movements speed up, and we thrust against each other frantically. Seeing him like this is a whole new experience. The concentration giving way to need is the most expressive I've ever seen his face, and this weird sort of claimy feeling passes through me as I realize I'm the only one who has ever seen him like this. Novi gives me a side of him that he doesn't share with other people, and I don't know how I got so lucky, but I was right that sex with him isn't enough.

His scent, his touch, the way his head dips so our foreheads brush. I never would have imagined Novi had tenderness in him, but I can't escape it. Not with the way his fingertips stroke my shoulder blades or in how his lips brush my temple. Every exhale feels like he's waited a lifetime for this, and I listen intently as they get faster and shallower.

And just as I think he's about to spill over, I rasp, "Look at me."

He opens his deep whiskey-colored eyes, and then he stills. His lips part, and he shudders a few times, but before he can come down completely, I reach between us again to get myself across the finish line too.

He swats my hand away and wraps his fingers around me, taking over, and the second he does, I have to throw my head back and groan.

That feels so good. So fucking good.

His hand speeds up, and I'm moving toward release like a speed train.

Then, when he leans forward and sucks hard on my neck, I can no longer hold back.

Ropes of cum land between us, and that blinding white heat passes through my body as I ride the wave.

Whether or not this will turn out to be a mistake in the future, it doesn't matter. All that matters is that when I open my eyes again and meet Novi's gaze, he's smiling in a way I've never seen him smile before.

It's official. I'm claiming it.

That smile belongs to me.

CHAPTER TWENTY-ONE

NOVI

One day, I will have many children running through my house. I saw it as soon as I bought this place because it screams happy family home. All those polished floors to protect their little toes, dark walls and cabinets to hide their grubby fingerprints, and overgrown land outside for exploring. A line of happy, dirty faces looking back at me from the other side of the long kitchen island.

I ache for this future.

It is not surprising, though, when I am a very big kid person.

My eyes are closed, and I'm half dozing, picturing my retirement, when Colby stirs beside me. Cum has dried on my pubes and abs, and I know we have to get up, but I am not ready yet. Our talk and the sex have opened more questions than it answered.

Starting something with him is terrifying when I consider my family, how it will banish me from my country, and how deeply I'll become used to this new normal and never want to give it up.

Not just it.

Colby.

His lips cover my chest with kisses before trailing up over my shoulder. It is pleasure greater than sex, an affection given through want and not need.

Both my hands run up his back as I pull him closer and let my eyes sneak open.

"I'm a mess," he croaks.

"That's okay with me."

He laughs, thumb brushing over my nipple. "We should probably shower."

"Later." I pull him closer. This is everything I've needed for years, and I'm not in a hurry to let it go. His face is all happiness as he leans in and rubs his scratchy cheek against mine.

"Who knew you were such a cuddle slut?"

I pull back and eye him in surprise. "I have always been very affectionate."

"Considering half the time you look like you'll kill anyone who touches you, and the other half the time you're in fights with anyone who does, I'm going to go with no."

Poor, sweet Colby. The man clearly does not know what affection looks like. "Don't worry, I will be cuddle slut with you always." I drop a kiss on his nose, and he gives me his serious eyes.

"Not *always*."

Urgh. Reality. Apparently, we're jumping straight to it. "I have protected my family for most of my life. My sister has made her choices, and I will not come out and put a target on her, but I … I can't keep pushing down who I am. *This*." I marvel at how he feels against me. "This is right. I want a chance to be with someone and see where it goes, and there's no one else I trust like you. No one else I would risk everything for. If you do not feel the same, that's okay."

"When it comes right down to it, risking my career seems like nothing compared to you risking your sister's safety."

My lips tighten. If it were a matter of her safety, we would not be doing this at all. "I'm scared for that. A future where the laws change again. But I have always been living for the future, and I'm starting to see that the future isn't something that is set. I thought I would get my whole family to move to the States, and they would just move. It didn't happen. I thought I would finish my career and be done with it. Go private and start the rest of my life. Then more and more players joined the Collective, and I saw how happy they were. How full their lives seem. The closer I get to the end of my contract, the more I don't want that to be it for me and hockey. You coming back into my life feels like a sign. That it's time."

"Time for?"

"For me to have everything. I want to show off to you when I play. I want to kiss you goodbye before a game. I want to know I have my person cheering for me, even if you can't do that in public. Then I want someone that I can start building a future with, if that's something you want at all." I search his eyes for answers. "What do you want?"

That crooked smile jumps onto his face. "I've always wanted you, Novi. Obviously. With our time apart, I might have moved on from the crush I had, but the second I saw you again, it was as if nothing had ever changed. For me, I'm comfortable with the see what happens stage. You tell me you're ready, and I believe you, but I'd hate if you're outed because of me. I'd hate to lose my career because of you. Those aren't ideal ways to start a relationship."

"I understand."

"I think, at least while you're playing, that we be careful. It's smart."

"Smart."

"Exactly."

"Right." I smile at him. "And kissing me again is smart too."

He gives me what I want, a lazy afternoon of kisses and orgasms and being smart. Colby is my favorite addiction.

We will be smart because we have to be. And when it's time, we will be everything else.

-

I'm showing my team who's king as we run drills on the ice. I am outskating them all, having fun and showing off, well aware of Colby watching in the front row.

He's not just watching me; he's doing his job and taking notes on everyone, but I do everything I can to keep his focus. As soon as Coach switches our lines over, I speed toward where he's sitting and pull up sharply, spraying ice over the boards.

"Impressive, *da*?"

"Your left knee keeps bending the wrong way on turns."

I fold my arms over the divide and lean toward him. "You couldn't keep your eyes off me."

Colby's eyes shine with amusement, but he keeps that flat, professional expression. "That *is* my job."

"Did you check out my ass?"

He chokes on an inhale and glances around. "What happened to keeping this on the down-low?"

"My voice is down very low."

"I mean, subtle, Novi."

Got him. He's been harder to pull into my game lately, and I think he's caught on to what I'm doing. "I am the king of subtle." I switch my stick to the other hand. "It would be very obvious if I avoided you."

"Actually, it would fit perfectly with other people's perceptions if you avoided me."

I brush off his statement with a wave of my hand. "Only for people who don't know me. My teammates know I'm way too charming for that."

"Uh-huh." He doesn't look like he believes me as he turns his attention back to the ice.

"It is fine. We are at training, and you are my coach. It is normal to talk to coaches at training."

"Yeah, talking." Finally, I get a spark of something out of him. "But what you're doing is flirting."

"There is no difference."

"There is when you look like you're about to leap the barrier and maul me."

That tickles a laugh from me. "You are very dramatic."

Colby gives me an indulgent once-over. "Careful, you almost look happy."

"See?" I give him a wink. "Totally normal, no one will suspect a thing."

Coach Whelan calls me back over, and I join the line on the opposite wing to Turkey. He is the only thing getting me down today, and I am trying hard not to let myself pay him attention, but every time I see his face, I am reminded of what a coward I am.

And right now, he's watching me, confusion etched onto the lines around his mouth. "Atatürk down the left, Novi, cut across in front of Landers. I want to run it again."

Apparently, 'again' means forty times until Coach is happy with the play, and we finally get to head off the ice to shower. My training gear is heavy and sweaty against my skin but holds the same comfort that my game day uniforms do. I love this job, and I know why Colby loves his job too. As long as we're careful, there is no reason why we can't have both.

I'm swimming in thoughts about him, but as happy as I am, there's sadness there too. Sadness that this is all something I have been denying myself for so long. Could I have been this happy for years? Without Colby, I doubt it, but I might have had something close.

This swimming, giddy feeling in my gut is a lot of fun.

Turkey tears things from his game bag and grumbles something under his breath.

"What is wrong with you?" I ask him.

His head whips toward me, scowl etching deeper before he shakes it off. "You know what? Forget it, Novicov."

I watch as he slings his towel angrily over his shoulder and stalks off. He sounds angry with me, but I am not the one who stopped us being friends.

Sort of.

Maybe.

My denial slowly seeps away, and I let the guilt and hurt come back. It doesn't stand much of a chance against my Colby happiness, but there is room for both, and if I'm honest, after Turkey cutting me off, I miss him.

All because I couldn't give him a little something to prove our friendship is real.

Instead of heading into the showers with the others, I strip off to my base layers and then sit at my cubby and wait. My muscles are aching from practice, and I stink, but those things don't feel important.

The room clears out as my teammates head for the showers, and a moment later, Turkey returns. He's still pissed, wrapped only in a towel, and he pulls up short when he sees it is only the two of us.

He gives me the cold shoulder as he reaches his cubby next to mine and doesn't say a word as he gets dressed.

My mouth is doing the clamming-up thing. For someone who is an easy conversationalist, it is a foreign feeling for me to get all tongue-tied and lose my words. I'm also overly aware that the rest of the team could be back at any second, and I might miss my chance.

With the effort it takes to stop a third-period game-winning goal, I unstick my tongue from the roof of my mouth.

"I am sorry."

Turkey freezes. The locker room cools, but he doesn't say anything.

"You were right. Mostly. All those things you said, all those things you thought about me. You're the closest to the truth anyone has gotten."

Finally, his face tilts toward me. He is wary but no longer looks angry. "What are you saying?"

I let out a long sigh and put all my effort into staring at my hands. "I would still be friends with you." I blindly reach for my towel and stand, clinging to it like a lifeline. Then I meet his searching gaze, hoping he understands without me needing to say the words. "Now I'm asking you the exact same question. You stand up for Kessinger. Will you stand up for me, too, when I need it?" I will him to catch on, and it's like I can see the thoughts turning behind his eyes. The moment drags on so long I feel sick.

Turkey's mouth drops suddenly, eyes blinking rapidly. "Novi …"

"I deserve to exist too, even if in secret," I force out.

"Jesus, Novi." Turkey grabs my shoulder and pulls me into an aggressive hug. He squeezes me tight, not caring he showered and I stink like a dog. "I didn't know. I'm sorry, I didn't know. I've got your back, brother. Always."

CHAPTER TWENTY-TWO

COLBY

As much as it's tempting to reply to Novi's message: *Coming over tonight?* with a "Hell yes," I don't. He's not entirely grasping this subtle and down-low thing. It's not like he's outright screaming that he and I are sleeping together, but like I told him, the more we sneak into each other's places, the more he flirts out in the open under the guise of getting coaching advice, the higher the chance of getting caught. I am all in on this, but I'm determined to be smart about it.

I have a video meeting to prepare for in the morning. Why don't you ask Turkey to come over if you want company?

Because I can't fuck Turkey.

And you don't want to... right? I might have caught your half naked hug in the locker room earlier.

Someone sounds jealous. If you come over, I can give you fully naked hugs.

Not jealous. And I'm not coming over. But I thought Turkey was mad at you. Did you make up?

I came out to him. Sort of.

Jesus. I hit Call on his number because I know he hates texting.

"You on your way yet?" he answers.

"No. You came out to Turkey?"

"Sort of. A little."

"How do you come out to someone *a little*?" I'm proud of him, but isn't he supposed to be the one who's used to keeping quiet? If Turkey knows about him, then it's not going to be a big leap to figure out our history and that we're together now. I guess he really has decided he's ready.

If it weren't for my position with the team, I'd be ready for more too.

"I simply told him that he was mostly right about me, but not in the way he thinks, and then I asked if he would stand up for me like he does with you."

"Like for me?" I'm trying not to panic, but also mentioning me in his coming out speech? He might think he's being subtle, but he really isn't.

"I pointed out he was willing to cut ties with me to stick up for you. So I told him that I deserve to exist too, even if it's in secret."

My panic completely dissipates at that. "He took it really well, I'm guessing by that hug."

"You are so jealous, but that's okay. I would be too."

"If I hugged another man?"

"No. If I were you. I'm a sexy man. As soon as I come out, men will fall at my feet, and I will have to say, 'Sorry. I have very jealous boyfriend.'"

I snicker. "I can't wait to see that."

"It's true," he says vehemently. "I will have to beat off with my stick."

"You mean beat them off." Even if that also sounds wrong.

I swear I hear him smile. Damn it. I corrected him again.

"Back to my question. Are you on your way over yet?"

It's so tempting, but I really do need to prepare for this meeting in the morning, and I'm not going to let Novi learn that he can ask for something and I'll immediately give it to him. He can figure that out at a later date.

"You have an early skate and then a video meeting tomorrow. A video meeting that won't be ready if I go over to yours."

"Fine. Tomorrow night, then."

"You have your game."

"I mean after game."

He's so pushy, and if it was any other guy and not Novi, I would think he was being way too clingy, but just like I can see his actual bubbly personality under his I-will-kill-you face, I know he's only trying to tempt me.

"How about this? You have home games through this weekend, but I'm on the road with you next week. We can wait until then."

"I do not approve of this plan."

I snort. "Maybe file your complaint with management."

"You don't play fair."

"And your face isn't built for pouting."

"It is too. Have you not been listening? Very handsome. Very approachable."

"There's that delusion. I'll see you at work tomorrow."

I end the call before he can protest and ask me to come over again because I'm dangerously close to caving in.

A few seconds later, my phone lights up with a message.

> I will definitely see you at work.

Why does that sound like a threat?

-

When I arrive at the office while the team is still on the ice for their morning skate, I find Ackerman throwing things around the room.

"Where the hell is it?" There's paper strewn everywhere, and he looks like he's about to tear his hair out.

"Missing something, boss?"

He turns to me wide-eyed. "You know that stash of electrical tape you got me a few weeks back? It's gone."

"I brought you three rolls of it. What do you mean it's"—Fucking Novi—"gone …"

"You didn't move it?"

No, but I have a pretty good idea who did. "Maybe the cleaning crew moved it. I'll go grab some more."

"Thanks. It has to be here somewhere, but I give up. It was right here yesterday." He taps our small storage cabinet. "I know because I used it."

I came in through the employee entrance, so I didn't walk past the ice, but if I had to guess, Novi isn't out there doing his job. He's waiting for me.

"No sweat." I drop my bag at my desk. "I'll be right back."

I charge down the hall, not because I'm eager to see Novi—I am, but that's not why I'm moving fast—but because the next person to walk through that storage closet door will wonder why Radimir Novicov is in there. He probably has his "Sorry, I don't speak English" excuse ready.

Only when I open the door to the small room, the light is off, and there isn't a single sound coming from inside.

I flick on the light and head down the aisle between shelves, and when I turn the corner to where the electrical tape is kept, there he is, in his sweats, hair freshly washed and wet from the shower, and his smug "Got ya" face on his mostly emotionless expression.

People might not be able to read him, and maybe if I hadn't spent that season with him, I wouldn't be able to either, but I know him, and I know how he thinks. Like right in this moment, he thinks he's being smart.

He's not.

"I bet you weren't expecting to see me," he says.

"Actually, you were exactly who I was expecting." I walk over next to him. "Were you seriously waiting in here for me with the light off? Aren't you supposed to be on the ice?"

"I start early, finish early."

I hold up a roll of tape. "By the look of it, you got started extra early."

"Good invitation, no?"

I cock my head at him. "It is subtle, I'll give you that. But what if Ackerman came instead of me? What would your excuse be?"

"Ran out of stick tape, so was going to use this instead." He picks up a roll and hands it to me.

"That's better than the *I don't speak English* excuse I was expecting you to say."

"That was going to be my second excuse when he tells me I can't use electric tape for my stick."

I laugh. "I should be flattered that you went to such lengths to see me, but you're being reckless again."

"Not reckless. Romantic."

"I don't think you understand what that means in English."

"Locking you in a room so I can kiss you without you getting away is not romantic?"

I pretend to think about it. "It's one of those things where it's only romantic if the other person wants it. Otherwise, I think it's called kidnapping."

"Why would someone nap on a kid?"

I point at him. "You know that's not the right phrase, and I'm not going to play your game anymore. Don't think I haven't noticed you writing notes in your phone whenever anyone corrects your English."

Novi unleashes one of his amused smiles, which is really only the quirk of his lips on one side. "Now, that's romantic."

"What? No it's not."

"Not me keeping score, but you noticing that I do it."

"I still don't think you know what romantic means."

"I do. It means this." He wraps his arm around my back and pulls me to him, pressing his lips to mine.

I don't hesitate to kiss him back, but I'm not completely present for it because my ears are on high alert. Anyone could walk in, and while we have some coverage from the shelves stacked with office supplies, being in here at all with a player is an odd occurrence that has already happened once. Twice? Totally suspect.

I break my lips from his. "Novi," I whine.

"You are cracking already."

Cracking, melting, same thing.

"You're going to ruin me," I whisper.

He kisses the tip of my nose. "Only in the right ways. I promise."

And stupidly, even if he's being reckless, I believe him.

I hold up the electrical tape. "I need to get this to Ackerman." I turn on my heel before he can make me forget what I was doing in here with his lips.

He follows me. "But you can't. The lock is broken."

I get to the door and turn the handle. "I hate to break it to you, but Ackerman got it fixed after the last time we got stuck in here."

Novi mutters under his breath. "Damn him and his competence."

CHAPTER TWENTY-THREE

NOVI

All through the video meeting, I'm distracted watching Colby. He is so sexy. The athletic sweatpants might not be gray and cotton, but they're tight and slutty, leaving nothing to my imagination.

And he calls me a flirt.

A few times, our eyes meet, and he has to quickly pull his gaze away, eyes taking on those cute creases in the corners as he tries not to smile. Agreeing to a relationship makes me happy, but it has a side of sadness too.

Colby was my first, and always will be, my oldest friend. The sex is something I am hungry for with him, especially if we spend afterward wrapped around each other, but now that we've agreed to it, he is very tense about being seen together.

I understand, but I hate it.

I want to spend time with him. Making him laugh at my witty jokes, learning more about him, and being in his presence seems impossible now. I remember the boy I'd race, tease for being a turtle, who'd throw ice at me, and learned a handful of words in Russian because he'd wanted to be able to speak to me in my own language.

Right before I freaked out and ruined everything.

I want to bring relaxed Colby back. Seeing him so filled with tension whenever we're together in public only reminds me that while he's making me happy, I'm doing the opposite for him. Stress can also lead to heart attacks. I don't want him to have a heart attack. I need his heart. I'm going to win it one day.

With how distracted I am, it is a surprise we hold a 2-2 score at the game and don't lose until overtime.

I'm determined to do better for our game tomorrow, so instead of following through on my *Operation: friendship* plan, I take my ass home to bed and try to push Colby out of my brain. Kind of hard to do when he should be sleeping next to me.

When I get to the arena for a skate the next morning, I leave the electrical tape alone, have a skate, review game tape, and keep my gaze firmly away from him. I will see him tonight, and then I can look all I want, but my team and the fans are who I need to focus on right now. It's hard *not* to focus on him when a good part of the footage review is Colby picking out that I was in the wrong position play after play.

This is a very mental game, and I dropped the ball last night. I will not do the same tonight.

It only takes me one minute and forty seconds to sink my first goal against Chicago, but from there, it's an uphill battle. Coach gives our younger lines more ice time, and they're talented but green. They play like I played last night, and every time I hit the ice, it's like I am chasing our tail trying to gain back control. Chicago keeps building momentum until they have us 2-1 going into the third.

It is not an easy game.

And I love it.

The mad scramble for the puck, being locked out of plays, messy hits and messier attitudes. The more aggressive and frustrated both teams get, the more calming it is on me. I live for this chaos. I live for the moments our plays don't work and we have to get creative. The defense is matching us, and other than that lucky goal at the end of the second, Dotrosky has had a good game.

Chicago's goalie is better though. We have had almost double their shots on goal, and Gabrov is ready for every single one. Whenever I am on the bench, my eyes are locked on him and the way he moves.

Then I remember something Colby's ass said earlier. Well, not his ass. But that was all I was focused on. *If you get deep on his right, his left side is unprotected.* It's what we've been trying to do, but as I watch him save another, I see what Colby meant. He gets his stick up in time but leaves a wide-open gap between his stick and his helmet.

I can make that shot.

I lean toward Turkey. "Next shift, you get the puck, go down the right."

"The right? That's my bad side."

"*Da*, but I do not need you to make the shot." I gesture for our assistant coach to give me the whiteboard and marker, drawing my play. "Bring Gabrov to here, then pass to me over here. But I need you to get the puck high."

"How high?"

"Aim just below my shoulders. Fast as you can."

He laughs. "You say that like it's so easy."

"Don't worry. I won't miss."

Coach calls for our shift, and we power out onto the ice. Chicago takes possession and tries to slow play down by making long passes across the ice and holding down the puck. Landers blocks a shot, but they get it back on the rebound and pass it to defense before sending it to Edgers, who tries for a breakaway.

Turkey is there.

He clips Edgers, steals the puck, and takes off down the right.

Here we go.

The play will have seconds in it, and if I am too slow, we miss our chance.

I'm too slow.

I curse as I dig the puck from the boards, take a hit, and then send it back to Edgers. He passes to Landers, who sends it straight back, and I try to get into position again.

Gabrov sends a heavy blow to my shoulder because I'm dangerously close to his crease. I hold ground, and his jab is harder this time, but I am not in the blue paint. I refuse to move, even with the love taps he sends my way. Then Turkey gets the puck.

Gabrov's attention shifts, and he crouches like I knew he would. Turkey gets it close, looks set up to take the shot—and for a quick second, even I think he's going to—before he flicks the puck my way.

Fast enough to break my ribs if I weren't wearing all my padding and I missed this shot.

I am ready this time. I bat the puck out of the air as Gabrov turns and gets his stick up, but it is too late. The puck hits the net with satisfying finality, and the horns go off.

Our fourth line sneaks one more past him late in the third to get us the W.

And when I leave the ice, I am happy and ready for my friend date tonight. That Colby knows nothing about.

Damn video coaches and their late-night schedules. I went home to sneak in a few hours' sleep and woke up to the email footage from the game tonight. I take that as a good sign he is done with work and is home.

When I jog up to his front door, his car is in the driveway, and all the lights are off. He is going to be blown away by my thoughtfulness. I use the key I snuck from his bag earlier—they really should lock that coaches' office—and make my way inside.

He does not even have an alarm system. I will have to talk to him about that; anyone could sneak up on him.

"Colby …" I call out, starting up the hall. The first door is a powder room. The next is the kitchen. It is a very nice house. Too bright to be homey, but all the color reminds me of him.

"Colby …"

A door down the hall opens, light spilling out into the shadows, and my man walks out of his bathroom, wrapped in a towel, black hair damp from his shower.

He jumps a foot in the air when he sees me.

"Novi? What the fuck?" He dramatically clutches at his chest.

"Is it stress? Are you having a heart attack?"

He watches me with wide eyes. "I don't think stress is the reason my soul almost left my body."

"Then what is it?"

"You scared the shit out of me!"

I frown. "Me?"

"You're in my house. Creeping around in the dark."

Oh good, he noticed. "Romantic, *da*?"

"I don't think breaking and entering qualifies."

I approach him, tempted to touch, but I promised myself I wouldn't. Colby said no boyfriend stuff until we're away next week, so tonight is purely friends. "But I did not break." I hold up his key. "I unlocked."

He curls forward with laughter. "*You* stole my key? I thought I was losing my mind when I couldn't find it. You're lucky I had a spare hidden ... somewhere I'm not going to tell you about if this is going to become a habit."

"I wanted to surprise you, and I couldn't stand on your front step, knocking at 2:00 a.m. Imagine if someone had seen."

"Imagine if someone had seen you let yourself into my house at 2:00 a.m.?"

"That is why I did it quickly. With my hood up. And did not turn on any lights."

"I'm sure any peeping neighbors would have been very comforted by literally all of that."

I give him my most charming smile. "I have come to whisk you away for a night of friendship."

He eyes me. "Friendship?"

I hurry to nod. "I have missed you. The friend I used to have. I don't like not being able to spend time with you. So I came to sweep you off your feet and kidnap you."

"Aww ..." He steps right toward me, teasing creases by his eyes. "That was very nearly romantic until you brought felonies into it."

"See? You admit I am romantic."

"I admit you are almost romantic."

"I stole your key for you."

"*More* felonies. You really should have stopped while you were ahead." He leans in to kiss me, but I quickly catch his lips, and they meet my fingers instead.

"No boyfriends tonight. This is a friendship date. I know I am irresistible, but you will have to try to control yourself."

"No boyfriends, huh?" His eyes take on a challenging glint. "So absolutely no funny business?"

"Correct."

"You broke into my house—"

"With a key—"

"In the early hours of the morning—"

"You want *private*—"

"To kidnap me—"

"Sweep you off your feet—"

"And I'm not even allowed to kiss you?"

It's hard because I really, really want to kiss him. "These are your rules. Next week, you said. You might not think I know romance, but I do know boundaries."

Colby cups my face, large hands still warm from the shower. He presses his bare chest against me, and it is almost impossible not to touch. "Novi. Babe. Trust me when I say that you really, really don't." He swipes his thumb across my stubble. "But I'm starting to think I might like your brand of romance."

"See? You're coming around."

"The same can be said for Stockholm syndrome, so don't get too excited." His expression softens. "But how many other men would sneak up on me in the dead of night to jump-start my heart like that?"

"See? I make your heart race. Like you do me."

"And I can promise you *no one* has ever made my heart race like that."

"So you're saying I'm one of a kind?"

"Something like that." Colby steps back. "But since this is all friendship, I guess I better get dressed."

Then the teasing bastard flicks open his towel and lets it fall to the ground. My gaze immediately tracks over him, remembering all those times in the locker room I secretly wished for this to happen. He's half-hard, his body still as sexy as ever, and when he turns to walk up the hall, displaying that delicious ass, I have to bite my fist against the need.

"Put on clothes," I beg. "Lots and lots of clothes."

"Warm clothes?"

"Don't care. Just lots. Many clothes."

Colby's laugh rings out behind him as he disappears into his room.

"And not those slutty fucking sweatpants!"

If Colby's going to spend the night teasing me, I will never survive it. Maybe this wasn't such a good idea after all.

CHAPTER TWENTY-FOUR

COLBY

"Wow. This really is a friend date," I say as he pulls into the employee parking lot at the practice rink. "Nothing says unromantic like going to … your place of work."

"*Da.* Friendship only."

"What are we even doing here? And how can we get in when it'll be all closed—"

Novi smiles, and I slump.

"You stole a key for here too, didn't you?"

"Of course not. Big corporations notice when those types of things go missing."

My gaze narrows.

"I had one copied."

"There it is. And how do you propose we stay out of trouble with security checks and CCTV cameras everywhere?"

"Everyone loves me. No trouble." Novi parks in his favorite spot and turns off the car.

"You've done this before, haven't you?"

"Once or twice."

"Novi …"

"I like to come here over summer and skate while it's closed, okay?"

"Over the summers? Why aren't you with your family?"

"I go see my parents in Canada, but this is my home. I'm comfortable here. They sometimes come stay with me, but they can only come on tourist visa. If I could have gotten them residency in US, I would have, but Canada was easier. So even though we're apart, and I rarely get to see them, I at least know they're safe where they are."

We get out of the car and walk toward the employee entry, which he easily unlocks. Novi hasn't spent his entire career here; it's only been a few seasons. He's played for three different teams over his career: Anaheim, who drafted us, Winnipeg, and LA, so I guess he must like LA the best to have signed with another team here.

"Why do you like LA so much?" I hate the traffic, I hate the bustle, and don't even get me started on the cost of living in California, but I suppose Novi doesn't have to worry about that part. My job pays me sufficiently well, and while I'm comfortable, I'm not exactly swimming in extra cash because rent, utilities, and everything else costs double the amount of where I was living in Pennsylvania. Outside of Hawaii, California is the most expensive state to live in the whole country. How people on minimum wage do it is beyond me.

"I like it does not snow," he says.

I laugh. "You're a hockey player. Who plays on ice."

"That doesn't mean I like being cold."

"Ah, that's the real reason you don't want to go back to Russia, isn't it? It's not the threat of being arrested—you don't want to deal with the snow."

"*Da*. You got me."

At least he can joke about the shitty position his government has put him in. That's something.

We make our way through the back halls, and he brings me into the locker room of the team.

"You still size ten in skates?" he asks, holding up a pair of Landers's skates.

"I am, but I have my own in my office."

"I did not steal … I mean, I don't magically own a key to that part of the building."

Of course he doesn't. "Landers's stinky skates it is. I hope he doesn't have athlete's foot."

"Wear two pairs of socks. Condoms for your feet."

The things this guy says, I swear to God.

"Feet condoms. Got it." I take the skates from him, and he throws me two pairs of socks from his cubby. I wish I could say they smell clean, but I can't smell anything in this room other than body odor. That smell never goes away. It lives in the walls, in the carpet … everywhere. I'm going to have to trust him. It's not like my feet aren't disgusting after years of squashing them into skates anyway.

"So, what's the plan?" I ask as we lace up. "Going for a very unromantic skate in the middle of the night with no one else around?"

"It will be very unromantic. I want to see if you can still outskate me."

"You know I can't." I'm on the ice less as a coach for the NHL than I was coaching D1, and I haven't had the time to sleep, let alone skate for the fun of it, since I moved here.

"Making you puke. Very unromantic."

"Good to know you have some standards. Felonies are romantic, but you draw the line at puke."

"*Da*."

I can't tell if he's saying yes or duh. Could be both.

I lace up and stand. "Okay, I'm ready to be humiliated."

"You could use some. You've gotten so much bigger head since you were drafted as a top ten pick."

Whether he's pointing out how much of a cocky ass I was back then or he's trying to bring me back to that moment, it works. It's suddenly seventeen years ago, and I'm obsessed with his attention. Mocking me or being nice, I didn't care.

I still don't.

It's the middle of the night, and I should be bone-tired, but I'm not. I knew going into this video coaching role that I would be one of the first to arrive in the morning and the last to leave, but Novi breathes new energy into me by being in the same room. Who needs sleep when I have those whiskey-colored eyes shining at me in amusement?

On our way out to the ice, he stops by the electrical box to turn on the lights to the ice.

"It's not going to be smooth. When was the last time a Zamboni was out here?"

"Bumps make it more fun." Novi takes to the ice like a duck to water.

I don't show off quite like he does, smoothly gliding across the uneven surface. Though it's not as bad as I was expecting. They would have resurfaced this evening, but it's melted a bit since then.

Novi skates backward away from me while I follow him, not bothering to try to catch up. "You know, as one of your coaches, I should probably tell you to take it easy. You just played back-to-backs."

"I'm not tired."

"You might not be, but your body—"

"If you call my body old again, I might have to take back all my romantic grand gestures I've given you."

"Oh no. Don't take away breaking into my apartment and dragging me out in the middle of the night."

"I feel like this is American sarcasm, but then I remember how much you want me, and I am mistaken."

I would hate him if it wasn't true.

We may not be the same men we were as young adults trying to find our place in the world, but my feelings toward him haven't changed since then. If anything, getting to see this relaxed and open side of Novi has only made them grow into so much more.

We skate around, and I refuse to race him because I know I will lose. I wasn't joking when I said I shouldn't be encouraging this. He needs to rest up because we go on the road in two days.

And even though it wasn't his intention, this does turn out to be a pretty romantic date. If only we could show affection freely, but I know this place is covered in cameras.

If we're caught here and now, it could be put down to working through Novi's issues with his knees or Novi being pedantic and me trying to tell him that we won tonight and he can stop wanting to correct his mistakes from the game.

If we were to touch or kiss and then get caught on camera, it's all over. Everything we've both worked for.

We take a break and rest against the side railing.

Novi looks so happy. So carefree. He never looked like that back when I knew him.

"When did you know?" I ask.

"Know what?"

"That you were gay."

His lips flatten as he thinks about it. "There was something that always made me feel a bit different, but I didn't know what that was or why I felt that way for a long time because I never saw it growing up in Russia. I didn't know two men could ..." He hangs his head.

"I'm sorry. I shouldn't have asked. I was just thinking that since ... well, since owning who you are, you're happier than you ever were back then."

"I am. I am not all the way happy yet, but once I get everything I want, I will be happiest man on Earth."

"Your sister out of Russia?"

"Among other things." Those light brown eyes meet mine again, seeing right through me and deep into my soul.

My throat is dry as I ask, "Like what?"

He averts his gaze first. "A family. You know, kids."

"Like, for breakfast? Fee fie foe fum style?"

"I don't know what this means. I want to have children. I want to raise a whole lot of kids to believe they are supported and welcome and can be anything they want."

At first thought, yeah, Novi being a dad is a ridiculous notion, but looking in his eyes and how genuine and exposed he is, with those angry walls down, I could see him being the best kind of dad.

The kids would be too scared to do anything naughty, but with how Novi's talking right now, I know he'd be completely open with his kids, which means they'd be comfortable coming to him with any confusion or questions they had about being themselves.

"You think I won't be good dad?" Novi asks.

I shake my head. "Not at all. I was thinking that any kid would be lucky to have you for a father."

And that I would love to be there to see it happen. But that's getting ahead of ourselves.

CHAPTER TWENTY-FIVE

NOVI

I've never been this excited for away games. We win our first one, which puts me in an incredible mood, and after one drink with the team, I head back to my room. Colby should be back at the hotel by now, so while I'm riding the elevator up to my floor, I send him a text, written, so the two other people beside me don't hear it.

I m bak

Restless energy sits on my shoulders, and I thought I got it all out during the game, but the closer it gets to seeing him again, the more the energy builds. These stolen moments where we get to be a couple breathe new life into me.

As soon as I'm in my room, I shuck off my suit jacket, tie, and take off my shirt. They're thrown over the back of a chair as there's a knock on the door.

And even though we have hooked up a couple of times now, I am nervous. My palms are clammy like I'm on my first rookie season of the NHL. That same season where I refused to think about everything I left behind in the AHL, and now what I left behind has caught up to me anyway.

My smile is completely uncontrollable when I pull open the door and see him standing there. His button-up has the top two buttons undone, revealing beautiful, silky skin, and his sleeves are shoved up to his elbows. He looks chaotic and messy, and it makes my gut twist happily.

"I've never worked faster in my life," he says, voice dry like he has not spoken in hours.

I pull the door wider, and as soon as he steps through, I slam it closed with one hand and back him up into it.

"No shirt, Novi?" His hands run over my pecs.

I watch the way he practically drools. "Should I go put it back on? Maybe a sweater? Mittens? Beanie?"

"Shut up." He leans in and catches my mouth with his.

His mouth is like a morning coffee. A zap of high followed by a deep, simmering calm. I will never get enough of how he tastes, how he feels, the way his tongue wraps so deliciously around mine. My hips pin him to the door, and I'm eager to get us both naked, but the kissing is too good. Couples get to experience this every day, and I can barely wrap my head around the luxury.

"Novi ..." He pulls back, touching his forehead to mine. Then, his fingers move to his buttons. I swallow as he follows the path down, undoing each one and revealing more skin for me to drool over. "You still want to fuck me?"

"Very, very much." The second the last button is open, I push his shirt from his shoulders and tug it down his arms, then I bring our bodies together.

I hold him against me, face dropping to his neck, where I breathe in the scent of his shampoo and leave kisses beneath his ear. My cock is straining in my pants, and the need for him deepens with every second. Colby Kessinger makes my body hum with an electrical awareness that's only ever belonged to him.

His fingers run over my shoulder. "Is this from that dirty hit in the third?"

I pull away reluctantly to see what he's talking about. A bruise is blooming from my collarbone to my shoulder. "*Da.*"

"Ouch."

"I like it. It is like decoration."

Colby's laugh tickles me. "Decoration. Okay. Why don't I give you something amazing to like instead?" His fingers thread through mine, and he tugs me away from the door. Being separated from him feels like going backward to me, but when he pulls me over to the small couch and orders me to sit, I sit.

"What are we doing here?" I ask, looking up at him.

"Hopefully not going to destroy any hotel furniture for one thing. Second … I'm confident this is going to give us a good angle."

"Oh really?" I'm curious about what he has planned. I extend one arm along the back of the couch while I pop the button on my suit pants with the other. My eyes don't leave Colby's body. He's still got beautiful shoulders and pecs, less clean-cut twenty-year-old body, more filled-in man. The dusting of hair across his lower belly runs into his pants, and I follow the trail all the way down as Colby drops his pants and pushes his underwear down with it.

"I was going to prep before I came here, but someone was too *thirsty.*"

The way I downed that one beer proves his point. "I was not thirsty," I tell him, drinking in the sight. "I was very, very hungry."

Colby inhales deeply, expanding his chest, before letting it all out in a flood. "What a coincidence." He folds to his knees. "Me too."

I watch as he tugs down my fly, then yanks my pants from my hips and over my thighs. He doesn't stop until he's stripped me completely, and I spread my legs, letting him see everything.

"Damn …" he breathes, tongue sneaking out to flick over my cockhead. "I knew you were hiding an amazing dick under that towel, but it tastes even better than I imagined."

"You thought about my dick?"

"Constantly." He licks a wet stripe up my shaft. "I've dreamed about this goddamn thing and how it would feel splitting me open."

"We should compare. Quickly. See if you came close to the real thing." My hand finds his soft hair as Colby buries his nose in my balls and inhales. I have been on the receiving end of many blowjobs, but none that make me feel as wanted as Colby's.

"So impatient."

"You are not the only one who has dreamed."

His eyes soften, and he presses a kiss to my inner thigh. "See? You can be sweet sometimes."

"I am sweet all the time."

He climbs up onto me and straddles my thighs. "You're really not. Your whole thing is condescension and this weird sort of playfulness I'm half convinced you've created to fuck with everyone else. And it's all of that, plus the glimpses of your big heart, that attracted me to you in the first place. The moments you are sweet? I'll take them when they come because they're all a bonus."

I like being a bonus, but I want to be sweet as well. Colby deserves sweet. And adoring, romantic, and someone who makes him happy. I want to be all of those things.

I brush his lips with mine. "You're like my second gift, and this time, I know how to appreciate you properly."

Colby hums, then lifts two of my fingers to his mouth and sucks on them until they're wet. "Start now, then," he says, sliding my hand down to rest on his ass, then guiding my fingers between his cheeks. "Be gentle, one at a time. Get me stretched and ready for you."

I pull him back into a kiss. My cock is leaking out onto my abs as I skim my fingertips over his hole. I'm flooded with arousal at the touch, careful not to go too fast, but when I press gently forward and my finger sinks inside, it's one of the hottest things I have ever done. Colby rocks back onto it, nudging my cock with his own, and I have to clamp my free hand down on his hips to stop him rutting against me. With the way he's tugging my hair as he eats my mouth, that would all be too much.

I take my time stroking in and out of his hole before I add a second finger. It's fun to tease him, to feel the way his body reacts to me and opens for my thick fingers.

He's panting when he pulls back. "Where did you put the lube and condoms?"

After the last time we were cockblocked, I made sure to pick some up and sent him a photo earlier of them tucked away in my suitcase.

"There," I point to where my luggage is open on the floor.

Colby climbs off me and heads in that direction, and the whole time he's gone, I'm fighting myself not to touch my dick. The ache building in it is begging for attention, and I'm sure I could get away with a little tug, but I'm worried I won't stop. Nothing is going to prevent me from sinking into his gorgeous round ass. He might be unfit on the ice these days, but he hasn't lost that butt.

"Hold this." He tosses me the bottle of lube, then rips the condom open. My greedy stare doesn't part from him as he rolls it down my length, teasing touch leaving me desperate to have him wrapped completely around me. "You're a perfect size," he says, taking the lube. "I'm gonna enjoy this so much."

"If I can last." I'd like to think I have the stamina to fuck him all night, but I've never done this before. I'm going to be fighting myself the whole time.

"You will." He kisses me softly as he spreads lube over my cock, then climbs up over it again. "And we're going to have plenty of time to practice this. Over and over and over." Colby tosses the lube aside. "Hold yourself steady until you're inside me."

"Fuck …" I wrap my fingers around the base, and Colby lowers himself, finds the position … and sinks down onto me.

My eyes roll back the moment I slip inside him. His body pulls me in, closes tight around me, and I sink into the man I've fantasized about from the moment I met him.

Once he's fully seated, I let go, hands finding his hips instead, and when I look up at Colby, he's grinning. "Feels good, doesn't it?"

"Indescribable."

"Does it make me a bit of an asshole that I love being the only one you've ever done this with?"

Colby staking his claim on me? Hot as hell. I could be bitter that I've waited my whole life for this, or jealous he got to experience it before me, or annoyed that he's bringing it up, but when it comes down to it, I wouldn't change this moment if I could. Anyone he's had before doesn't matter because he has me now. "No, it makes you perfect for me."

Our eyes catch as he moves, rocking slowly up and down, and I have to tighten my grip to stay in control. Every roll of his hips, every downward grind, every time his leaking cock slides against my body, I'm ready to let go.

He picks up speed, and it gives me the confidence to join in. All his weight is on his knees, and I tug him down into every thrust, chasing that moment where it all gets to be too much and I can't hold out anymore.

"I never thought this would happen," he rasps.

"I'm sorry." I kiss my way along his jaw. "I was a stubborn man who missed out on so much."

His laugh is husky and drenched with lust. "*Was*?" He kisses me before I can dispute it. "Just fuck me, Novi. Fuck me like you always wanted to."

Our mouths slam together so hard that pain shoots across my lip, and our kiss is sharp and messy and driven by pure need. He keeps one hand in my hair, holding me close, while the other reaches down for his cock. The glossy tip passes over my skin as he strokes himself in time with my thrusts, the steady hum of his moans and grunts mixing with my own.

I want this to go on forever.

I never want to let Colby go.

What we have is risky and fragile and has the potential to blow up in our faces, but it's also worth it. Worth every minute waiting and worth all the sacrifices I've had to make to get there. I only hope that when it comes to it, when reality pierces our bubble of hope, Colby will think I'm worth the same.

I've had too many years without him. I never want to go back to that again.

Never.

I pull back from the kiss, sweaty and flustered and so ready to come, and when I glimpse his blissed-out face, I make myself a promise.

If things ever come down to Colby or hockey again … I'll choose him.

"So close," he pants, head dropping back as his eyes close.

"Me too, *Kotik*." *Kitten*.

I give him everything I have left, snapping my hips up to meet his thrusts as he strangles his cock to the end.

My blood is on fire with need, cock bridging that moment between pleasure and pain where it all gets too much. My balls are aching with the urge to come, and I'm worried I won't get Colby there. Worried I'll let go too soon and ruin everything.

The first splash of cum on my abs is like being doused in relief, and feeling it is permission to let go. I stop fighting, relax into the bliss, and my orgasm washes over me with cock-throbbing finality.

Colby lets out a long exhale before falling against me, like his whole body has deflated. I'm still lodged inside him, not yet soft, and I seal our hips as close as possible to drag this moment out. The sex was incredible, but this, after, the connection is deeper than I could have imagined it went. My chest is light and bubbly. I've never been so happy.

His lips press to my temple, and I close my eyes against it.

I'm wrung out to every limb.

This is how life should be.

CHAPTER TWENTY-SIX

COLBY

If it were up to me, I'd spend every night wrapped around Novi, but the more we do it, the more chance there is of everyone finding out. So I've been good. I've implemented rules. Only on road trips, one night a week at his place, and no more trying to lock us in the storage closet at work.

Yet, all he has to do is tease me with a naked picture message, headless, of course, in case they ever got out, and I cave. I forget the rules.

I'd say it's because he wants to spend as much time with me as possible as well, but a part of me thinks he does it because he likes making me break. He loves knowing how hard it is for me to keep my distance.

Which is how I've ended up at his house, in his bed, after only spending one night apart after their road trip. In my defense, Radimir Novicov is irresistible, especially now he's more confident in his skin. His naked skin.

The same skin pressed against me as he spoons me.

Yeah, I'm totally gone when it comes to Novi. I can't get enough, and neither can he, consequences be damned. Unlike me, he doesn't seem to worry about what will actually happen if it gets out. I know he *is* worried, but he doesn't show it, and it makes me wonder whether he's refusing to let himself picture it.

I think with Turkey and the Collective guys knowing, Novi is getting to a point where he'll want to be out, and I don't want to hold him back, but even if he came out and didn't mention he's currently fucking his coach, it will be messy. It would put a spotlight on him, and it would be more difficult to sneak around.

If it wasn't for his sister, he probably would have done it already.

For me, I don't want to ask him to keep holding on to secrets when he's finally gotten the freedom to let go of all of them, but the reality is, if he comes out, we'll have to take a step back. Considering I can't even last two nights without him, I know I won't be able to keep my distance.

All these worries don't matter at this point and won't matter for a long time, but as I lie here in his arms, I can see myself repeating this situation over and over again.

I made the rules for a reason, yet I know I'm going to keep breaking them.

I can see us getting serious. I can see a whole lot of things with him that I shouldn't be picturing this early. I should have enough control to hold out for him because this has the potential to be life-altering for both of us.

I need to talk to someone about it. Someone who isn't Novi. Especially not a naked Novi. Because if I tell him I want to pull back because I'm scared of falling for him, it will either make him run away screaming or only encourage him to keep chasing me. I can't afford the latter, and the former … that's something that should happen, but I don't want it to.

My head is a mess of chaos running in two different directions. But then Novi stirs and holds me tighter. Just like that, all those worries dissipate once again, and I'm tempted to push back and rut against him until he comes on my back. If it weren't for Novi needing to get to the practice rink, I'd trap him by wrapping myself around him and staying here all day.

And right on time, his phone blares through his minimalistic bedroom.

"*Nyet,*" he says, but his phone only gets louder.

"I don't think your alarm is voice activated."

"I meant I'm not going to practice. I'm very sick." He reaches behind him and stops his alarm.

"You don't sound sick."

He fake coughs and then comes back to me, pressing his hard cock against me and sliding it along my ass crack. "See? Very sick. Can't skate."

"Fuck," I hiss. He's doing it to me again, making me forget my priorities and his. "You can't miss practice."

"I can be late to practice."

My cock is hard, my self-control is nonexistent, and as I give in to Novi once again, I make myself a promise: I need advice, and I need it sooner than later.

"Fine, but make it quick."

"Now who's romantic?" he says in his signature dry tone, but he does as I say.

He grinds against my ass and reaches over me to wrap his hand around my cock. It's quick, it's messy, but goddamn, it's so good. It always is with Novi.

It doesn't take long for both of us to reach breaking point, and we fall. His warm cum lands on my back while I fill his hand.

Breaths heavy, spaghetti limbs, we're boneless while we come down from our high. I'll never get over the intensity in which he makes me come. I'll never get enough. He recovers first and slaps my ass.

"Shower. We can't be late." Novi jumps up, but I roll onto my back with a lazy, happy smile.

"You'll be late. I have one of those things we never get."

He pauses. "Is this English I don't understand?"

"I have a day off."

"I still don't understand. That's not a thing. Summer is days off. The rest of the year is work."

"Maybe for you, but you're forgetting one thing. Us coaches don't need to be in top form like you athletes do."

Novi puts his hands on his hips. "I'm starting to see why you chose to become coach. Staying fit was too hard."

"Something like that."

His comments don't get to me like they might have fourteen years ago when I did have to give up being an athlete because I couldn't cut it. The thing is, I accepted it a long time ago, and I love being a coach so much that I'm certain my life turned out the way it was supposed to. In all aspects except one.

Why couldn't this opportunity have popped up in two years' time instead of now? Hell, even one year from now. I could keep it in my pants for three hundred days. I'm sure of it. But two years? It's almost like I know it's impossible, so I'm not really trying.

But I should try.

"What are you doing with your day off?" Novi asks, and I don't want to tell him.

"Go shower already. You're going to be super late, and then Whelan might bench you."

"Please. I'm on a streak. He won't bench me."

"That doesn't mean you can't be respectful and lead by example."

He huffs. "You're in coach mode." He heads for the bathroom as I sit up in his bed.

"I am your coach." My authority would maybe hold more weight if I wasn't naked and covered in our cum.

-

My phone vibrates in my pocket as I reach the entrance to the restaurant Lane agreed to meet me at for dinner. At first, I think it's him to let me know he's here or running late, but when I take it out and check the message, Novi's name is on the screen.

What you doing?

I quickly type out: *I'm at dinner with a friend, and no, I'm not coming over afterward.*

We'll see.

I'm not.

Okay.

I hate you.

I'll leave the door unlocked for you.

He can do that, but that doesn't mean I'll go over there.

A hand lands on my shoulder, and I jump a mile high. I'm quick to put my phone away.

Lane eyes me with amusement. "Off in your own world?"

Did he see that message? Do I lie here or be vague instead?

"Yeah, sorry."

"You been standing out here long?"

"Not at all. You're right on time." I gesture for him to enter the restaurant first, and I follow him in.

Once we're led to a table that's in a quiet corner and we sit across from each other, Lane merely stares at me.

It's kind of unnerving, but I get it. Since going out for drinks in the beginning of the season, where we promised we'd catch up, seeing as we're in the same area blah, blah, blah, we haven't made the effort. Not once.

I bury my head in my menu. "The salmon looks good."

Lane doesn't reply, and when I tilt my menu down so I can stare at him over the top, his lips purse.

"Are we eating, or …" My voice cracks.

"We can. Or we can talk about why you messaged to randomly catch up with me. Not me and Oskar. Just me."

I drop my menu. "This isn't a date if that's what you're asking."

He laughs. "Didn't even cross my mind. I was thinking more along the lines of you wanting something with a certain person because you have history, but you also can't go there because you're his coach, and that would cross a lot of lines, so you reached out to the PR manager who fucked his hockey player and got fired because of it."

I blink at him. "Okay, you're good. I'll give you that."

"You can't have sex with him."

A throat clears as a server steps up to us. "Uh, do you need a few minutes? I can come—"

Lane turns to him. "He'll have the salmon, I'll have the rib eye, medium rare, and we'll both have whatever single malt scotch you have, neat."

"Very well." The server disappears.

Now I know why the Collective say Lane has Daddy vibes.

I lean back in my seat. "Lucky this isn't a date, or that would've pissed me off."

Lane smiles. "Ordering for you? I only did it because you said the salmon looked good, you need a drink to have this conversation, and I wanted to get back to my point. You can't have sex with Novi."

Hearing that from someone who already crossed the same lines I have doesn't make this any easier. "See, logically, I know this, but ... there's a slight problem with that."

"You already did, didn't you?"

I lower my voice and mumble, "Multiple times."

Lane takes a deep breath, holds it, and then lets it go a couple of seconds later. "Are you two together?"

"Sort of? I mean, yes, but we both know it can't get out. At least not until he retires. And I tried. I tried so hard to wait the two seasons he has left before asking him out—"

Lane cuts me off. "It's November."

"Don't come at me with time math. Have you seen that man shirtless? It's impossible to stay away."

He softens at that, and at least it doesn't look like he's going to lecture me. "I can't judge because I can relate. Not with Novi, obviously, but it was the same for me with Oskar."

"So, what you're saying is I'm fucked either way?"

"Sorry." Lane takes a moment, tapping the table with his thumb. "Do you, uh … did you hear how that worked out for me?"

It takes me a moment to know where he's going with this. "As we already established, you were fired."

"Not only fired. It affected my hireability. My entire reputation was damaged because of it. No NHL team in the league would've offered me a job, possibly any team in any sport. I was lucky that I'd made a connection with Damon King, but if I hadn't and he didn't offer me a role at King Sports, my career would've been dead. I want to make sure you know what you're getting yourself into. I wouldn't trade Oskar for anything in the world. You need to decide if Novi is worth the same to you."

CHAPTER TWENTY-SEVEN

NOVI

Colby is good at resisting me, but some nights, I am better.

Thankfully, last night was one of those times, and today, I get to wake up next to him again. He runs hot, so we are slightly sweaty pressed together, and his morning breath is directed right toward my face, but it only makes me smile. For so long, I worried I would never have this, and now that I do, I want it all.

I know he wants to be cautious, but I am … tired. Everything we have together is so good, and after so long, we deserve this. I know the real world is waiting for us outside this bubble, but I'm getting to experience for the first time what so many people do growing up, and I selfishly want it all.

Our deal for away games only is mostly going strong, but apparently, I am needy in relationships, and Colby lets me be that way. I honestly thought this would be enough. The time together, the closeness, the sex. Having someone to text when I am lonely or bored or excited or teasing. Being able to look at one man and know he's mine should be enough for me.

But between our stolen time in hotel rooms, reluctant home visits, and stiff professionalism at work, it has left me wanting more than ever.

Coming out has always been important to me, but I was convinced I could wait. My amazing career is so close to ending, but instead of being comforted by the thought of drifting into anonymity, I am frustrated.

I don't want to hide.

I want hockey. I want responsibility. I want to be a role model and spend my days giving people hope. Infecting them with my happiness and positivity. I'm a people person right down to my core, and my natural charisma would make me great at it.

I don't think I can wait anymore. But if I come out and something happens to my sister or her family, how do I ever forgive myself?

Like I've summoned her with a mere thought, a text comes through on my phone, and Elena's name crosses the screen. I click on the message.

> What do you call this, leaving your favorite sister waiting on the doorstep?

Waiting …

Surprise lights me up as I throw off the covers and jump out of bed. I quickly dress, jog down the hall, and when I pull open the front door, three of my favorite people on Earth are there waiting.

"Elena!" I wrap her in a hug before diving down and scooping Mischka and Alexei up into my arms.

"Ah, *Zaychik*! Put me down."

In response, I blow a raspberry on Mischka's cheek. Alexei is much more subdued, but he is younger, and it has been months since I have seen them.

"If I knew you were coming, I would have bought presents," I say, setting them down.

"And that's why I didn't tell you." Elena presses a kiss to my cheek and steps past me into the house, dragging a large suitcase behind her.

"How long are you here for? Also why?"

"Two weeks."

"That doesn't tell me why."

She turns her attention to the kids and tells them in Russian to go and play.

"The toy box is in the second bedroom," I yell after them. It feels good to be speaking in Russian again.

When they're gone, Elena pins me with her big sister stare. *"I am worried about you."*

"You could have picked up the phone."

"Yes, because that worked so well for us last time when you called drunk and depressed."

That's a fair point. *"I wasn't depressed …"*

"Hmm." She looks around. *"Wonder what gave me that idea? Oh, yeah. You said you were depressed."*

"I was joking."

"I know you're melodramatic sometimes, but I also know there was a bit of truth to it. Plus, it's been a while since I visited and told you all the ways you're not looking after yourself properly so—"

"Ah, Novi?" Colby's voice precedes him down the hall, and for a moment, I'd completely forgotten he was here. "I know we're official and everything, but please tell me that I'm hallucinating and you didn't steal us two ki—" He cuts off as he steps into the foyer and catches sight of Elena.

Her smile is positively evil. *"Who is this?"*

"No Russian," I say, switching to English. "It's rude."

"Fine," she repeats. "Who is this?"

"Colby, this is my sister, Elena. Elena, this is Colby."

"Hi." He holds out his hand, almost looking scared, but Elena is a second away from laughing.

"It's lovely to meet you."

"You too. I'm guessing those kids belong to you and that Novi didn't actually steal mini humans?"

"Steal?" She actually does laugh. "My sweet little brother has never broken a rule in his life."

"Sweet …"

Elena jiggles the suitcase. "I'm unpacking in your kitchen. Our clothes are in the hire car." Then she leaves us together, and Colby turns to me with wide eyes.

"Her?" he asks. "That's who you're worried will be in trouble if you come out?"

I nod solemnly. She might be my older sister, but she's shorter than me by a head and looks far too positively at the world to remember to protect herself. "She is an idealist."

"*Her*?" Colby almost sounds confused.

My eyebrows knot. "Are you okay?"

"I'm terrified. I have the strangest urge to grab the suitcases and deliver them to her on bended knee."

"That is an odd thing to say."

"Novi, please know that I say this from the bottom of my heart … your sister might look even scarier than you do."

I can't work out what he's saying. Elena? Scary? "I don't think you got enough sleep last night."

"Whose fault was that?"

Colby and I grab the suitcases from the car. I leave him with Elena's and grab the two teeny tiny ones.

"Look how small they are," I say. "They're adorable. Like they are for dolls."

"Please don't put the idea of Chucky in my head while I'm dealing with your niblings."

"It would probably be accurate," I tell him. "Those two are pure evil at times. I am wrapped around their tiny fingers."

I'm not sure, but I think Colby shudders.

We get the bags inside, and the sound of Elena with the kids deeper in the house just feels right.

"You okay?" he asks.

"This is what I want it to be," I tell him. "Them—and Ivan—here where they're safe. Where I can see them always. Where my children can play with their cousins and grow up together."

"That does sound pretty special." His hand rests on my lower back. "Do you want me to go so you can catch up with them?"

"What? No." I grab his hand before he can run away. "She'll already be cooking for us both. You need to stay. If you don't let her feed you before you leave, *then* she will be scary."

For some reason, the thought of my sister's cooking doesn't delight him. Colby still looks worried, but getting this gift of having them all here with me is something that won't happen again in a hurry.

I swallow. "Can you please stay?"

"Of course I will." He squeezes my hand. "On one condition."

"Anything."

"You have to promise that if she runs at me with a kitchen knife, you'll dive in between us."

And Elena calls *me* dramatic. "You're an idiot." I give him a soft kiss. "Let's go."

Colby trails after me. "Can't help but notice there was no promise."

I drop his hand as soon as we reach the main living area. The kids have found the toy chest, and there's already scattered LEGO, puzzles, trucks, and teddy bears all over the living room while Elena looks on from the kitchen. The sight fills me with so much happiness that I join Mischka and Alexei on the floor, overly aware of Colby creeping into the kitchen to talk to Elena while he keeps the enormous island between them.

He has nothing to worry about though. The reason Elena was so successful where so many people aren't is because she's social. Can carry any conversation and make people feel drawn to her. We both inherited our father's big heart.

Alexei drives his truck into my thigh, and the little fucker hurts.

"Ouch." I take the toy and toss it across the room. "Fetch, you cretin."

"Help me build a castle," Mischka says, shoving LEGO pieces my way. Her English is improving a lot. I wish I'd learned English when I was their age. Kids are like sponges. It's why I encourage them to speak it when they are with me.

"Play. Trucks!" Alexei says, pegging the one he has at my head. I catch it right in time.

And for the next half an hour, I build with Mischka and toss the truck across the room for Alexei, feeling filled and happy in a way that only happens with them.

"Is Novi ... playing fetch with your son?" I hear Colby ask.

Elena goes back to chopping something loudly. "Maybe it will tire him out."

Their voices drop to murmur about something. I hope she is telling him about the time I was five and ran down the street naked. Or when I was sick and sneezed so hard I covered my desk in snot. Or that time she chased me because I found her diary, and I fell over and broke my arm. It is a sibling's job to embarrass each other to their partners, so she sure as hell better be doing it for me.

"Uncle Radi, who is that man?" Mischka asks.

My whole good mood immediately slurps down the drain. "He's …" My partner. My lover. The man I will hopefully marry one day. But none of that can be said to a child who will repeat it innocently in places where she shouldn't. "A friend from work."

"Is he mean to you? Sometimes my friends are mean to me."

My attention locks onto her, and I lean closer. "Who do I need to kill? I want names."

Mischka tuts. "Mommy asked the same thing."

"Good. I will get the list from her later."

My distraction costs me though. Alexei gets back, and the truck *whacks* against my temple. The pain is sharp and short, but I pin him with my stare. "You will pay for that."

He squeals and goes to run, but I am much too fast for him. Before he can get a few steps, I leap up, grab him, and hang him upside down by the ankle.

Laughter racks through him as I head toward the kitchen.

"Open the trash," I tell Elena. "This one is defective."

"Help, Mommy, help!" His English is forgotten while his brain is upside down.

Elena approaches us, then hums and leans in to inspect him. "Yes. He's a lot noisier than I remember."

"You can get a new one?"

When Elena glances up at me, I see it. The real reason she's here. A spark fills her eyes as she gives her stomach a pat. "Already working on it."

My jaw drops, and I only remember Alexei enough to gently set him back down again before I'm pulling her into a hug. "Number three?"

"It took us long enough."

"You're having *another* evil gremlin?"

"They are chaos. But I love them."

I squeeze her tight, so happy I'm ready to lift *her* up by the ankle. "Will you finally call this one Radimir?"

"Not on your life."

When I glance back at Colby, he's smiling at us. "Do you still think she's scary?"

"He thinks what?" Elena pulls away.

"What? No. I didn't—Never said—"

Elena looks stunned for words. "But I am delightful."

A long sigh falls from me. "I say this all the time."

We exchange a look. *"Americans."*

CHAPTER TWENTY-EIGHT

COLBY

Eating with Novi's family is a surreal experience. It's easy to see why Elena has her own cooking show because her food is delicious, even if it's a dinner meal at breakfast time. She argued it's dinner time in Russia, so I shut my mouth. One, because I want her to like me, and two, I wasn't sure a knife wouldn't fly at my head.

Sitting at this table with her and Novi, plus the two devil children who are somehow adorable yet terrifying, that fear of flying knives is still in the back of my mind.

One thing I have noticed, though, is the way Novi's hardened features soften around his sister and niblings. He's more relaxed, there's no tension in his wide shoulders, and he smiles more. A genuine smile that anyone could pick up on. And looking at Elena through that same lens, I realize they both really are the big-hearted softies Novi claims them to be.

At least, I think. If I'm going to stay over again while Elena's visiting, I'm still going to lock the bedroom door to be safe.

But I shouldn't stay again. Because rules, damn it. Plus, Novi deserves to have family time without me distracting him or taking away from their visit.

The little one, Alexei, turns to me and asks something in Russian. I only pick up on the word "hockey."

"Use your English," Elena says sternly. Or sweetly. I give up on trying to decipher the Novicov tone.

Alexei hesitates before saying, "You. Hockey. Play?"

"Ah. I used to, but I'm now your uncle's coach."

He looks confused.

I try to think of another word for coach. "Uh, teacher?"

Alexei thinks for a moment. "Teach. Lesson."

"Hockey lessons. Yes."

He goes back to his food. Elena's food is so amazing even the kids eat it. My diet at their age consisted of nuggets and fries and not much else.

I don't actually know what I'm eating, but it's some kind of soup with vegetables and meat, and it's the most delicious thing I've ever eaten.

I go to tell her exactly that, but when I meet her eyes, she's got that scary-ass look on her face again.

"And you are at my brother's house. Early in the morning."

"Coach Kessinger makes sure to give me extra attention because I'm at a level of amazing that very few coaches can teach."

Elena rolls her eyes.

But from that moment and for the rest of the day, I notice every time she looks my way. And she does it a lot.

I'm self-conscious as Novi and I do the dishes after we've finished eating because I can feel her watching.

Novi doesn't notice or doesn't care. He's determined to be cute and annoying by covering me in soap suds whenever he can.

I duck away from his attempt to put a dollop of bubbles on my nose. "At this point, I think it would be more efficient if you let me do the dishes on my own."

He nods solemnly. "Efficient but less fun."

"That's true." Doing anything without him lately is less fun.

Like sleeping. Showering. Even watching TV. Not that we've really had time to do that with our fleeting trysts and sneaking around. I just know that being at home and watching TV feels so empty now.

Is this what obsession looks like? If we were to spend all of our waking moments together, would this craving I have for him dim? Would the need to constantly see him and be with him be replaced with needing a break?

When I step back up to the sink, Novi steps in behind me and presses himself against my back.

My gaze goes right to where Elena is in the living room, playing with her kids, and yup, she's staring right at me.

I elbow Novi in the gut and whisper, "Your sister is watching."

"It's not like she doesn't know about us."

I twist to look at him over my shoulder. "You told her?"

"No. She's observant. Like she said, you were here early in the morning."

"But you told your nephew that I was a friend from work."

Novi grips my hips and turns me toward him. "I didn't realize you heard that. He might be little, but he has a big mouth, and he wouldn't understand the need to not talk about the man who shares a bed with his uncle."

I swallow hard because the pain of having to lie to his nephew makes everything in my body tense up.

"If it's too hard for you—"

He presses against me again, his hips meeting mine. "It's very hard."

"Not. That." I grit my teeth and use all the restraint I have to playfully push him off me because if we can't show affection in front of his niblings, he can't be pushing his hard cock against me.

Novi's genuine smile appears once again as he steps away and adjusts himself. I love what happiness looks like on him, but it only reminds me that behind closed doors is the only time I've ever seen it.

He deserves happiness, damn it, and I wish I could be the one to give it to him, but it's something he has to do for himself. I know he's close to wanting to tell the world—I think he's been ready for it for a long time, but he's only now admitting it to himself—but there's one thing holding him back. Two if you include me, but even though I would be more comfortable if he stayed closeted so I wouldn't lose my job, I would never ask him to stay in there for me.

Once he does come out, it will only be a matter of time before our relationship becomes public. We can't stick to the rules now where no one would even jump to those conclusions. If everyone finds out Novi isn't the homophobe they think he is … how long will it take them to put two and two together?

Player suddenly comes out only mere months after a gay coach started with the team?

"Who wants their uncle to take them for ice cream?" Elena asks with the same expression Novi has when he's excited. The same expression that makes people think he's threatening them, not asking if they want to do something fun. But the kids obviously know their mother, and I'm guessing they know the English words "ice cream" because they scream with glee.

Maybe the threat is against me. Because while I'd love to escape with Novi to go get ice cream, it seems Elena has already clocked that we can't be seen in public together unless in a professional capacity. Which means I'm stuck here. With her.

Alone.

Where all the knives live.

Novi looks back at me, then at his sister, then at the kids. He says something in Russian, and Elena tsks him.

"What happened to speaking English?" she asks.

They start bickering in Russian, but Elena steps closer to him and turns to me. His arguments die on his tongue.

"You're not really scared of me, are you? You'll survive without my little brother protecting you."

My lips part, but no sound comes out.

"See? He's happy to stay here and keep me company while you take my children and give your overworked, pregnant sister a break from the chaos."

I wonder if she considers murder a form of chaos or an everyday nonevent.

I'm still standing in the kitchen, frozen at the sink.

Novi's eyes meet mine, and as if having a silent conversation, they ask if I really am okay with it, but it's not like I can say no. She might kill me even harder.

"Go be with your niblings. I'm fine." I'd probably be more believable if my voice didn't crack.

"And if he's not, you know who to blame," Elena says.

This time, I hear the playful tone in her voice and am able to recognize it for what it is. Just like Novi, Elena loves being feared, but I trust Novi when he says she's as sweet as he is. Not many people get to see that side of him, but I do, and I'm going to remind myself that she's exactly the same as he is.

She's not intimidating. She's not.

"Need me to take all the knives?" Novi lowers his voice, but Elena must hear him because she snorts.

"Of course not," I say. Loudly. But my eyes must say something else because Novi picks up the knife block and tucks it under his arm.

"Let's go, kids!"

They leave, but I can no longer be nervous about being left alone with Novi's scary sister because now I'm worried about what the public will think when they see Radimir Novicov carrying a block of knives down the street with two little kids trailing behind him.

I hope he has bail money stashed around here somewhere.

Because I'm too chickenshit to approach Elena, she comes to me. I figure as long as the kitchen counter is still between us, I'm safe. Only, she rounds that and keeps coming.

Even though my flight instinct is telling me to run, I force myself to stay still.

Remember, Colby: she's not intimidating.

She raises her arms, and just when I think it didn't matter if Novi took her knives away from her, she's going to kill me with her bare hands, she wraps her arms around my shoulders—my shoulders and not my neck—and hugs me.

Through my confusion, I'm able to stiffly hug her back, and when she steps away, her eyes are glassy.

I want to make more jokes about her wanting to kill me and crying because she feels sorry for me over it, but there's something in the way she casts her gaze down, her head low, that tells me now's not the time.

In a shaky voice, she says, "Thank you for bringing him out of that closed-off way about him."

I'm … confused. "You think I did what now?"

"I didn't know why my brother was suddenly so adamant on wanting to come out, and I realize now. It's because you make him happy."

"I know it might seem like it's because of me, but—"

"Maybe now he will not care what Russia has to say about him when he does. He will just do it."

I suck in a deep breath and send up a silent "see you soon" to all of my dead relatives because Elena might be scary, but she's also misguided, and I want her to know what her reluctance to denounce him does to him.

"The thing is," I start and then have to take another breath. "He doesn't want to come out for me. Even if he does come out right now, we can't tell anyone we're together because I'm his coach. I would lose my job, it would be a huge scandal in the hockey world, and even when he retires at the end of next season, we're still going to have to keep us under wraps for a while so no one thinks anything inappropriate happened while we were working together."

"But that has happened."

My gut sinks. "I know, and yes, we both acknowledge that it's a morally gray area, but …" I flash back to Novi locking us in the storage room, to him recreating us playing quarters like we did all those years ago, and how it almost seems inevitable that we ended up where we did. Like it's fate or something.

"But …?" she asks.

"We couldn't help ourselves."

"You're in love with him," she says.

If I'm not, I'm mid-fall with no safety net. "I'm falling hard."

"Then if he's not coming out for you, why—"

I make sure to stare her in the eyes as I say, "He doesn't want you or your kids to suffer because of him. He's been ready to come out for a few years, Elena. He hasn't, though, because even if you refuse to leave Russia, you also refuse to denounce him, and he won't—"

"I wouldn't get arrested for not doing it. He's being overprotective of us."

"It doesn't matter if the chance is only small that something could happen to you or your family. Because if there's any risk at all, he won't do it. He's selfless to a fault."

"How can he ask me to give up my career?"

"He's not."

"He is though. I can't not stand up for my beliefs that the best person I know in this whole world should get to be happy with whoever he wants. I won't pretend to hate him when all he wants is to be himself."

"I understand that, I do, but have you thought about an alternate plan where you get to keep your career and not denounce him?"

She thinks about it for a beat, her lips pressed into a flat line. "You're talking about leaving Russia."

"I know Russia is your home and you love it there, but there are cooking networks in the US who might want to snap you up. Or in Canada. The UK. Hell, anywhere else in Europe."

She folds her arms. "I thought you were scared of me, and now you're telling me to my face that it's my fault my brother is so depressed."

"No, it's not your fault. He's depressed because he *chooses* to protect you. Personally, I think you could take on the Russian government all by yourself. But yes, until he can know you're one hundred percent safe, he will continue to hide his true self from the world."

Just as I think I'm getting through to her, she hugs me again.

"Then I can't express how glad I am that he has you to scatter happiness and light amongst his darkness."

It might be official: Novi's sister is him in woman form. Terrifying, subtly sweet, but most of all, bullheaded and stubborn.

CHAPTER TWENTY-NINE

NOVI

I love Elena and the kids being here, but I end up with a run of four days away right in the middle of their visit, and then yesterday, we were in Anaheim for the day. It's one of the downsides of this career. We are so busy and play so much that during the season, we have little time in our lives for something that isn't hockey.

I have a lot of respect for my teammates with kids who try to be present in their lives, but I know it is hard on them. This is why I will adopt once I've retired and can spend my entire days teaching them to play hockey instead. It would also be a lot easier if I had a certain coach beside me to do that …

"I made sure you have excellent tickets for tonight's game," I tell Elena on my way out of the house. "And if you see Colby there, remember that you do not know him."

"Who?"

"Exactly." I kiss her head goodbye and leave. In two days, they're flying to Canada to visit our parents before heading back home again. It's the part I hate most. Yes, I will maybe convince Colby to stay over more once they're gone, but the kids are growing quickly. I miss them. It's also been too long since I've seen my brother-in-law.

If I come out, I will likely never go to Russia again.

Then it's all on Elena to visit. To take the children and the flight. How often can she do that with a newborn?

The frustration is getting too much though. Hiding, faking, being accused of homophobia.

It used to be so easy to ignore.

The difference is that I don't want to ignore it now.

I get in my morning skate, go home to a quiet house for a big meal and a nap, then head back to the arena. The buzz is infectious, people everywhere as they get ready for the game. My teammates are either quiet or too loud, and the coaching staff have last-minute meetings and check-ins. Making sure they're happy with the lines. Going around and giving pep talks and checking we're ready. I love all the buildup.

Colby approaches where I'm sitting in front of my cubby, iPad in his hands, professional "we barely know each other" mask that he wears so well in place. "Knees," he says, not looking at me.

It's so cute when he plays coy.

I tap his foot with mine, and he drags his eyes up to meet my gaze. "I have *very* good knees," I reply, and he knows better than anyone how good I am on them.

"You do." Amusement flares in his gaze. "So look after them. Especially the right."

He walks away before I can say anything else, and Turkey chokes back a laugh. "Subtle, Novi."

"I do not know what you mean."

"Poor Coach Kessinger. He's just trying to do his job."

"*Da*. He does it very well."

"Please don't tell me how well."

"Very, very well."

Turkey swipes his hand over his face. "Lucky me, being the one you get to share gay sex jokes with."

"We had a moment. We are bonded now."

"Did I get a say in that?"

"People are begging to be best friends with Radimir Novicov, and you're the chosen one."

He gives me a dry look. "Are those *people* in the room with us?"

"I am a fun-loving guy." I pretend to sigh. "It is a curse sometimes. To be so popular."

Turkey pats me on the shoulder. "Delulu as always. Never change."

I feign confusion. "Who is this delulu?"

"It's slang for *delusional*. Which you are, my brother."

Ha. Another point for Turkey on my list. Life is sweet.

"Novi?" Coach Whelan calls. "Visitor."

There's not long before we need to get ready for warm-ups, so I'm clueless about who would be waiting, but when I step out into the hall and find Elena with the kids, I'm immediately concerned.

"Was there a problem with your seats?"

"Nope," she says and then switches to Russian. *"There is a problem with my brother."*

"Rude."

She smirks and holds something out to me. *"I have been researching."*

My gaze drops as I reach out and take the rainbow stick tape from her. *"What is this?"*

"I know you won't come out. I understand why, and it hurts me. I want to be here supporting you as you, not as this straight man you pretend to be."

"But—"

"I'm the older sister. I've been a grown-up longer than you, and I know you think I'm a bit of a silly idiot sometimes, because I am, but I can protect myself—even Colby said so. I can make my own choices, and so can you."

"I don't understand."

She flicks the tape I'm holding. *"People use this in warm-ups, yes?"*

"Yes …"

"Then I want you to use it. I want to see my whole brother on that ice. If you won't come out, at least give me that."

I'm shocked into silence for once. *"I …"*

"I'm not asking. If you're not ready, that's one thing, but if you are … please. I love you. Let me see you happy."

"People will talk."

"Straight players show their support with it all the time."

"Yes, but most of those players don't have a reputation for being homophobic." I turn the tape over and over in my hands. There have been so many moments in my life where my teammates used this, and I had no interest in playing that game. Now … I want it. I want it so much it physically hurts me.

She wraps her hands around mine. *"You can do it, Radimir."*

I can do it. Sure, people will talk, but I don't have to answer them. I don't have to give an explanation. I don't have to do anything other than put some tape on my stick and warm up for the game. That's it.

"*Time to go, kids,*" Elena says, and I watch her gather them up and head along the hall.

I have no clue how she got down here, but that's my sister for you.

The locker room has the same big energy as it did earlier, but I block most of it out. I rub my thumb over the rough tape, still debating with myself, but then a flare of indignation takes over.

Fuck it.

I'm allowed this one thing.

I keep my gaze on my stick the whole time I tape it up, not wanting to see any of my teammates' reactions. I'm going to be confident but silent about it.

Only the second I set the tape down beside me, Turkey snatches it up again.

Without a word, he wraps his stick as well.

Then he presses a kiss to his work. "What a sexy-looking stick," he says, tossing the tape at Landers, who shrugs and tapes his up too.

This warm feeling in my chest is usually only reserved for Colby.

I can feel some of the looks being sent my way, but I'm too focused on the guys beside me, who, without even knowing it, have taken the pressure completely off my shoulders. It's one thing to be the only one out there; it's another when I'm part of a group. There will still be speculation, considering how against this I've been in the past, but it's a start.

What straight men don't realize most of the time is that it's literally *that* easy for them. No overthinking. No questioning every choice.

It's a word. An action. An adjustment to their belief.

With something so easy, they've not only made me feel safe but human.

I wish everyone understood the impact they could have by doing so little.

We get dressed, lace our skates, and then it's time for the warm-up skate.

I refuse to let myself be nervous because it's the first time I'm ever getting to take the ice as myself. That is a freeing feeling, knowing that my sister and Colby will both see me.

The arena is filling slowly, expected to be almost full by game time, but I ignore the fans and focus on what I'm here to do. We trade passes, shoot bullets at the net, stretch, and get our muscles loose while adjusting our mindset. It's the biggest part for me.

And every time I glimpse that rainbow at the end of my stick, it makes me smile.

This might not be a big moment, but it's my moment.

I look around at the crowd, and it hits me: I don't want to wait until I retire.

I want to play as my whole self and inspire people like me, and if it makes the homophobes mad, that's even better. One of my biggest regrets was not getting to play in the charity hockey game a year ago. I don't want to regret this too.

Warm-up is over too soon, and I leave the ice feeling hopeful but tired. Wanting something doesn't mean that I can have it, and while that felt great, fundamentally, nothing has changed.

On the way back to the locker room, I'm stopped by a reporter. "Novicov, that rainbow looks great on your stick. You've always been so resistant to anything Pride related in the past. What's changed?"

In my mind, I picture myself opening my mouth and telling her that nothing has changed. That I've always been gay, and I love it.

In reality, I fall back on old tricks. "Sorry, I don't speak English."

Then, I walk away before she can ask anything else.

Back in the locker room, I retape my stick, and with that, the moment is a memory, and I'm Radimir Novicov again.

And I have a game to win for my sister.

CHAPTER THIRTY

COLBY

I'm equally proud of Novi and terrified, but my eyes are only watery because of the pride I have for him. I don't approach him in the locker room after warm-ups or while everyone's getting ready for the game to start because I can tell he's trying to sink in on himself. A couple of the others are already bringing attention to him more than he'd like, so I don't want to add to that.

But because I'm on the bench tonight, receiving plays sent from Ackerman, who's cutting tape as the game happens, it's really difficult not to approach him. I'm on iPad duty, and all I'm hoping for is for Novi to fuck up somehow or for me to need to go to him so I can tell him how moved I am by what he did tonight. Though maybe it's better I stay where I am. I don't trust myself to refrain from wrapping my arms around him.

This isn't the place for that, and I need to remember my professionalism, which is nonexistent thanks to Novi.

The main thing keeping me from saying anything is that his play is flawless, and I don't want to take that away from him. He hasn't scored yet, but it's only the first period, and he's leading in shots on goal. He wants it bad, and as long as he keeps the puck inside that offensive zone, one's bound to go in.

My eyes are glued to him as he skates up to a face-off with Anton Hayes. I saw Ezra have some words with him in between plays before, and I can imagine Ezra telling him he's proud of him too.

It was only rainbow tape on a stick, but for someone who has never been able to show his real self, it's a symbol of something bigger than him, bigger than the NHL.

Novi and Anton exchange words, and whatever Anton has to say makes Novi pause for that fraction of a second long enough for Anton to get the jump on the puck. Anton passes to Ezra, who passes to Deidrich. Their playing is top-tier, and it's obvious they've been playing together for years because it's so seamless.

Like it always does when I think the opposing team is going to score, my stomach jumps into my throat. The home crowd gets on their feet, anticipating the worst. Boston keeps passing between the five of them on the ice, the puck moving so fast it's difficult for even me to follow. I have no idea how Flores keeps up, but he does, and when Anton shoots backward to Ezra, and Ezra goes for his famous slapshot that's almost impossible to stop, he's ready. Either that, or it's a fluke when the puck bounces off his body and rebounds right onto Novi's blade.

There's a bit of a scrum, Anton and Deidrich trying to get control of the puck again, but Novi and Turkey have this. Novi passes to Turkey, pushes past Anton, and then Turkey passes back to him.

Ezra and his defense partner, Kosik, try to stop them, skating backward better than most people can go forward, but Turkey and Novi become an unstoppable force. Novi knows the exact moment to pass backward to Percy, our D-man, while he breaks Ezra and Kosik apart. And in that moment, Percy achieves what Ezra attempted only thirty seconds ago.

His slapshot doesn't miss, and we're the first to get on the board. My man gets a point for the assist.

My man.

I don't know when exactly I started thinking of him that way, but it makes sense. I want to spend every free moment I have with him. I want more with him, while at the same time, I know it's next to impossible.

Why does timing have to be a cruel bitch?

It's the same ol' argument I've been having with myself, and I don't see it changing anytime soon. Not until our situation changes.

The biggest problem with that is it's difficult for me to see how it could possibly change for the better. There are all these things I want with him: public dates, a relationship that we don't have to hide from the media or team management. But with Novi and me already fraternizing behind everyone's backs, I don't have high hopes that they'll allow us to have our happy ending. Not without the consequences of either losing my job or Novi being pushed out before retirement. It'll most likely be the former.

Oskar and Lane left San Jose because of past managements' actions after their relationship came out, and we're in a very similar situation. Maybe if we went to the organization first, there'd be a chance they'd be okay with it, but we can't do that until Novi comes out to the world. And it might be too late because lines have already been crossed.

While being too much in my head, Boston retaliates with a goal of their own, but Head Coach Whelan wants to review the play. It's not until his hand lands on my shoulder that I snap out of my Novi trance and get to work bringing up the replay on the iPad from one of our many cameras.

We only have a small window to challenge the goal if it's offside, which Whelan thinks it is. But if we challenge it and it's deemed to be good, we'll have to go on the penalty kill because it'll be classed as a delay of game and wasting time.

Because of my fumble, we only get to watch the footage over once, but Whelan is confident it was offside.

We challenge the goal, and the entire team holds a collective breath. When those magic words are spoken, "After review of the play, it is deemed Boston was offside, so no goal," we all finally breathe again.

After that, Boston is rattled and can't seem to land another one in the net. They do, but not until well into the third period, and we've scored twice more in between. Pulling their goalie in the last three minutes doesn't help them because Novi scores on an empty net.

We walk away with the win, and lightness beams from Novi's smile.

Of course, his teammates comment how psycho he looks and that he should be happy, ignoring him when he says, "This is my happy face. I am always happy."

Lately, because of him, so am I.

-

By the time I wrap things up with Ackerman in the cutting room, Novi is nowhere to be seen. I have texts from Ezra telling me to meet them at Oskar and Lane's house for a Queer Collective catch-up, and I'm assuming Novi got them too.

I love that they're including me even though I'm not a player, but I was kind of hoping to have a Novi night.

Alone. Naked. I want to show him with my mouth how proud I am of him.

I text Novi to see if he'll be at Oskar's, but he doesn't respond by the time I get to my car, so before I turn the car on, I pull my phone out again to call him.

That's when his hand lands on my shoulder, and I drop my phone and jump a mile high in my seat.

"Payback's a bitch?"

Even if he scared the crap out of me, I'm happy to see him. "Aww, we have a running bit already."

"Our bits run?"

"You know what I mean. Stop trying to get another point on your little scorepad."

"I forgot you know my game."

"I can't believe no one else has ever picked up on it."

"No one gets me like you do."

I both love and hate how he makes it sound like I'm special. That I'm the only one who understands him. Like I was made for him. He's making it more and more difficult to protect my career over my feelings for him.

"We going home to your place?" I ask.

"I have to go to Oskar's first."

"Is Ezra forcing you? I've heard he can be demanding when two queer players are in the same city. Like the world will implode if they don't combine their queer powers."

"No. Well, yes, he threatened violence, which is cute, but no, I have to go see my bestie so I can gloat about kicking his ass and tease him over the unallowed goal."

I will not be selfish in this moment. I won't be. "How much trouble do you think I'll be in if I skip it? I'm not really in the Collective. I'm like the adoptive puppy following them around."

"You have to be there. This is why I hijacked your back seat."

"I'll go. If you want me there."

He scoffs. "Now who speaks bad English?"

"How was that bad English?"

"Because it makes no sense. I want you everywhere with me."

Aww.

"Besides, we'll be at Oskar and Lane's house, which is technically in public but also within the safety of the Queer Collective, who are vowed to silence when it comes to me."

My lips twitch. "You made them take a vow of silence?"

"No. They super nicely offered it to me. It was weird."

"Were you, by any chance, smiling at them when they did it?"

"I was! How did you know?"

"Just a hunch." A hunch that they were scared to death by him. "Okay, let's go make an appearance." The thought of walking into a social gathering with Novi on my arm like we're properly together makes my heart beat faster. In a good way. And who knows? Maybe in the long run, this could be our loophole. We may not be able to have a public relationship until he retires, but this might be public enough.

I pull out of the parking lot, double-checking no one is around to see us leave together, but all the players are gone, and the only one who might still be around is Ackerman, but I left him finishing up the video files for the morning meeting.

"Oh, you should play my game with me," Novi says when we're on the road. "Everyone in the Collective is good at correcting me. They think they're doing me a favor. They're some of my highest point scorers this season."

I shake my head. "Does anyone ever not fall for it or ignore you?"

"Coach Whelan. He is no fun."

I love the way he pouts. Actually, I love the way he does most things.

When we pull up outside Oskar and Lane's house, Novi practically jumps out of the still-rolling car to get to the front door.

I'd like to think it's because he's excited we can be like an actual couple here, and God knows I'm dying to be able to kiss him for the first time all night. But as I catch up to him and the door swings open with Oskar standing there with Ezra's and Anton's voices filtering out from inside, Novi says, "Did they already tell you how badly I kicked their donkey?"

Oskar cocks his head. "You mean ass?"

"This is what I said." Novi pats Oskar's shoulder and lets himself inside, but not before winking at me over his shoulder.

I go to step past Oskar myself when he cuts me off.

"Arriving together?"

I wonder how much Lane has told him. "We do work out of the same arena. Carpooling is good for the environment."

Oskar nods solemnly. "I've heard that. So is showering together. Saves water."

Ignoring his blatant prying, I say, "It's true. It's why hockey players shower together. Or so I've heard."

"Lies. We all shower together for the orgies."

"Heard that," Lane calls from the other room.

"That man has the hearing of a bat." And even though Oskar says this on practically a whisper, Lane's retort is loud.

"Only when it comes to you and group sex."

"He's such a jealous man," Oskar says.

"I'm starting to think the real reason I didn't make it in hockey is that I am not ridiculous enough. You and Novi sound practically the same."

We make our way down the hall to where the others are sitting at a high-top kitchen counter, but Oskar says, "Can confirm. It is a prerequisite to be ridiculous to make it in the NHL."

Anton clears his throat, but Oskar waves him off.

"You don't count. You fell for one twice as ridiculous as the normal hockey player, so you cancel each other out."

Novi pats the stool next to him, and the second my ass lands in the seat, Ezra turns to both of us.

"Have you fucked yet?"

Anton backhands him, and Oskar laughs.

"Exhibit A."

Yet, every single person in this room is staring at us, waiting for the answer, but it's not my place to say, so I wait on bated breath for words to come out of Novi's mouth.

Any words.

CHAPTER THIRTY-ONE

NOVI

I knew this question was coming, and I'm perfectly ready for it. It has taken me months, but I finally understand why this group exists and why so many queer men have joined it.

I trust them. I can be myself here.

"*Nyet*," I say, feeling the weight of their disbelieving eyes as I grab Colby's stool and drag him closer with a tile-protesting *krrrr*. Then I add, "Well, not today."

Ezra and Oskar break out into increasingly louder versions of "I knew it" as Lane releases a long sigh, throws back his nip of amber liquid, and sets the glass on the counter again.

"I'm happy for you both," he says, but the searching look he gives my Colby makes me think it's not their first conversation about us.

"We're happy for us both too." I'm speaking for Colby, but it has to be true. I could not be happy if he is not. "And we're keeping this on the down-loud, obviously."

"Down-loud?" Ezra asks.

"*Da*. Like it is a secret."

"Oh, down-*low*."

Under the counter, Colby holds up his hand, and I high-five it. See? He's happy.

"So this is one of the great Collective meetings, huh? I know I've had dinner with a couple of you before, but this is the first time it's been a group thing," Colby says, looking around. "It's tamer than I was picturing."

"Don't challenge them." Anton is sitting two stools away from Colby, sipping on a beer. With his black hair and square jaw, he reminds me of Colby, but in more of a clean-cut sort of way. The creases in Colby's forehead, the smile lines around his eyes, and his messy hair speckled with grays turn me on way more than the catalog-model type.

All he needs is some missing teeth to be my perfect, rugged man.

"Did someone say challenge?" Ezra asks.

"*No*." Anton and Lane are so perfectly in time.

"So what you're saying," I begin, pretending to be confused, "is there will be no naked runs or tables dancing or ordering five hundred pizzas at midnight?"

"Are you purposely trying to give us ideas?" Oskar asks, leaning his crossed arms on the counter. With the jagged scar down one side of his face, he is the type of handsome I can get behind. Mostly. He is still too pretty.

"I have heard so many things, and none of them involved talking around a kitchen counter like we are a book club."

Lane pins Colby with a pleading look. "Make him stop."

"I'm only saying, maybe it is right to never meet your idols."

"Awww, I'm your idol?" Ezra asks.

"I think he was talking about all of us," Anton points out.

"I'll get you into a thong again," Ezra promises him. "Don't you worry."

"There's a story there," Colby says as Lane makes a slashing motion over his throat.

I put the poor man out of his misery. "Is there food here? I am so hungry after such an incredible win where there was no competition and I showed why I am one of the greats."

"I think you've forgotten English again." Ezra jumps up to sit on the counter. "You mean to say the win where you barely beat us and only got that last goal because I was feeling friendly toward you after the whole gay stick thing."

"You cannot tell people Novi has a gay stick," Colby says.

"Rainbow rod?"

"Nope."

Ezra's eyes squint up. "Magic unicorn staff?"

Colby face-palms, and Lane takes over. "Speaking of rainbow tape and making a statement, have you checked to see what the online response is?"

"I don't need to," I say. "The people who care will be split between homophobes and others debating if it means I'm queer, while others will say it doesn't matter after my years of being silent—it's still too little too late in their eyes. I'm not in a hurry to see all of that."

"It'll die quickly," Anton says. "Despite what your ego thinks, no one really cares all that much about us."

"What do you mean? I'm Radimir Novicov. Everyone cares about me."

"In hockey circles, sure. But when I was trying to come out subtly, literally no one noticed. Ez and I would be holding hands or going out to dinner, and it was completely ignored. Unless you kiss Colby in the middle of a game, what you two are doing is a nonevent."

"It only takes one person though," Lane cautions.

Anton laughs. "Remind me how you and Oskar were found out again."

Something smug crosses Lane's face. "We were fucking around in the arena."

Colby immediately turns to me. "No."

"But—"

"No."

I turn to Ezra in support. "You see how he ruins my fun?"

Ezra hooks a thumb at Anton. "I'm married to the most boring person on Earth. I get it."

"I wore a thong bikini for you!"

"Again, I'm very interested in hearing about this thong," Colby says.

"Besides," Ezra continues, eyeing Colby with suspicion. "Even we're not dumb enough to fool around at work."

"Is dumb the right word?" Lane almost sounds offended as Oskar wraps an arm around his waist.

"It's exactly the right word. But I'm also happy everything worked out how it did. Anaheim is having an okay season, but more importantly, they're not a bunch of assholes. No one even reacts when I suggest a locker room OnlyFans."

Ezra perks up. "A what now?"

"*No.*"

The way Anton and Lane have perfected the unison really is sort of creepy.

While they bicker about that, I tease them again. "Only fams is about families, yes? This sounds like a perfect thing for the locker room and team bonding."

Colby shakes his head, and at first, I think he's forgotten the game. "It's Only *flans.* Lots of baking."

"Why would they bake in a locker room?"

He shrugs. "Sounds sort of unhygienic to me."

Ezra's mouth is somewhere around his ankles. "What in the great gay gods are you talking about?"

"You want to start a baking show with your team?" I answer. "My sister can give you tips."

"Oh my God," Lane mutters.

"It's porn," bursts from Oskar. "You want your sister to give us tips with porn?"

"I don't think cooking prawns is baking, but I'm sure she can—"

Ezra all but leaps over the counter to seal my mouth with his hand. "I'm doing you a favor."

When he finally lets go, Colby and I high-five under the counter again.

"Moving on from whatever that was," Anton says. "*Are* you planning on coming out, Novi? Is that what tonight was?"

"It was my sister's idea. A way for me to go out there as myself. She was very pushy about it."

"Was she?" Colby asks, voice strange. "Was she pushy? Your sweet, funny, delightful sister?"

"It's hard to believe, I know."

He takes my hand. "I was very proud of you."

"I was too. It felt really good. Like I didn't have to hide anymore."

A slight frown settles between Colby's eyebrows. "So you *are* thinking about coming out?"

That's a difficult one.

Ezra switches to Russian. *"What about your sister?"*

"She is very determined that I stop thinking about her and do it."

"And how do you feel about that?"

It takes me a second. *"Unsettled. But hopeful."*

"Wait, wait, wait." Colby turns to Ezra. "You speak Russian?"

"I also speak Polish," I say.

Ezra gives me a look of betrayal. "You told me you didn't. All this time I've been trying to remember the Polish word for the English word and then the Russian word for the Polish word. You made me speak Russian when I didn't have to?"

I shrug. "You say that like you can actually speak Russian. You needed the practice."

Ezra switches to Polish. *"Fuck you."*

I blow him a kiss.

"I want to learn," Colby says, ignoring us both. "I started, but …"

But I went AWOL and ditched out on him before he could. "I'll teach you."

"Thanks." It doesn't sound like he means it. "I'm not sure you have the patience for it."

"But I am very patient."

"Last time you told me that if you spoke it constantly around me that I'd pick it up. Then refused to speak anything else."

"*Da.* It's how babies learn."

"I'm not a baby."

Anton is laughing. "You think Ez will be more patient? Ezra? I've seen him eat a banana *through* the skin because peeling it would take too long."

"I wasn't trying to eat it. I was trying to seduce you."

"Trust me when I say there's nothing sexy about a man trying to deep-throat a banana, peel and all."

"But it was a big one."

"The little stalk bit at the end was still attached!"

One side of Ezra's mouth kicks up like he's remembering. "Yeah, that tickled the tonsils a bit."

Colby tilts his head to one side. "Just how big was this banana?"

"Don't encourage him."

"All I'm saying is that if it really *was* big, I'd be impressed."

Ezra turns to Oskar. "Quick, where's your fruit kept?"

"I could tell you that, but it wouldn't matter anyway."

"Why?"

Oskar hooks a thumb over his shoulder. "Lane hid everything phallic-shaped before you got here."

"The audacity."

Lane pours himself another drink. "I stand by my decision."

Anton tilts his beer Lane's way. "Thank you for your service."

"Yeah," Colby says. "You have to nip this behavior in the butt."

"I think you mean bud. But yes. I've learned." Lane pours himself another drink.

"Careful, Ezra is ready to curl into the feeble position," I add.

"It's fetal, and no I'm not." He plants his hands on his hips as Colby and I high-five twice under the counter. "Bet I could find the stash though."

"Good luck."

"They're in your nightstand, aren't they?"

"Despite the numerous edible things in there, no, we did not stash the food with our sex toys," Lane says.

"Numerous?" Ezra looks around at each of us. "Be right back."

"Is he … going to paw through our personal items?"

Oskar pats Lane's shoulder in pity. "You *just* said you've learned, and yet you dangled that in front of Ezra anyway."

"Lube, massage oil …" Anton counts things off on his fingers. "Underwear …" He pauses and squints at the wall. Then he abruptly stands up. "Ah. I'm going to go and … check on … something. Not Ezra. Be right back."

I reach across Colby to scoop up Anton's half-finished beer and take a long drink. "He is going to help Ezra. You know that, right?"

Oskar looks at Lane, who holds up a fist. At first, I think they're going to fist bump, but then they start rock, paper, scissors. Oskar loses.

"Fine, I'll go. But I still maintain this is your fault."

"It's about time you cleaned up one of my messes. Equal partnership and all that." Lane watches Oskar go before immediately turning back to us. "Before the three stooges get back—"

"You're including Anton in that?" I ask.

"Yep." Lane doesn't even hesitate. "Give it time and you'll understand. He's just as ridiculous as the rest of them. But quickly: I know I don't work for either of you, but I'm here. Anything PR, you're welcome to come to me to talk through it, and I've already made this offer to Colby, but I'm making it to you as well, Novi. Coming out isn't going to be a stark before and after for you that some of these other guys have faced. I'm not minimizing or saying it was easy for them, but not only do you have to think of your mother country, you also need to think about Colby and his job. Coming out could mean that people draw the line between you two, and I know that's something Colby is worried about."

I turn to him, hating that he worries about anything. "You're worried?"

"Hey, no need to yell."

"I am not yelling."

"Sorry. Your death glare confused me."

I huff. "I don't glare. And you should not be worried."

"In a perfect world, I agree with you. But we've been seeing each other for a while now, and we couldn't tell anyone because you're not out. Telling them *after* you come out isn't an option either because if they find out we've been crossing boundaries already, it will cost me my job."

Lane drums his fingers on the counter. "He's right. Seeing Oskar cost me mine, and I hate to agree with San Jose's team management, but they didn't really have a choice in that matter. A team has to protect its players. We can say it was all consensual and above board until we're blue in the face; it doesn't change the power dynamics. I do maintain they could've handled it better, but I knew the risks when I started sleeping with a player."

That almost makes me laugh. "Colby? Have power over me? But he's like a cute polar bear, and I am the puppy following him around."

Colby squeezes my thigh. "That metaphor doesn't make the point that you think it does."

I still don't see the problem.

But between my sister and the team finding out that Colby is my boyfriend, it's sounding less and less likely that I can come out.

The others get back, and Lane straightens as Ezra walks up and stands beside him. He doesn't say anything, just looks at Lane in a way that looks unhinged.

"Well, well, well," Anton says, walking in behind Oskar. "We had no idea you had it in you, Lane."

"Didn't you?" Lane only downs his neglected drink. "I guess you're all forgetting that Oskar proposed to *me*."

Colby and I glance at each other.

I have no idea what they mean by any of that, and I don't think I want to know. Toys? Edible things? What is more sexy than enjoying Colby's body? I don't need anything fancy in order to do that.

While they all continue to tease Lane about what was in the drawer, I lean over and press a kiss to Colby's cheek. "Do not worry about anything. I will make it all work."

And I'm determined to.

CHAPTER THIRTY-TWO

COLBY

I'm not mad at Lane for bringing up legitimate concerns, but there's a reason I haven't gone into too much detail with Novi about worrying for my career. Seeing Novi with the others from the Collective, where he's comfortable enough to show me affection in front of them, him taking a step by using rainbow tape on his stick, he's slowly gaining that confidence he's been lacking. At least when it comes to his identity. He has more than enough confidence in every other aspect of his life. Maybe a little too much.

He's been attentive and sweet all night, as if that's what I need to ease my worries. They only make them worse. But when he's touching me, looking at me the way he did that very first night seventeen years ago, everything else floats away.

If I'm completely honest with myself, the fact I so easily turn off my thoughts about my future when I'm with him already tells me that I'm willing to make him my priority. That doesn't mean it's a smart decision. Especially when I don't exactly know where Novi's at emotionally.

We're together, and we're exclusive. I've met his sister and niblings, but past being able to be an out couple once he retires, we haven't exactly said we're in it for the long haul. Then again, if we're talking about being together two years from now, that should be indication enough for me.

But it's not.

Because I'm putting everything on the line here. Before, it was Novi, but with Elena's stubbornness resembling his, I have no doubt he'll come out before Elena leaves Russia. I get the feeling she won't leave at all.

Novi's happy to have us the way we are, and he's eager to come out, but once he does, will he really be happy settling for the first guy he's been with?

If I think back to the first guy I ever tried to date after I came out, I'm not filled with good memories. Back then, I thought all relationships were filled with insecurity and holding on so tight they'd get claustrophobic and disappear for days.

Turns out, no, he was just a fuckhead who wanted his cake and to eat it, too, and always made me feel like his cheating was my fault.

Not that I'd be that kind of toxic with Novi, but shouldn't he experience that before realizing I'm the ultimate catch? Shouldn't he make dating mistakes so he knows for sure if I'm the one for him?

"You are still worried," he says as I pull up to his house. Usually when I come over, I park my car in his garage so no one can see, but he won't have his clicker with him seeing as he left his car at the rink.

"Worried isn't the right word." Don't ask me what the right word is.

"If you lose your job, I will get you new job. Better job."

"I appreciate that, but if I get fired during my first season in the NHL, there's no coming back from that."

And I've already given up on one dream job. I don't want to lose this when I just got the opportunity, but I'm also at the point where I don't want to give up Novi either.

"We're making this secret work. We can keep doing it."

"Maybe not if we're seen sitting in your driveway at odd hours of the night."

"I'll go open garage." Novi jumps out, and I take a deep breath and try to convince myself not to freak out about everything yet.

Novi's right when he says we're acing this secretive thing. I don't have to worry about the consequences right this second.

The garage door slowly opens, and even though I'm sitting here, clouded by doubt, I realize that Novi not only deserves happiness, but he also deserves honesty.

So I pull into the garage, climb out of the car, and follow him inside.

"You want drink first or go right to bed?" Novi pulls me toward him by the lapels of my suit, and as tempting as it is to choose to go to bed, I need to give him something more than that. Even if it's putting my heart on the line, I want him to understand that my fear comes from losing both things I care about more than anything else.

"Let's have another drink first."

"Are you trying to get me drunk? Because you don't need to. I am what they call a sure thing."

"It's not that. Trust me when I say I'm eager to get you naked so I can make you forget the rest of the world with my mouth—"

Novi groans. "I take back my offer for drink. No drink. Only sex."

I grip his hand. "How about talk first. Then sex."

"Is it more about your worry?"

"Sort of."

His hands land on my shoulders and make their way down to my biceps, where he squeezes. "We will work something out."

"It's easy to say that, and I want to have that kind of faith, but the truth is, I'm worried because I'm risking everything for something that might only be a fling. If you really see a future with me, then you are worth the risk of my career. If you think you might want to date around after coming out, then … I can't keep playing this game."

"What game?"

"The one where we're together but only in secret because we have too much on the line. I wish I could see into the future and know that everything will work out and that I'm not about to have my heart broken or get fired, but I don't know that either of those things won't happen."

"You're worried I'll break your heart? Does that mean you are putting it in my hands?"

"It means I want to, but I'm terrified it won't be worth losing everything for."

He lowers his forehead to mine. "I will cherish your heart always."

I swallow hard. "Always? What if I get fired, and then I grow resentful, and I treat you like shit, and—"

"That won't happen."

"How do you know?"

"Because the same way you need to trust I won't do anything that could hurt you, I need to do the same. Because you don't have my heart in your hands: you already own it."

My breath is stilted as I try to suck in air, and he's making that thing happen again. He's making all those doubts disappear until they're so far in the back of my mind I can't even see them anymore.

I lean in and take his mouth with mine, plunging my tongue inside.

Images of our futures with each other flood my brain, taking up space where my worries were. I see us with our family—his sister and niblings, his parents, my parents, and us adding our own additions of tiny humans and fur children. I can see Novi staying home and teaching them how to be big and scary like him while I'm on the bench as a head coach. It all looks perfect. It feels right.

But if I truly needed all of that, I'd have the strength to stop this. Right here. Right now.

I want that future with him more than I have ever wanted anything else in my life. More than *anything*. Including the NHL. Including coaching. Because if I could have that future with Novi, I'd be willing to compromise what kind of coach I could be. I loved D1 hockey. I also loved teaching the younger kids. I love being a coach, and with Novi all but confessing he's falling for me as much as I'm falling for him, the level at which I do it doesn't seem so important anymore.

I don't want to give it up, but I will. For him.

"Please tell me we're done with the talking now," he says against my lips.

I pull away from him and reach for his jacket at the same time, shoving my hands inside and slipping it off his shoulders. "So done."

"Thank the hockey gods."

It's a messy trail of discarded shoes and clothes on the way to his bedroom, but while we're frantically pawing at each other, it's not about rushing this. It's about needing that closeness, skin on skin, hard body against hard body. It's about promising each other through physical touch what our mouths aren't ready to say yet.

It's giving each other the trust needed to let ourselves free-fall into love.

We continue to kiss. I grab his ass and push our hips together, trapping our hard cocks between us.

Novi ruts against me, and it steals the air from my lungs. It feels so good to be like this with him. Tingles shoot all over my body, and goose bumps fill my flesh.

He runs his hand down the middle of my back, and his fingers slip into the crease of my ass. I pant into his mouth as my hips surge forward, trying to get his hand lower. The anticipation of his fingers stretching my hole makes my body warm all over, but it never comes.

Novi removes his hand and places it on my hip. He gently pushes me away from him, and when I open my eyes, he's already staring at me.

"What's wrong?" I ask.

"I want to bottom for you."

That idea excites me, maybe too much, because my dick throbs at the thought, but I want him to be sure. "You don't have to."

"I want to."

"Because you've thought about it or because you want to prove a point about how serious you are about me? You don't have to bottom for me to believe you. I do believe you." I cup his cheek. "And I would never want you to do something outside your comfort zone because you felt like I needed it. I don't need it. I only need you."

"Then have me. All of me."

I suck in a sharp breath. "Then get on your hands and knees."

I don't mean for it to sound growly, but it comes out that way, and Novi shudders.

"It's official," he says and steps out of my arms. "I will not be able to take direction from you at work without getting hard."

"I'm offended you don't already. All you have to do is be in the same room, and I ache for you."

Novi gets on the bed, and I grab supplies from his nightstand.

Not going to lie, it's been a while since I took someone's ass virginity, so I'm nervous as hell, but I'm glad he's chosen to do this with me and not some random guy in a glory hole somewhere. I'm going to make sure he enjoys it, even if it means taking our time.

I approach him as he looks absolutely sinful with his ass in the air while resting on his elbows.

My knees hit the bed behind him, and I crawl my way in between his legs. I lean forward and plaster my front to his back, then kiss along his shoulder blades. "If you don't like any part of it, tell me, okay? I want this to be a good experience for you."

He looks at me over his shoulder and says, "I trust you."

And in this moment, I realize I trust him too. With everything. Even my heart.

CHAPTER THIRTY-THREE

NOVI

This isn't something I've had long, deep thoughts about, but Colby moving inside my body feels right. It's only his finger for now, yet I've never been more connected to him. I can feel the way he cares and wants to make this good. It connects with a deeper part of me that needs the tenderness of his kisses, his hands, the way his nose drags over my spine.

Colby is my partner in everything, and I hate that he doubted how deeply my feelings go, but with him, I'm ready for the world. He makes me feel invincible because I know I will always have his support, so I want to give him the same. I want us to be a power couple. The greatest that ever was.

My head coach husband living his dreams while I talk about hockey and play with our kids. This sounds like magic to me.

"You okay?" he checks, finger stroking in and out of my hole.

"*Da*." It feels strange but good. This thrill of something unstoppable between us. "I want more."

"Of course you do." His voice is all smiley. "Let me guess, you want to be the best at this too?"

"Want? There is no want. I know I will be incredible."

"Based on all that past experience?"

I love the way he teases me. "You will see. I'm going to drive you wild." I press back onto his finger. "Now, more."

Colby thankfully listens as he kisses along my neck and pushes another finger inside. It's a tighter fit, but still nothing I can't handle.

"More."

He chuckles. "Give me a second."

I twist my fingers in the sheets to try and be patient. Needing him always doesn't make it easy though, and in no time at all, I'm pressing back into him again, tilting my hips as a silent beg for him to give me what I want.

"You're so fucking sexy," he says, mouth bringing the sensitive skin at my throat alive. My whole body craves his touch, including my very full cock hanging very heavy between my legs. That part of me really, really needs him to touch it.

He bites down on my earlobe, and the short, sharp pain distracts me as he fills me with another finger. This time, I notice the stretch. The fullness. Being worked open makes my balls ache pleasantly, and I'm impatient for it to be his cock.

His fingers stroke over something deep in my ass that sends a ripple of pleasure through me.

"There we go," he says at my long moan. "That's what I want you to sound like."

"Keep doing that and I will keep making those noises," I rasp.

His fingers are magic. I've heard about a prostate and how anal can be anything from uncomfortable to painful to amazing, but I never expected this. This steady buzz of building want, spreading out to all my limbs and making me hungry for Colby to keep going.

"I can't wait to get inside you. It's going to feel so good."

"Do it already."

He peels himself away from my back, up onto his knees, and spends a moment stretching me with his fingers. The noise he makes is deep and rumbly, just like those words he growled at me earlier.

I've never been so turned on.

"Yeah ..." His voice is strained. "You're ready."

Finally.

"If you could see yourself from this angle ... Fuck, Novi. This is seventeen years of fantasies come true."

Suddenly, I'm thrown back to those days, all the times I'd looked at Colby and wondered. Longed for his touch. We're no longer the grown men we are today but those two scared boys, too cautious to act on our urges.

"Colby," I whine.

His fingers disappear, only adding to my desperation, and he grabs the condom wrapper from the bed. I don't like it. Being open and waiting. Like my body knows this isn't right. Colby should be with me always, and I'm ready for him, needing him to hurry it up so I can feel myself wrapped around him.

"Your ass has always tortured me, but this is something else."

I look over my shoulder at him. "You can do everything to it that you ever wanted to."

"There isn't enough time in one night for that," he says, rolling on the condom. "But this is a good start."

Colby moves between my legs, both hands rubbing over my ass before he reaches for his cock. I can't see what he's doing, but I can feel it. Feel his hesitance, his excitement. Feel the way he wants this so desperately but is trying to make it last.

I feel it in him because I'm the exact same way.

He inhales deeply. "Okay, you ready?"

"Always."

His cock presses against my hole.

I relax into the intrusion, hungry for it, loving the way his tip is forcing me open. Deep in my gut, this feels right. The man I care about more than anyone, the man I've wanted always, the man who I might be falling for, filling me in a way no one ever has before.

It's torturously slow. Careful. I can't wait for the day that we know each other's bodies completely and can have all kinds of sex. Quick and dirty, slow and sensual. Sloppy, drunken, fun, and deep, meaningful, drawn-out. I want all of it with Colby, and if I try to picture a future that doesn't have him in it, the sadness is unbearable.

He's the only one I've ever wanted, and I hope that never changes.

Colby lets out a long exhale as his scratchy pubes reach my ass. It doesn't hurt, which is surprising. The desperation in my cock has waned, but as soon as I wrap my hand around it, interest floods back into it. I stroke myself until I'm hard again while Colby's hands run up and down my sides.

"Let me know when I can move."

I squeeze around him, and he chokes over a breath. I wish we were face-to-face so he could see all the ways he's making me smile. "I'm already good at this."

"Fuck. Good. Yes."

His wrecked voice makes my balls ache. "You can move."

Colby settles his hands on my hips as he pulls slowly out and pushes forward again.

It's a weird, different, amazing feeling. The way the movement ignites all the nerves in the area and has lust sweeping through me again. Each controlled thrust, each stuttered breath, the way his grip is steadily tightening on me.

And that spot he keeps passing over is making me lose control. Like my arms and legs might melt and I'll become a puddle beneath him.

All discomfort is gone. All worry about pain has passed. The craving for more is filling my gut with force, and when Colby falls into a rhythm, I push back onto him.

This is the sex of my dreams. How I always imagined things would be with him. I'm trying not to regret how I let him slip away the first time, but if I didn't, would we be here now? I was so young and stupid and scared back then, I'm positive I would have ruined it. So while I don't think the regret will ever leave me, at least I know this is right. We came together when we were both ready, and now that I know what it's like to lose him, I'm never going to do it again.

Colby is the only man who can match me. The only one I'll ever be satisfied with.

The forearm I'm leaning on is stiff from my weight, but I don't want to let go of my cock to ease the kink in my shoulder either. I'm painfully hard, balls tightening with every thrust, and the noises Colby is making drown out everything else. His balls skim mine with every thrust, and it's almost too much. The whole area is ignited. My ass, my balls, my cock, and everything in between is being worked in the most mind-numbing way. Colby knows what he's doing, and I trust him.

Sex couldn't be easier than that.

"You okay?" he manages to get out.

"*Velikolepno.*" *Great.*

"You know I don't have any idea what you said, don't you?"

"*Da.*"

His husky laugh is so sexy. "Good. Carry on."

How he expects me to be able to make a thought, let alone remember English, is beyond me. My brain is scrambled and soupy in the best possible way. All I need is to get off, to relieve the pressure building in my balls.

The way Colby groans, how he grips my ass, thrusts getting deeper and more forceful, tells me he's getting close.

I finally let go of my cock to spit into my hand, and this time when I jerk off, I'm not holding back. My dick is swollen and ready, right on the edge, tip so sensitive that every time it slips through my palm, my ass clenches tighter.

"So close," I choke out.

"Me too, Novi. *Nrg*, close. Fuck."

I bounce back onto him as he fucks me, the sweet, loving Colby replaced by pure need. Neither of us is trying to be quiet, and it's lucky we are down the other end of the house to the guest rooms so we won't be overheard.

My hair is plastered to my forehead with sweat, the slap of his hips meeting my ass is loud and fast, my palm is slick with precum, and I'm sure I'll have bruises left behind from his hands, and every part of this is perfect.

I speed up my strokes so close to letting go, and just when I think it's taking forever, I finally hit that moment. That moment where everything is too much, feels too good, but it barely lasts for a second. I crash over that high, cum flooding my hand as my arm holding me up finally collapses.

Colby stills behind me, letting out a choked moan as he grinds against me before finally stilling, giant inhale piercing the suddenly silent room.

We're both panting, and he runs one hand down my sweaty back. "You okay?"

I turn toward him and overexaggerate my smile so there's no doubt how happy I am. "My sheets need changing."

"That's what you're thinking about?"

"It's my only complaint. Everything else was perfect."

The soft look he gives me is exactly how I feel in my soul. Colby slowly pulls out, and when I'm empty, it's strange. Like it doesn't feel right. He pulls off the condom, ties it up, and dumps it in my bathroom.

He drops back onto the bed, and I crawl out of the wet patch to cuddle up to him. His chest is warm under my cheek.

I think I love you.

The acknowledgment settles over me, welcome and happy. The thought might have been sudden, but the feeling has always been there. Like when I look at Colby and feel at home. He's my person.

And I need to take this worry away so we can be happy like this, always.

CHAPTER THIRTY-FOUR

COLBY

The more Novi and I sneak around, the more comfortable I am with it. Sure, I have moments of paranoia, but we're able to keep it professional at work, and that's really my main concern.

Turkey knows, but he really is a true ally, and I have no worries about him saying anything to anyone. Having a trans sibling, he's probably had his fair share of keeping other people's secrets.

Being with Novi makes the cloak-and-dagger stuff worth it. That, and the sex. Dear fucking God, the sex. I think I've fucked Novi on every surface of his place since his sister left for Canada. Walking out that morning after I'd first topped him was awkward as fuck when I remembered she was still there.

In my defense, I was too engrossed in everything Novi to register the small reminders around his house, like the kids' toys, Elena's purse, or anything that contained a color other than beige, black, or gray.

But since his family left, all my rules have gone out the window. We're still careful, and we still take any and all precautions so we don't get caught, but the number of times I end up at his house instead of my own … well, there's no more limit on that.

I don't want there to be.

One side of me is screaming that I'm being careless, but I'm getting addicted to how good it feels to be with him. It makes it impossible to enjoy this completely, and I hate that I'm getting in the way of my own happiness—in both aspects of my life.

I want to spend every waking moment with Novi, and he's taken advantage of that. Not that I'm complaining.

Here, with him wrapped around me, naked skin against skin, my back to him while I lie on my side … it's peaceful and … right. I'm content.

Even if I am being poked in my lower back by Novi's morning wood. I wouldn't normally complain about that, but last night, he claimed to have missed my ass so much that he had to use it every which way he could. Ever since discovering what a prostate orgasm feels like, he's been needy for it. Demanding even.

I was looking forward to switching back to me, but after a night of being fucked fast, hard, slow, long, my ass is more than a little tender this morning.

Yet, as Novi begins to stir and moves his hand down my stomach and pulls me against him harder, my well-used hole contracts as if searching for his cock.

"Are you too sore for more?" He grinds against me, his cock slipping in between my ass cheeks.

"Good morning to you too." My comment might be sarcastic, but I'm smiling as I ignore the ache in my ass and push my hips back.

"You too sore?" he asks again, his deep voice more desperate than before.

My skin is sticky, but I can't tell if it was from the mess we made last night or if he's leaking precum into my crack. Either way, I don't care if I'm sore. "I need you."

He lets go of me for a second, then reaches between us and lines up his freshly lubed cock, slowly pushing in. It's only been a few hours, and while it's a tight fit, I stretch open easily for him.

We ditched condoms after that first night I topped him. We've had physicals, we're exclusive, and that's good enough for me.

Novi's hand creeps down further on my stomach, and he wraps his fingers around my dick. He strokes in time with his thrusts inside me. He's slow and gentle, and he murmurs how good it feels into the back of my hair.

Despite being spent, despite being sore, I love what he does to me. He turns me inside out in the best ways, makes me feel sexy and cherished and *owned*.

Novi's phone goes off on the nightstand, and he pauses to reach for it.

"Really? You're checking your phone while you're inside me?"

"I … lost track of time. We are late for All-Stars meetup with Collective."

He goes to pull out of me when I reach behind me and grab his ass so he stays right where he is.

"Do not start something you can't finish, Radimir."

"Ezra will be mad. He's super clingy, and whenever I don't reply, he reminds me I am his best friend, and if I keep him waiting, he will think I have defected our friendship."

"You are both ridiculous. Tell him we'll be there in an hour."

"I will tell him we're getting in the car. One hour gives him time to come over here, and we're in LA. If you can't use traffic as an excuse here, when can you?"

"Hurry up and reply so you can get back to what you were doing."

"You're so demanding of me. I am only one man. It is not my fault I'm so popular."

"We really are in a relationship now. We've gotten to the pause-during-sex part to look at our phones."

And even though I'm dead serious and my dick is crying, is it weird that I'm okay with it? It's like a new milestone in this unconventional courtship.

"Done. Now to make you come." Instead of going back to fucking me in that slow and caring way, he pulls out of me completely.

I almost complain until he pushes me on my back and then leans over me and swallows my dick. He jerks himself off while he sucks me down, and considering I'm still spent from hours ago and I'm no spring chicken anymore, the orgasm that rocks into me is hard and fast.

With Novi's mouth on me and the way he licks over my tip on every upstroke, I come faster than a teenager. He follows me over the edge, but only after I lift my head and watch as he drinks all my cum.

I relax back into the pillow and try to catch my breath, but he doesn't let me.

Novi taps my thigh. "Up. We need to get in the shower and get on the road."

The only reason I comply is because I like hanging out with the Collective. They're chaotic and fun, but most of all, Novi and I get to be a real couple with them. Hiding our relationship might be necessary, but that doesn't mean it's not triggering sometimes. I have closet PTSD from when I played in the AHL, and this feels a lot like putting myself back inside those teeny tiny four walls. Novi more than makes it worth it, but it's still nice to step out every now and then and breathe the fresh air.

The Collective is my fresh air.

I'm ready for the chaos.

-

I'm so not ready for this type of chaos.

We walk into Oskar and Lane's house, having lucked out that's where the Collective decided to host their annual All-Stars meetup, and the first thing I see is Ezra pinning down Turkey in the middle of the living room. Turkey is on his stomach, Ezra is straddling his back, and he's pulling Turkey's hair and yelling something in Polish. I assume.

Novi turns to me. "See, I told you I am popular man."

"This is over you?" I don't mean to sound doubtful, but oops.

"I'm the only teammate who knows about him," Turkey yells.

"I was the first to know about him," Ezra boasts.

Connor Kikishkin raises his hand. "Uh, actually, that was me."

"Don't make me come for you next, Kiki. I've claimed him as my best friend."

"What am I? Chopped liver?" retired NHLer Westly Dalton says.

Anton sighs. "Ez, you're in your thirties. Don't you think you're a little old to have a best friend?"

"No. Everyone must love me."

"Sure, he goes from adamant no one will love him to everyone must love him," Anton mutters.

I shake my head at Novi. "You're a terrible influence on a group of guys who are bad enough as it is. Make this stop before he hurts your winger." I wave my finger in the direction of the living room.

"You are no fun." But he does as I say and pulls Ezra off Turkey. "Never fear. There is lots of me to go around, but I have sad news. Best friend status has been taken from you both." Novi's whiskey-colored eyes meet mine across the room. "Colby wins that, hands up."

"Hands … up?" Connor Kiki asks.

"He means hands down," Turkey says.

Novi smirks. And there's another point for Turkey.

I'm still smiling over Novi calling me his best friend though. Because that's what partners should be: each other's number one.

"Eww, you'd choose your partner over me?" Ezra asks.

Novi throws his arm around him. "Don't worry. You are a very close second. Third at the most."

"What about Elena?" I supply helpfully.

"Shit. Then fourth. But you're a very close fourth."

Ezra turns to West. "Westly Ann Dalton, you know how I love—"

"Nope." West puts up his hands. "Don't come crawling back to me now."

"Ugh. Fine. Turkey, how about it?"

Turkey throws his hands up. "Sure. Seeing as Novi discarded us so easily."

"Why are you even here?" Novi asks. "You are not in Collective."

"I invited him," Ezra says. "When I'd heard that he'd tried to steal you, I had to have words with him."

"Plus, my sister. I'm a true ally."

Ezra shakes his head. "Nah, mainly the best friend thing."

"So you two are really together, then?" Connor asks, his gaze flitting between me and Novi.

I've still barely stepped inside the house, so I move over to where Novi's standing in the living room with everyone else.

He wraps his big arm around me. "*Da.* We are in a very serious relationship too. He said so today, while we were having sex, and—"

I cover his mouth with my hand. "Do. Not."

"I knew you lied when you said you were getting in the car!" Ezra yells. "First, you choose him over me, and now you're lying." Ezra points my way. "You are a pest."

"Keep pointing that finger at him, and you will be down to nine," Novi threatens.

Not going to lie, it's hot as fuck.

Ezra quickly puts his hands in his pockets.

"You done peacocking yet?" Anton asks. "Skills is starting."

We take our seats around the living room, some of us on the floor, others on chairs they've dragged in from the dining room.

We end up right by Connor, with Novi taking the seat on the couch next to him while I sit on the floor between Novi's legs. He plays with my hair as we watch All-Stars and he and Connor talk.

I try not to eavesdrop, but it's not like they're attempting to have a private conversation.

"Doing the secret thing too, huh? How's it working out for you?"

"It's ..." His hand pauses in my hair. "Not our first choice."

Connor nods. "Neither. I can't tell you how much I'm holding out for this off-season."

"Why aren't you and your man flaunting it?" he asks. "You no longer play hockey."

"No, but we agreed to a full year of me being out of the league before we announce I'm dating my old team's owner. We wanted that big enough gap between leaving and announcing, you know? Otherwise, it opens a bunch of unethical doors we don't want to deal with."

My heart sinks, and my gut lands in my throat. Because we didn't think of that. We've been saying we can hold out until Novi retires, but what are the chances anyone will believe us if we say we only started dating after he left if we announce our relationship the day after his last game?

It's impossible to know if our relationship will survive that long in the shadows.

Something's got to give. I just … haven't had the balls to open my laptop and look for another job. Maybe this is the kick in the ass I need to protect my future.

Our future.

CHAPTER THIRTY-FIVE

NOVI

My days are spent waking up with Colby and falling asleep with Colby—on the days he is finished work early enough for him to meet me before I crash. We eat together and celebrate together and squeeze in games of golf in a few free moments. Turkey comes with us to play golf because we can play that off as actual teammates and an assistant coach being friends. One day, we'll be able to go out and play by ourselves without the paranoia of someone asking why, but if this is what being in a relationship is like, I am obsessed.

That said, every time we talk about his coaching career or what happens next, he closes off to me. I think it is subconscious from him, but I am a very intuitive man, and I can tell when he's trying to hide something.

I know what that something is as well.

His worry.

He is still worried about what my coming out will do for his career.

The thing is, I might have decided that I want to come out, but I haven't figured out how to actually do that. Elena and the kids are back home, Ivan is busier than ever with work, and I get their happy family photos of her growing belly every week.

I'm a very proud uncle, and one day, Colby will also be the uncle to my gremlins as well. Even if they do still scare him.

I'm heading for the locker room, and I smile as I pass the supplies closet. Maybe I mastermind getting him alone somewhere again; the thought of hooking up at work is hot.

As much as that fantasy teases me though, I know it won't happen. Colby has been even more distant at work than usual, and I understand that he is trying to protect his job, but I wish that it didn't need protecting.

Our relationship is beautiful and wholesome—we should be allowed to flaunt the perfection and make everyone insanely jealous of our love.

Even if I still haven't said it yet.

I'm not scared. I'm waiting. The last thing I want is to go flinging that word at him and have it get lost under all his worry.

My phone buzzes with a dramatic text from Ezra about their game last night. They lost to Buffalo, and Asher Dalton has been texting him photos of different animal poop all day.

Seriously, where is he getting all these photos?

I laugh at the message and tap the microphone button.

His social media has him checked in at the zoo. There is a photo and everything.

He went all the way to the zoo just to taunt me?

It says he has a day with his siblings. Maybe it was lucky timing?

You don't know how evil he is. I'm willing to bet he called them all after his win last night so he could put this evil plan into place.

You could stop opening his messages?

Leave them … unread? When someone is giving me attention? I thought you knew me better than that, bestie.

I snort and tuck my phone back into my pocket because I do know Ezra. I know I will be texting him all day unless I put an end to it, and with practice about to start, I don't think Coach would be happy with me running drills with my stick in one hand and my phone in the other.

I am talented enough to do it, of course, but it wouldn't be sending a good message to the others.

We're having a strong season, are in grasp of making it to the playoffs, and it's hard to think that my second last season is almost half over. More than half over if we don't make it to the playoffs. I've had a long and successful career, but it doesn't stop the ache behind my ribs at the thought of it all being over and behind me.

This must be what Colby is struggling with. Unlike me, his career is only beginning, and how would I feel if I'd been thrown out my rookie year? If I'd never had the chance to prove how great I am?

Much like Colby in his short AHL career. He's already lost one dream, and while he wasn't NHL player material, he is head coach material. He's great at his job. I've seen him in action, I've watched past games from Penn State last year, and I know deep in my bones that he's going to be one of the best.

So long as he gets that chance.

I need to make sure that happens for him.

I reach my locker and dump my bag in my cubby. Turkey is testing his ankle beside me. During our last game, he was taken off the ice in the second period, and he did not come back.

"You good?" I ask.

"Yeah, I've been getting too aggressive in my stops. Coach Kessinger said this would happen and look at me now."

"Over-rotated?" That's what they were speculating when he injured it.

"Looks like it. But the pain is gone now, so they're just being cautious."

"Good. I need you out there." I'm about to say more when my phone vibrates again. I assume it's Ezra and am about to ignore it when the buzzing continues, and I pull it out to find a call. From Elena.

"What's up?"

"What? I can't call to talk to my little brother?"

I laugh and switch to Russian. *"You can, but if you're calling to bully me into using more Pride tape, it isn't going to happen."*

"You underestimate how convincing I can be."

"And you underestimate how stubborn I can be."

Elena makes a *pfft* sound. *"No one could underestimate that, Radimir."*

"We are getting ready for practice. Can I call you back later so you can finish insulting me then?"

"Nope, this won't take long."

Something in her voice catches my attention. *"Is the baby okay?"*

"The baby is fine, Ivan is fine, the kids are fine, and so am I, thanks for asking."

"Obviously, I know you're fine." Why would I bother asking about her when I'm talking to her? Besides, it's Elena. Nothing gets to her.

"You'll never guess where I am now," she sings.

"If you're calling me from the toilet—"

She huffs. *"Move on, that was one time."*

"I am scarred."

"You're an idiot is what you are. Besides, I was in the bathroom, not using the bathroom. When you're a parent, you'll understand it's the only place you can hide, and even then, it's not a guarantee."

"Why would I want to hide?"

"You'll want to hide. Trust me on this."

From her demons? I'd understand it. My children will be perfect.

"I can hear you thinking about how perfect your children will be—you're not subtle. And I can't wait for the day you admit you're wrong."

"I don't think I've ever admitted that."

"Well …" I finally place the tone of her voice. Excitement. *"Hopefully, you'll be able to admit it sooner rather than later."*

"Why?"

"I'm in London. I flew in yesterday, had a meeting today, and … I think this is it."

I'm sure I know what she's saying, but I also don't want to get ahead of myself. *"This is what?"*

"After I got home, Ivan and I had a long talk. We've always wanted to travel. He needs to take a step back from working so hard, and with the baby, and you and—"

"Get to the point."

"I've been offered a job. When we agreed that I could see if there was any interest for a TV chef in other countries and leave it up to the universe to decide, neither of us realized how much interest there would be. I don't know if you know this, but apparently, I'm kind of a big deal."

"Of course I know this," I say, trying not to get too excited. *"You're related to me."*

"I can hang up at any point. Just so you know."

"Fine, fine. You are wonderful and amazing and so talented. Why are you in London?"

"I've been offered a celebrity judge position on a cooking show. They flew me in to talk numbers. I had to get an agent and everything. It's overwhelming and strange, but they offered me a lot. Like, a lot. Like, move the whole family here, give Ivan a year off with the new baby, a lot."

I'm stunned. Yes, I've always been proud of Elena and everything she's accomplished, but this sounds like a whole other level. *"I offered you that kind of money,"* I remind her.

"And I said no. I don't want your money; I want my money."

"I'm very proud."

"Careful, little brother, or I might be the most successful Novicov before long."

"I'd be worried if you weren't a Kuzmina now." It's still taking me a minute to process it all. *"I didn't think you wanted to move from Russia."*

Her sigh is long, and it gets quieter in the background. *"Honestly, I don't. I'm struggling with the idea of packing up our home and moving somewhere that we'll be the different ones. Alexei's English isn't great yet, so daycare will be hard for him, but …"*

"Yes?"

"How can I not do this? We're happy at home, but we can be happy here too. Ivan will work so much less. He'll have more time with the kids, and … this way, you get to be happy too."

I drop down onto the bench, elbows on my knees and hands in my hair. *"You're serious?"*

"Yeah. I've already accepted the offer. It's happening."

It's happening.

It's fucking happening.

A lightness hits my chest that I've never felt before, and it takes me a moment to realize how stressed I've been over my decision. Elena might not be coming here with the rest of our family, but she's always done her own thing.

"Why … why now?" I choke out.

"Colby, obviously. It's not fair that the two of you have to be so careful, and I've never seen you as happy as you are with him. Plus, we're getting older. I selfishly want nieces and nephews for the kids to grow up with, so you need to get a move on."

She's serious about this. It's just such a mindfuck to try and wrap my head around. Elena is finally leaving, and once she does, I have nothing else holding me back.

I get to have it all.

The Pride tape.

The advocacy.

Being a role model to the kids who need it.

I can volunteer and make social media posts and walk in Pride parades, but even more than that, I can be me.

"Thank you," I say in English, throat tight.

"I love you."

"I love you, too."

"Okay, I better go because I'm not going to let my little brother make me cry. Bye." She hangs up before I can say anything else.

My face hurts from smiling as I set my phone beside me.

"What was all that?" Turkey asks.

"My sister is moving to London."

It takes him a second, but slowly, the awareness fills his eyes. "Oh, wow."

"Wow. Yes, wow." I stand up, feeling so happy I might burst. "I want to say something," I shout over the conversation in the locker room. It immediately pulls attention from my team. All I want to do is laugh, but if I start, I won't know how to rein it in or control it. Giving some long, big, heartfelt speech isn't me.

So instead, I pull up the words I've always wanted to say and never could.

"I'm gay, bitches!"

CHAPTER THIRTY-SIX

COLBY

While we coaches have a meeting in Coach Whelan's office, a commotion from the locker room grabs our attention. Not just any commotion, a Novi commotion.

"Did he say what I think he said?" Ackerman asks.

Them not knowing Novi the way I do, I can see why they'd be shocked, but this … this is very Novi.

I have no idea what made him say it that loud—so loud we can hear it through a closed door—but I'm stunned.

And trying not to be pissed off. Or scared.

But with the way Ackerman and Whelan are staring at me already, I don't know how else to feel.

Novi couldn't give me the heads-up?

I knew this was coming, but I didn't realize it was coming right now. I'm a mix of pride and anxiety—and a whole lot of confusion because what the hell? Why now?

"Did you know?" Coach Whelan asks me.

"Uh, what? What's happening?" Can I really play dumb when everyone in this room heard the thicker-than-usual Russian accent say, "I'm gay, bitches"? I wish I could use Novi's *I don't speak English* excuse right about now.

"We should get in there," Whelan says, and a second later, the entire coaching staff files into the locker room.

The news obviously hasn't shocked only the coaches but everyone else too. Well, other than Turkey, who's sitting next to where Novi stands, his arms still stretched out, which is how I imagine he announced it. He's probably waiting for the shock to wear off for everyone to jump up and give him a hug.

I desperately want to go give him a hug, but paranoia over management watching me has me rooted in place.

Novi's eyes meet mine across the room, and I force a smile.

"You heard the good news too," he says to the group of us coaches. "Am I fired?"

Coach Whelan splutters. "For being gay? No. Why would you think that? Unless this is some homophobic joke, then we're going to have issues."

"Not for that. For this." He waves around the room, where the rest of the team is still in shock. "I broke them. Sorry."

Finally, snickers break out around the players.

Turkey stands and puts a hand on Novi's shoulder. "I, for one, am proud of you. I know it was a difficult thing to do with your home country being behind the times."

"It's not so much the entire country. Just the government. My family supports me, and they always have."

"So, that's why you've been so anti-LGBTQ?" Grady, our captain, asks. "I think I can speak for everyone here when we say we're happy for you, but it's a bit of a shock. You've always been so anti … everything. Why couldn't you have said you were an ally?"

Because it's not that simple, I want to argue, but again, every single part of me is frozen in place. I'm probably too outwardly blasé, and that could bring even more attention.

Ooh, look, a new level of paranoia has been reached: selfish asshole level. Where I can't bring myself to speak up for what I know is right and a good thing.

"Being gay in Russia is no longer illegal, but anything pro-LGBTQ is considered an extremist act and can be punishable by imprisonment." Novi hangs his head. "Even something like me taping my stick. Which is why I had never had the guts to do it until recently."

"What's changed?" my mouth blurts without permission. Thank fuck it wasn't something like "I love you."

"I have a very stubborn sister who refused to leave Russia, and she called to tell me that she's moving to London. This obviously won't be immediate, so I do ask all of you to keep it quiet for now, but I wanted you to be the first people to know because we're a family here."

Wherever Ezra is right now, he just got the shuddery shiver down his spine and feels like he's being stabbed in the heart, and he has no idea why.

My confusion and annoyance at the sudden announcement disappears.

Novi doing this makes me happier than anything else could. Elena's safety—and her husband's and kids'—was the last obstacle holding Novi back from being himself.

People seem to be looking at me for how to play this. I'm hoping it's because I'm part of the community and not because they suspect we're already fucking. Which we are, but … that's not the point.

So I make myself think of the least telling thing I could say, step forward, and give in to the temptation to hug him. "I am so happy for you."

I want to hold on longer, but no, the hug was probably already borderline when it comes to being professional.

"Yeah, man," Everly says. "We're all happy for you."

While the rest of the team approach him to give him their support, I slink to the back of the room and try not to freak out about what comes next.

It's a strange feeling being so overwhelmingly proud and happy for him while at the same time crippled with anxiety for myself.

I never wanted him to have to be closeted, but it made our relationship so much easier to hide. Obviously, I'm not going to stop seeing him, but I also can't quit my first NHL coaching job if I want another one. Having said that, there's no problem with me looking for other positions. I told myself I'd be okay with it, and I will be eventually. It just stings right now, but that's my issue. Not Novi's. He deserves this moment.

He deserves everything.

-

I knew things would change once Novi was out. He's not even fully out yet—only to the team—and it has already affected things. Like my sleep.

Falling asleep is difficult, but staying asleep is harder, and even though I'm throwing myself into my job even more than before to prove I'm in the right place, the thoughts of it not being enough are what keep me up at night.

Which is why I'm up at the ass crack of dawn again, on my laptop and scouring the internet for possible head coaching jobs in NCAA, juniors, AHL, anywhere. But without being able to use my connections to ask around, it's mostly looking at current staff and calculating how long their head coaches might be away from retiring. Or looking at team stats and trying to pick out who might be on the firing line anytime soon.

It's starting to become unhealthy.

I sip my morning coffee, which must not be confused with my breakfast coffee, my mid-morning coffee, or my afternoon coffee. I'm a habitual coffee drinker now, thanks to working off very little sleep. The screen in front of me doesn't change.

I don't get a magical email from a headhunter who had a hunch I was in the market for a new coaching job. With it being the middle of the season, there would be no reason why they'd assume it's not going well.

The team might not be on top of the leaderboard for points, but they are almost guaranteed a playoff spot. Why would anyone want to leave that kind of team?

For love.

Apparently.

I can allow myself to think that with bitterness, but the truth is, I know the second Novi wakes and comes out here that I would do anything for him. Just his face is enough for me to feel soft inside.

And as if proving my point, he does just that, but I'm not prepared for him to see what I'm doing, so at the slightest noise, I quickly shut my laptop. Which doesn't at all look suspicious and make him raise his eyebrow at me.

"You don't want me to see your porn?" He yawns and helps himself to the leftover coffee from the carafe I brewed earlier.

"Exactly that."

"Why not? Could be hot."

"Umm …" Think of something Novi wouldn't be into … No, wait, don't do that in case he actually is into it and asks to try it and it's something I'm not into. Ooh, I know. "It has women in it."

As suspected, he screws up his face. "Ah. I will pass."

Why he doesn't question that a gay guy like me would watch porn with women in it, I'm not going to ask, but good for him for being so open-minded about where I land on the sexuality spectrum. That's what I'm going to assume is his reasoning.

"You're up early," I say.

"Because you are. You have been getting up earlier and earlier."

"Yeah, well … your snoring wakes me up."

"I do not snore."

He does, but it's a cute snore. Like a pug trying to sleep with their squished nose and tiny nostril cavities.

"If you say so." I stifle the yawn I've been trying to hold in since he yawned, but it breaks free.

"You are tired. Why don't you try to go back to sleep? We don't have to be at the arena for morning skate until nine."

"Okay. Maybe I will." I stand and make my way to the bedroom, but he stops me on my way past him.

"Wait." Novi pulls me to him, and despite my coffee breath and his morning breath, we share a kiss that fills me with the same content feeling that has me looking for another job.

I would hate it if I did have to leave, but I need to have a contingency here.

I've only just collapsed on Novi's bed when he comes barging through the doorway with my laptop in his hand. "Why are you looking at hockey teams that are not in NHL?"

I sit up. "Why are you going through my things?"

"Because you lied and said you were watching porn with women."

Oh. So he knew I was lying. That makes more sense.

"I'm looking at other opportunities, and I have to be realistic. If we're found out by management and I'm fired, I won't get another NHL gig."

"So you are going to look for another job when you don't need to yet? You're going to quit?"

"No. Just … if it comes to that, I have to know where I want to go or what league I want to try to get into. NCAA was good money, but the AHL might be a better fit for me."

Novi places my laptop on the bed and sits on the edge of the mattress by my side. "Why are you so sure we will get found out?"

"I'm not, but I'm saying if we do, I need to accept that I might not have a future in the NHL."

"But … you do. I will make sure of it."

"How? Even if they would allow us to date, the second they find out we've kept it a secret all this time, they'll fire me so fast I won't even have time to collect my stuff."

"They wouldn't do that."

"Okay, I might be exaggerating about not letting me get my stuff, but the firing part is true. It happened to Lane when San Jose found out about him and Oskar, whereas Vance went to team management before anything ever happened between him and Quinn. We don't know what could happen. So I'm trying to cover my bases."

Novi hangs his head. "I don't like this. We should be happy."

I sit up and put my hand on his back. "I am happier with you than in any job I've ever had—including playing hockey. So I don't want you to think I'm doubting you or us. I'm doubting my future with the NHL. That's all. I'll continue to coach. I'll find another league I love, but I have to readjust my expectations."

"You shouldn't have to."

"I know. And if I didn't love you so damn much, I wouldn't be de-prioritizing my career for you. But I do. And I am."

"Y-you love me? I mean, of course you do. I am very lovable."

I smile. "You are. Somehow."

"I love you too, by the way."

Yep. I don't need the NHL. I only need Novi.

CHAPTER THIRTY-SEVEN

NOVI

I stand over Colby, watching him sleep, letting the love I wasn't going to tell him about yet wrap around me. The fact that even in all this uncertainty, he still put that word out there proves more than ever that I have to protect him.

My Colby will have everything he wants.

Because why is he so sure that *he* will be the one fired?

Maybe it will be me.

It should be me.

The certainty hits fast and hard because, let's face it, I have lived my dreams. I've had the chance to experience all I ever wanted, and now it's Colby's turn. It has to be.

I won't settle for him being happy with a consolation prize.

Radimir Novicov doesn't settle, and neither will his future husband.

I let one last, loving gaze linger over him before getting changed, grabbing my gear bag, and leaving. His car is here, so he'll be able to make it to the practice facility when he wakes up, but I want to get there first.

I'm full of nervous excitement as I drive to work because this feels right. I'm not one hundred percent sure of what I'm going to say, but what Colby said gave me an idea.

Lane was fired because they weren't up-front, but Vance wasn't.

Obviously, it's too late for us to be up-front about what has already taken place, but unlike Colby, I am a fantastic liar. It's not something I do often; I don't see much point in lying, but I'm also not going to let him give up, and I'm not going to start our relationship with him not knowing what the future holds.

I know what the future holds for us. And that's everything.

When I pull into the parking lot, I take a moment to look around, wondering if this is going to be it for me. Sure, I wanted to end my career on a high, to be amongst the top point scorers on record, but I was banking on having another full year to get me there.

I might not get that chance.

But if Colby gets his chance, it is all worth it.

Besides, ending my career with him is as high as it gets.

Normally I face everything with confidence, but I don't think I've ever been so personally invested in something before. If I screw this up, it's not only me who will be affected. Ruining things for Colby would kill me.

Which is why I'm not pinning down any of the plans forming in my brain. I will go in there with the complete belief that everything will turn out perfectly.

It's still early, so no one else is here yet, and the locker room is empty and echoey in a way I've never noticed before. I dump my bag in my cubby, like always, and then make my way across to Coach's office. I knock lightly and wait for him to call me in.

"Morning," he says with a broad smile. Almost like he's been expecting me. "You're here early."

"I am." I hesitate a second before I close the door behind me and take the seat opposite him.

"Is everything okay?"

"For me? Everything is wonderful."

"Good. I meant what I told you last week—you have my full support, and if anyone isn't in line with that, I want you to let me know."

It's cute he thinks I couldn't handle that kind of thing myself, but I appreciate him saying it anyway. "You've always been a good coach."

His head tilts to the side. "Thank you?"

"So I am hoping you will continue to be a good coach when I tell you what I need to."

That finally clues him in that this conversation might not be going where he thought it would be. Where is it going? Who can tell. Even I'm not sure what the next word out of my mouth will be.

"You're free to talk."

I slide my chair forward so I can rest my arms on the desk. I'm nervous, yes, but I'm also excited. I'm about to talk about Colby and me. Us. This is the first step to us having freedom to be together, and I want that more than anything.

Even hockey.

"Well, I am out now," I tell him. "But I haven't been for a very long time. I've pretended to be straight, knowing exactly who I am, purely because I was happy having hockey as my whole life, and it meant I didn't have to worry about my family. It worked for me."

Coach is nodding. "What part of that do you think I'm going to react negatively to?"

"I'm getting there," I promise him. "You know that Coach Kessinger and I were in the minors together?"

His eyebrows lift. "No. I knew you both came from the same AHL team, but I didn't realize it was at the same time." There's a pause I don't like. "He didn't mention it."

This is the part I cannot fuck up. "I'm not surprised. I was a dick to him then, and I bet he wanted to keep things professional." I hold out my arms. "I am your star player, after all. New coaches do not want to get on my bad side."

The suspicion disappears as he laughs. "I don't think anyone wants to get on your bad side, and it has nothing to do with you being my star player. Why were you a dick to him?"

"I knew he was gay." Flawless lie. "I hated him that he could be out when I couldn't."

"That must have been hard."

"It was. But not as hard as the part where I really wanted to sleep with him."

It's hilarious watching Coach fight with himself over not reacting to my complete honesty. "Okay ..."

"We didn't, obviously. He thought I hated him. But him being here and me being out, I really want to sleep with him now too."

Coach is nodding slower this time, obviously picking his words carefully. "And you know that can't happen. He's your coach. It would be inappropriate."

"Then you will have to fire me."

That catches him totally off guard. "What?"

"I'm not asking you. I'm letting you know, out of respect, that I have feelings for Coach Kessinger. I am going to ask him out."

"He'll say no."

"Then I will ask him out again. And again. And again—"

"Novi, you need to stop talking before you end up sounding like a walking harassment charge."

"I'm not going to harass anyone, but between you and me, I am very attractive to queer men. One hundred percent success rate." I hold off from mentioning that my seduction technique previously involved shoving my dick through a cubicle wall. "I'm ready to live out and freely. I want a relationship. A partner to come home to. Kids to raise."

Coach looks like he's losing control of his patience. "And you can do all that. But not with a member of my coaching staff."

"I'm sorry, I've already chosen."

"You can't club him over the head and carry him back to your place. It's not how this works. Relationships are between two people, and if he encourages you, he'll have to be let go."

"But poor Kessinger is only human. How do you expect him to say no to all of this?"

"Because it would be unethical for him not to."

"It would be unethical for you to fire him and not me."

Coach opens his mouth but quickly swallows his words. "You need to think carefully about this. This is your career. You're going to throw that all away?"

"*Da*. I've dreamed of this man for almost twenty years. So if you want to stop me, you need to fire me."

"You're on a contract."

"Feel free to pay me out. Think of the dates I can take him on with all that extra time and those millions."

"It's not even 8:00 a.m. and I already have a headache."

"I wonder if he would like Venice …"

"Dear God, Novi."

"Maybe Portugal. Russia is obviously out, but Switzerland is beautiful. Amsterdam. Greece."

Coach scoffs. "And between all this travel, when is he supposed to be here working?"

"You told me we'd both be fired, so I'm planning ahead."

"I didn't say that."

"Oh, so you will only fire him? That's okay. I'm sure his discrimination lawsuit will pay out millions too. Maybe he will take me on dates."

Coach glares at me. "I don't need the threats, thank you. I'm trying to think."

"What threats? I do not threat. Maybe I'm getting my English mixed up again."

He laughs, fingers rubbing his eyeballs roughly. "Why did I choose to work with hockey players? Why?"

"Miscalculation on your part?"

"Sure, your English is bad, but you can manage *miscalculation*. Why are you trying to make my brain explode?"

"I'm not. I just want to be happy, and I'm telling you what I need to make that happen."

"Why are you so certain he's interested too? And don't give me that *you're irresistible* shit."

I give him a pitying smile. "You really underestimate how attractive I am."

"Novicov."

"Fine." I prop my elbows back on his desk. "Maybe he does not want me. Maybe he says no, and this conversation means nothing, but I have two years to woo him, and I will spend every minute doing it. He doesn't know that I'm here talking to you because he loves his job, and we both know how good he is at it. He wouldn't risk it for anything. If I have to give up my career for him to have his, then I will. It's done. But I can't go one more day without getting a chance to make that man happy."

"You're putting management in an impossible situation. There's no way our GM will let me fire you without him turning around and firing me."

"Then what are our options?"

Do I feel bad about dropping this all on him and making him stress? Sure. But not as bad as I'd feel about Colby losing his job, so it's easy to ignore.

"No one will believe it if I put you on waivers; you're playing too well. Plus, you've just come out to the team, so the optics of that ..." He cringes. "Anything we do here is going to look bad."

"Worse than a coach fucking his player?"

"Okay, okay ..." His frown settles deep. "I'm thinking."

"What about a trade?"

"This close to making playoffs?"

"We are not at the trade deadline yet."

"Come on. We need you."

He thinks he needs me. I don't want to leave my team. They're great people, and I have good friendships, but I understand what this sport is. It's winning. By any means necessary. "The way I see it is that you fire me *and* your video coach, or you trade me for someone else who will be as big of an asset as I have been. I retire in a year, and there is some very good talent coming through."

I know everything that's going through his head. Who is going to have salary cap room for me? Who's going to pick up an old player in the final year of his contract? But more importantly: who is worth Radimir Novicov? That's a hard question to answer.

"Can you at least put off something with him until off-season? Give me time to talk to other management heads. GM. PR—"

"No. I have waited too long already. Out of respect for you, I will not be obvious about it, but if we start a relationship, it won't be a secret either."

"I guess I have to hope you're not as irresistible as you think."

That makes me laugh. "You're better off wishing for magic to save you."

CHAPTER THIRTY-EIGHT

COLBY

Novi's gone when I wake, but I don't think anything of it. He probably went to the gym before needing to hit the ice for practice, and now more than ever, it's important that we don't arrive or leave the arena together unless it's on the team bus.

It's not until I get to my office that something feels … off. Ackerman isn't where he should be, considering we have a game tape meeting in half an hour. He should be here cutting tape and preparing for it.

Instead, our corner of the building is empty.

I dump my laptop bag and head for the video review room in case I got the time of the meeting wrong, but that's empty too. The hallways are filled with players and some office employees, but all the other coaches are nowhere to be seen.

Not even the other new assistant coach, Nowak.

Now, paranoia creeps over me that I've forgotten a coach's meeting, so I rush to Whelan's office and open the door without knocking because I've forgotten my manners, and I'm also half expecting them not to be in there, but they are. All of them.

I pull up short, just sticking my head in. "Did I forget about a meeting? Am I late?"

Coach Whelan stands, his eyes wide like I've walked in on something I shouldn't have. And if all the coaches are in here except for me, maybe I have. Maybe they're talking about what bad a job I'm doing or … fuck, what if they've found out about Novi and me?

Where is Novi? I was too focused on Whelan's office door to take a look around the locker room on my way through.

"Come in, come in," Coach Whelan says.

I step inside the room, and that's when my eyes also land on the GM, HR representative, and Novi, who were hidden in the corner of the room.

"And close the door behind you," Coach Whelan says.

I'm so fired.

I don't dare glance at Novi because while I'm sure they already know about us, if they see the way I look at him, even for a second, they won't even need to ask me my side of the story. Not that I have an excuse when they do. It's not like saying, "Novi is as every bit irresistible as he thinks he is," is a good enough reason for sleeping with someone I'm supposed to be coaching. Neither is "New coaching technique I thought I'd try. You should try it too!"

"Take a seat," Whelan says. "We're sorry to spring this on you. We, uh, have a bit of an unusual situation happening, and we're still working out how to handle it."

I bite my tongue so I don't immediately break down and beg for my job.

Novi lets out a boisterous laugh. "Do not scare the man. He looks like he's expecting to be fired or something. Don't worry. This is a very good thing."

The HR representative, a nice middle-aged woman called Kirsten, glowers at Novi. "Please, Mr. Novicov. We spoke about you remaining silent."

"Is … is there a reason why everyone is here for this?" I ask. Whatever this is. I trust Novi enough not to worry, and his reassurance that this is a very good thing does ease my mind, but what has he gone and done? I'll yell at him later for blindsiding me again, but I can only focus on saving my career in this moment.

"Witnesses." Ackerman muffles his amusement.

Kirsten turns to Whelan. "I think this would be better handled without a large audience."

Whelan turns to my fellow coaches. "You're excused."

They look like they want to complain, but they get up and leave silently until only Novi, Whelan, the GM, and HR rep remain.

As much as I trust Novi's word that this is a good meeting, it's hard not to freak out at the seriousness of the situation. Though Novi doesn't appear serious at all. He's smiling—the type of smile everyone can see.

The thoughts running through my head are a lot—everything from they're about to fire me to they're offering me a job in their affiliate AHL team to this has nothing to do with me and Novi at all—and I try not to let them get away from me. Because there's no way to know what the fuck is happening until they tell me. I'm still ninety percent convinced it has to be about our relationship, but if that's the case, how can Novi look so unbothered if my ass is about to get fired?

Still, I try to remain as motionless as possible, even if my leg is itching to bounce and I want to bite my nails, something I haven't done since I was *playing* hockey.

"This is a delicate situation," Coach Whelan says.

"It's not delicate," Novi says. "I'm telling you, Coach Kessinger will want to date me just as much as I want to date him. There's no need for the human rights person to be here. Kessinger and I are friends, and he won't hold it against me that I am very attracted to him and want to ask him to be in a relationship with me. I have never had one before, and if Kessinger really is gay, then he will obviously be attracted to me too."

Kirsten tsks. "Mr. Novicov, again, please do not speak." Then she lowers her voice. "And I'm from Human Resources, not Human Rights."

Novi's mentally ticking off Kirsten's name in his notes app.

I'm both horrified and trying not to smile. Because he went and did this without giving me a heads-up. Again. But I'm starting to get the impression from what I can piece together that he hasn't let any real information get out. Yet.

In fact … it almost sounds like he's throwing *himself* under the bus.

"If you haven't understood all that," Whelan says, "with Novi having come out, at least to the team, he, uh …" He shakes his head. "This is going to be difficult to say without it coming across as inappropriate—God, what am I saying. This is a walking sexual harassment case—"

"I'm confused." I'm not even lying.

Coach Whelan continues. "We need you to know that no matter what happens here and what you decide, nothing will affect your employment."

"Okay." I draw out the word.

"Novi is under the impression there's something between you two, and he has come to us to ask for permission to pursue that, but we can't allow that to happen under our franchise. A coach and a player … we've never had to deal with this kind of situation before, but if it got out, it would not look good to the public."

I think I've finally worked out why we're here. "So you're saying that can't happen, and we should keep our professional distance from each other?"

"Look at how disappointed his pretty face is!" Novi throws his hands up before Kirsten turns to him sharply.

"*Radimir.*"

He mimes locking his lips.

"No, we're saying …" Coach Whelan looks at Kirsten for help. "Are we really sure this is even legal?"

She chokes over her words for a moment. "Who knows anymore? Here's the deal. Novi wants to date you, but because we said no, he has asked for a trade."

My gaze snaps to his. "You did what?"

Kirsten doesn't let him answer. "But until we know if that's even a possibility—"

"I already told them it was," Novi says. "I am sexy gay man. He is sexy gay man."

"Can we trade him anyway?" Kirsten asks Whelan. "It would make my job a lot easier at this point."

I shift in my seat. "You want a trade?"

"*Da.* I want anything that will give me a chance to make you happy."

Well, fuck. I refuse to look at him too long because there's no way they'll miss how in love with him I am. "So you want to know what my answer would be if he asked?"

"Yes," Kirsten says slowly.

"As much as it pains me to admit Radimir Novicov is in any way right, if …" I meet Novi's eyes. "If he were to ask me out, it would be difficult to say no."

I can tell it's not what Whelan wants to hear.

He hangs his head. "So, we're looking at a trade. Even though the optics of that would be horrible right after Novi came out."

"I could say no," I add. "If I had to. But isn't there some kind of HR form we could sign to say we wouldn't hold the franchise liable or sue for sexual harassment? Those are things, right?"

"They are," Kirsten says, "but it's more than that. It's about the team's public image, and if it comes down to a sex scandal or a trade of a gay man who only recently came out, the latter would be more acceptable to the public."

I don't know whether to be offended by that or agree. Sexual harassment should be taken seriously in the workplace, but the idea that the perception of homophobia would be easier for the franchise to recover from doesn't sit right.

We've come so far as a society, but we still need work.

Novi leans forward. "I had an idea about the trade, if anyone wants to hear it."

If I were him, I wouldn't have worded it like that because it's obvious by the scowls on everyone's faces that the answer to that is no.

"Great," Novi continues. "As you all know, I started my career playing for Anaheim. They're at the end of a rebuild, but they're not there yet. I would love it if my last year as an NHL player could be spent with the team I started this whole journey with. And that could be the media spin."

The GM, Hank Walter, who hasn't even said a word since I entered the room, says, "They won't give us any of their forwards who are of the same caliber as you. You might be old, but you're Radimir Novicov, Stanley Cup champion twice over and the owner of a lot of NHL records."

"I am not old." Novi pouts.

"Their goalie bench is deep," I say. "They have some amazing rookies who would be ready to step into that permanent backup role, and we could use that. Dotrosky only has one or two good years left as a starter, and there's no way Pike is going to be ready. He's an okay backup, but we need someone who's going to be our next big star goalie."

Hank rubs his chin.

Whelan looks to him for an answer.

My hope actually grows because if Novi could move teams—to Anaheim, so close to here—we would be allowed to be together, and—

"We'll work out logistics," Hank says and stands. "Until then, do you think you can keep the same level of professionalism you've had?"

"Same level?" Novi asks, hiding that cheeky smile of his behind his hard features. "I will behave. But I can't say the same for Coach Kessinger. Now he knows I am interested, he won't be able to stay away."

Coach Whelan turns to me. "Are you sure you want to date him?"

"Honestly, I'm asking myself that same question, but unfortunately, I've been curious about the man I half fell in love with seventeen years ago."

Hank mumbles, "You two better get married to make this migraine worth it," as he leaves.

Novi looks triumphant. "Who knew GM was a romantic?"

CHAPTER THIRTY-NINE

NOVI

It only takes Colby a couple of minutes to hunt me down in the storage closet. I still can't believe that my plan worked—not that it was a plan, exactly. More like a vibe. And I pulled it off anyway.

The second he walks in, I'm feeling the happiest I have ever been because we did it. All Anaheim has to do is say yes. Then Oskar Voyjik and I will be teammates, and Colby and I will be safe being together.

I should probably give my bestie, Ezra, the heads-up about that first part. He will be very jealous.

Colby's hands settle on his hips, and I can't stop myself from thinking how sexy he looks with his chest all puffed out like that.

"I'm a genius," I say before he can drop to his knees and worship me. "I've fixed all our problems."

Colby doesn't react, and it takes me a second to realize that something is wrong.

"Are you still worried about something?"

"You blindsided me."

"Blinded by my genius?"

"Don't pretend you don't understand me. I had no idea what I was walking into. What if I'd said something that completely ruined your whole story?"

"I made sure you didn't."

"But I *could* have. I thought I was fired."

I tip my head to one side, studying him. "You're mad at me?"

"Yeah. A bit."

"I can work with a bit."

I swear he almost smiles. "I'm serious. That could have been bad."

"But it wasn't. I don't understand the problem."

"The problem is that if we're together, we need to make these decisions *together*. You don't get to keep making all the choices for the both of us. This is my career."

My first instinct is to brush him off because everything *is* fine, so there is no point in worrying. But if I want to make him happy, I need to make him all the way happy, and this has obviously upset him. "It's also my career," I say. "And if I had told you I was going to tell him to fire me so I could be with you, you wouldn't have let me."

His jaw drops. "You told them what?"

I brush the question away. "But they didn't."

"But they *might* have. They might have fired us both."

Maybe this isn't the best time to approach him, but he looks like his head is about to explode, and his face is too pretty for that. I gently take his hands, and he doesn't pull away. "Coach and I have a good relationship, and you said if we'd been up-front, they would be okay with it."

"But—"

"So I was up-front." I tilt my head from side to side. "In a way. I told them I want to date you, and I do, so it wasn't a complete lie."

"It was a total lie, and you know it."

I drop trying to convince him. "Yes, I lied. I would have said anything I needed to in order to make this happen."

"And if they'd fired you?"

"I would have made sure they threw me a giant farewell party first."

"Novi—"

"Please stop." I stroke his cheek with my thumb. "You are my whole world, and as much as it's hard to admit, this team needs you more than it needs me."

"That was almost humble of you."

"Not humble, honest. I like to pretend I'm the best, but that's just my playful side. I got to achieve my dreams, and now I can't wait to see you achieve yours. I can't wait to be the one who supports you through it all."

Slowly, his anger fades. "This won't be the end for you. You're Radimir Novicov. Whatever you put your mind to, you're amazing at it."

"Including my wonderful plan to fix all our problems?"

Oops, shouldn't have brought that up yet. His eyes harden again, and he removes my hands from his face. "You need to understand I'm still not happy about you not talking to me first. You want us to be this power couple? To be happy forever? It starts now. With you promising me that every decision from this point forward will be an us thing. We'll talk it through."

"And if you wouldn't have let me?"

"There's no *let*. You're a grown man. But you need to trust that I'm going to support you too. Through the good … and the stupid. That doesn't mean we don't get to talk about it first."

Through the good and the stupid. That makes sense.

"And if it's something I'm firmly a no on, you need to respect that. No going behind my back. I have to do the same with you."

"Okay." After almost forty years of doing everything alone, it will be an adjustment to listen to someone else, but if I'm prepared to do anything for him, it includes that. "So we talk. Compromise. Then if one of us is firmly no, we say …"

"Anaheim."

"Anaheim?"

"Yeah. From now on, it means I love you, but I'm overruling this one."

I'm thinking it over when Colby finally smiles.

"And no. You don't get to *Anaheim* everything. Let me win sometimes."

"You have me." I cup his face. "You've already won."

He laughs and kisses me softly. Not enough, considering we're at work and need to get back, but I'll take it.

Before I let him go, I murmur, "But can we admit that my actual Anaheim idea was not so stupid?"

"Fine. You're amazing. But that's the last time you're amazing alone."

"*Da*. From now on, we're amazing together."

–

It's been a week, and I still haven't heard back about this trade. Colby won't stay at my house, and he told me I'm not allowed to sneak into his place either until it's settled. It's very, very hard not to go over anyway, but we promised to make choices together, and I'm going to master that like I have everything else in life.

Which means I'm having a terrible, lonely week, and we lost last night because I was so irritated. Not a good selling point when I'm hoping to be traded.

It's hard to admit, but I'm also nervous. What if I didn't pull it off? What if they're buying time as a way to fire Colby anyway? What if they trade me to New York? Or Winnipeg? Or even Florida? Anywhere other than Anaheim will be too far. Could we do long distance for the last year of my contract? Sure. Do I want to? Fuck no.

My phone buzzes on my kitchen counter, and a message from Colby flashes up on the screen.

> Coaches' meeting was called. Ackerman thinks it's about your trade.

Shit. Is this it? I immediately try to call him, but he hangs up after the first ring.

Fine. I will be patient. I'll get ready for practice and not go in there too early. It will be fine. I can wait.

Still, I'm ready about half an hour too early, and I drive to the practice rink anyway. It's not an unreasonable time to show up, and if anyone asks, I will say I'm here to flirt with Colby some more.

The nerves plaguing me are not something I'm used to. Leaving LA wasn't an option when I started the season, but here I am, willingly asking for it.

Even Radimir Novicov is wrong sometimes.

There are more important things than hockey.

I'm almost at the locker room when my phone starts to ring. It's Coach.

"Hey, when will you be here?"

"Miss me already? But you saw me last night."

There's a pause. "Is that you in the locker room?"

"*Da*."

"Creepy timing. Come to my office."

He hangs up, so I dump my bag and go through. The whole coaching team is there, and when I walk in, he points to close the door behind me. There's no hellos, no good to see yous.

"It's done." He doesn't look happy. "Not gonna lie, I'll be sad to see you go."

My eyebrows jump up. "Anaheim?"

"They jumped at the offer. Not surprised—they'd be crazy not to. A star forward for a backup goalie, a fourth-line forward, and a second-round draft pick? The fans are not going to be happy about this one."

He's right, of course. Our fans live and breathe hockey. They feel our losses and celebrate our wins right alongside us. On paper, this trade does not make sense, but I will keep everything crossed that he's vindicated next season.

"I really appreciate it," I say, no hint of the lovable joker in my tone.

"Then why do you still look like you want to kill me?" The spark in his eyes tells me he's joking. "We'll miss you. Other than this last week, you've been a joy to coach."

"I am a very lovable man. Will you cry at my farewell party?"

"What farewell party?"

"The one you will be throwing me."

He stares at me like I have sprouted a horn. "Tell you what: I'll send someone for cake. Best I can go."

"Deal."

"But you're going to do something for me. Press conference. This afternoon. You're going to tell everyone what a fantastic team this is, what an amazing coach I am, and that you love LA, and the only reason for this trade is because we support you finishing out your career in Anaheim. That's it."

All of those terms sound fair, and unlike some of my team, I love the attention from press conferences. "Of course." I wink at Colby. "Only reason."

"Right." There's a long, stale silence. "I guess this is it, then."

"Only one thing left to do."

Coach looks confused as I round the desk and motion for him to stand up. "What are—"

My hug cuts him off. "This is a fantastic team, and you are an amazing coach."

He laughs and hugs me back. "Just like that. But save the love for the press conference. We're going to need it."

"I disagree. You are going to need it when you tell the team. They love me."

He groans and pulls away, checking the time on his phone. "They should all be here by now. Guess we better get it over with."

Coach leads the way out, and when we get to the locker room, it's already full. My team—well, old team now—are in the process of getting changed, lacing up skates and talking smack with each other.

I'd miss it, but all locker rooms are the same.

"Hey, hey, listen up," Coach calls, making the room fall silent. "We have some, uh, news. Today is Novicov's last day with us. He requested a trade to finish out his career where he started it, and we've agreed."

"What?" Turkey exclaims, pushing to his feet. "He's leaving?"

"*Da*," I answer before Coach can. "It has been an honor working with such a fantastic team and amazing coach"—said coach sighs heavily beside me—"but this makes sense. I am sad to go, but I want to spend my final season where it all started."

"But we're a family," he says. "We're going to playoffs together."

My eyes find Colby's, and he gives a little nod. "We are a family, and I will cheer for you, but this is something I need to do to start my other family. Away from here and hockey. I have a new life to begin."

Turkey catches on to exactly what I mean. "Shit," he says, finally letting it sink in. "We're all going to miss you."

"I know. But it will be a lot easier to miss me with your names on a cup. So maybe put your focus into that and miss me during the off-season instead."

He grins. "Deal."

And I will miss them. All of them. But I meant what I said: this is the start of everything else for me. My heart will always be with LA.

As long as Colby is.

CHAPTER FORTY

COLBY

Novi and I might not have come up with the most convenient solution—and by we, I mean he—but it's a solution. Even if we don't get to see each other as much as before due to the two teams' schedules, knowing I can park outside his house or hold his hand in public has a weight lifted off my shoulders.

It's probably a good thing we aren't able to see each other every day because ever since he went to Anaheim, it's as if the shackles binding our relationship have been removed, and there's no stopping us.

There's no voice of reason telling us to slow down or be cautious. I'd hate that … if I absolutely wasn't head over heels for this man.

I'm finally able to enjoy being with him.

Back in the day, my fantasies about him might have been more about getting Novi into bed instead of the future I can't help envisioning now, but I'd be lying if I said there weren't similar thoughts back then too. It's as if a piece of me knew back then that Novi was my soul mate. The timing wasn't right, but the knowledge that one day he'd be mine was there. Even if I told myself that it was unrequited love and I'd never have the straight man.

That straight man is now mine, and I can't wait for this regular season to be over so he can be by my side every day. You know, when I'm not traveling with the team, because unlike Anaheim, we're actually going to make it to the playoffs.

They were doing well for a while there, and they looked like contenders, but it's all gone downhill. Since Novi joined, they have picked up a little, but it's too little, too late.

The team has just finished practice, so I make my way to the locker room to talk to those I've noticed have picked up new bad habits. Due to injury, due to muscle memory and comfort, that's what I have to find out.

"Stoltz," I say as I walk in, not looking for him but down at the video on the iPad.

"Yeah, Coach?"

I will never get used to that. I have over the years, of course, but being given the title of coach in an NHL setting, where the moniker is used with such respect … it is my literal dream job. And I get to have it because Novi was willing to step aside so I could.

I'm still smiling as I reach him.

"You look like you're about to tell me I'm being put on waivers or trade me. Stop looking at me like that."

"I, what? I'm smiling."

"If you say so."

Is it true what they say? That partners begin to look alike the longer they're together? Am I big and scary like Novi now?

"What am I doing wrong?" Stoltz asks.

I laugh. "Nothing. I've just noticed you've been favoring your right side today. You're slower on your left turns, so you've been leaning into the right. If it becomes a habit, other teams' video coaches are going to pick up on it. Are you hurt?"

"I ..." His brow scrunches. "I don't think so?"

Ah, hockey players. I remember those days. Being in so much pain I couldn't tell if I was injured or sore from exhaustion. Fun times. "We'll keep an eye on it, and maybe tomorrow for morning skate, we'll have you practicing turning left and see if it's a habit or if we need to get you to a doctor. In the meantime, go to the team trainers and get them to stretch out your legs and see if they can get those hips to open up, but let us know if there's too much pain or you think you might be injured."

Stoltz stretches out like he's testing his side. "Thanks, Kessinger."

I shrug. "It's my job."

"You're good at it."

I want to hug the man, but considering I've already made one player fall for me and leave, I don't want to get a reputation. Fuck, now I'm even thinking like Novi.

And as if mentioning his name, even only in my own head, he appears through the locker room doors.

"I am back, bitches."

That's my man, and I love him. Apparently. For reasons I'm forgetting at the moment.

"Hate Anaheim that much?" Turkey asks but gets up and pulls Novi in for one of those dude bro handshakes that turns into a hug.

"They are terrible," he says. "The people? Great company. The hockey? Even Kessinger could make that team if they had recruited him now instead of a billion years ago."

The room breaks into snickers, and I flip him the bird.

"Is that professional?" Novi asks.

"I'm not your coach anymore, so …" Double fingers now.

More laughs.

The thing is, this is probably the biggest step we're about to take so far. Yes, we're out and dating now, holding hands in public, being seen together, but … the world either hasn't noticed or doesn't care. We thought it might still be a scandal, with the conflict of interest between a player and coach on opposite teams, but both franchises aren't worried about us being professional, and that's what matters. We haven't made a public statement or announced anything. We haven't posted photos online. We've just been ourselves, and it's been great.

But I know Novi is ready for more than that, and with nothing standing in our way anymore, we're going to take that chance.

"No. You are just a chain on my balls."

Mouths drop in unison around the room. I think someone even chokes on a Gatorade.

I face-palm. Of course he breaks it to the team that way. He's gotten a lot better about giving me a heads-up when he wants to do something now—like announce our relationship—but I should've specified how we would do it. "Even though I know you're only playing your silly 'I don't know proper English' game, you mean ball and chain."

"There's a game?" Turkey asks.

"Oh yeah," I say. "Novi knows perfect English. Idioms and all. He purposefully messes them up to see how many of you will correct him."

"My boyfriend is a traitor." Novi folds his arms and pouts. Only, he's Novi, so he looks menacing and really, really hot.

"What can I say? You left this family, so now they're mine. I'm on their side."

When everyone on the team cheers and hoots at that, Novi relents. Because he knows how much I want to achieve with this team, and them knowing I have their backs is important for our working relationships.

"Are you two really together?" Stoltz asks.

"He loves me very much," Novi says.

I can't even dispute that. "Sadly, that's true. I don't know how it happened, but it happened."

"It happened because, as I told management when I asked for a trade so I could date you, I am very sexy and irresistible to gay men."

"Man," I remind him. "I'm the only relationship you've ever had."

"And you'll be the only one I ever have."

"Ah, so the real reason you asked for a trade comes out," Stoltz says.

"*Da*. Why else would I ask to trade to a team who has no hope of making the playoffs this year?"

"Not gonna lie. I thought you were trying to hook up with Oskar Voyjik," Tucheck, the up-and-coming goalie we traded Novi for, says.

Novi gasps. "And face the wrath of Lane Pierce? No. No way."

The room goes silent, and then Stoltz turns to me. "Is … is Novi actually scared of someone?"

"Why? Lane is a kitten," I say.

"Exactly," Novi says. "And kittens are bad luck and scary."

He's been spending too much time around Ezra Palaszczuk. Everyone knows he's terrified of cats. Especially black ones.

"Don't worry. I'll protect you from the big, bad Lane Pierce."

"How long have you been together?" Tucheck asks.

Coach Whelan enters the room at that moment and glances between Novi and me in rapid succession. "I'm going to leave the room in case information I don't want to hear is about to be spilled."

So much for us pulling off the greatest lie of all time, but I don't want him to mistrust me, so before he leaves, I say, "It's new."

Technically, not a lie. The last few months have been spent sleeping together thinking we probably didn't have a future unless we learned to have something called patience. We knew that was going to be a no-win situation because as hockey players, we don't know the meaning of the word.

"But we knew each other a long, long time ago, so it feels like I've been in love with him forever."

If I could go back and tell that scared kid with the pressure of the world of hockey breathing down his neck that pro hockey is not in his future—at least not in the way he thinks it will be—and that he'll find himself in an NHL locker room one day talking about how much he loves a man and that his team actually supports it … Past Colby would probably cry. Because this is the world I want to be living in.

It's the world every queer person should be living in.

We deserve happiness too, and I've found mine.

With Novi.

EPILOGUE

NOVI

We get to Aleks Emerson's house—though it's more of a mansion than a real house—and knock.

"Remind me why the Collective meetup had to be here?" Colby asks. "Technically, there are more of us in California. We should have overruled them."

"Aleks said here they have firemen on speed dial. Apparently, that is important, but I think they're overselling things. I have not seen mayhem from them yet."

"On speed dial? Isn't that just 911?"

I shrug and drop a quick kiss on Colby's lips, loving that I get to do that now. Whenever I want.

The door swings open, and Westly Dalton watches us for a moment, swaying on the spot. "You're late."

"Time is only a guideline."

He cracks a smile, going to lean against the door and stumbling when it swings wider. "Welcome! And I apologize for everything you're about to see here. I need to take a leak."

He disappears across the enormous entrance hall, and Colby and I step inside and close the door behind us. Music is blasting through the back of the house, and we follow the sound of it.

Now, I'm not sure what Aleks's house looked like before tonight, but I am almost positive it was not this.

There's what looks like fruit splattered all over one wall, spaghetti on the other, and in the middle of the cleared living space are boxing gloves, helmets, and way too many cushions to count.

"Ah … should I ask what that is?" Colby points to the roof above the blender, and I'm going to assume it's a Bloody Mary and not someone's blended body parts.

Which is a pity. That would have made for an interesting party.

And when we make it into the backyard, West's warning all makes sense. Oskar, Ayri Quinn, and Dex are in the middle of the yard, dressed in morph suits, while Aleks stands at the top of his patio with a paint gun.

I watch as he takes aim at the other three, who bolt, and a second later, there's a muffled *fuck* as Oskar's hit.

Lane buries his face in his hand, and Anton turns to him. "At least you'll be able to kiss his boo-boo better later."

"It doesn't make up for what a crybaby he is when he's sick or in pain."

Colby and I sit across from them.

"Drinking vodka?" I ask, nodding at their glasses.

"Water." Anton sends a dark look Ezra's way. "I still have PTSD from the last time."

"Bringing on the alcohol, I say!"

As soon as the words leave my lips, Tripp redirects where he's walking past and zeros in on me instead. "Alcohol? You said alcohol?" He shoves a glass each at me and Colby.

"What is this?" I ask, eyeing the fancy drink.

"My specialty margaritas."

"What makes them so special?"

He giggles in a way I've never heard Tripp giggle before. "I literally have no clue how to make them. Bit of rum, bit of vodka, bit of absinthe—"

"Absinthe?" Colby repeats, holding his drink out from his body.

Tripp pulls a face. "Probably better I don't tell you the rest, then. Bon Apple Tea."

I light up. "Oh, you know the game too?"

"What game?"

Colby sets his hand on my thigh and shakes his head at me.

"Oh …" I wink at Colby. Tripp is not playing my mix-up word game. He is just stupid.

"Bon Apple Tea!" I throw back his drink, and it burns the entire way down.

"Woo! That's the spirit. Now, where did Lachie go?" Tripp sways as he looks around. "I swear he had the other pitcher …"

Colby looks between us both, then to the water Anton is drinking, then back again. "Fuck it." He downs his drink, too, and gets through about half of it before he dry retches. "So … good."

"We'll take two more," I tell Tripp, and he cheers before stumbling back inside for them.

"My turn." Asher Dalton's boisterous voice cuts through the night. He appears out of nowhere like a ninja and takes the paintball gun from Aleks. Then he turns, his back to the spandex trio, and aims at where Ezra is leaning over an ice bin.

Before I can warn my bestie, Asher lets off a shot and hits Ezra right in the left ass cheek.

"Mother*fucker*," he cries as the hit sends him face forward into the deck tile.

Asher cackles with laughter. West, who's just stepped outside, takes a look at them both, then shouts, "What's that, Tripp? You need help with the drinks?"

"Traitor!" Ezra shouts.

Connor Kikishkin takes the chance to grab a fistful of ice and shove it down Ezra's shirt.

Things get wilder as the night wears on, and Tripp's lethal cocktails fill our bellies. Anton has given up on the water, the morph suits are gone, and now they are taking turns being moving targets in their underwear. The purpose of the cushions becomes clear as Ezra and Asher run at each other, as hard as they can, and send each other flying, and Tripp and Lane are trying to talk Dex away from the fire pit—something about the last time.

"Is okay," I shout, sounding more like my old self than ever. "They haff fireman on speed dial."

"Strippers?" Oskar asks, popping up from behind an outdoor couch.

"I haf never seen stripper."

It's like a record scratch the way they all stop and turn to me. I'm saved from being interrogated when Easton stumbles out of the house and almost runs into the couch I'm sitting on. "Has anyone seen Lachie?"

"Not since we got here," Colby answers.

East slaps a hand over his mouth. "Uh-oh."

"Uh-oh what?" Connor demands.

"Uh-oh, we've lost our baby brother?"

Considering baby brother is in his twenties, I don't know why that's such a problem. "He will be fine," I say.

"I'll call him," Lane says with the tone of someone who's been here a thousand times. It rings out. "No answer."

"When did you see him last?" Connor's eyes are wide with panic.

"In the kitchen with …" Easton trails off and turns to Tripp. Connor follows his gaze, and it takes Tripp a second to realize they're both looking at him.

"More margaritas?"

"You said Lachie has the other pitcher," Colby reminds him. "Tell me he didn't drink the whole thing?"

"He … didn't *not* drink the whole thing?" Tripp's innocent smile needs work.

Connor swears, pulling out his phone, but before he can call, a high-pitched scream pierces the air.

Ezra comes tearing from the house, and he throws himself behind Anton. "There's a demon animal in the house!"

Aleks staggers toward the open doorway then back-tracks quickly. "There's a demon animal in my house!"

I hurry to turn around as Lachie Kikishkin walks outside … pulling a llama with him.

"Where the hell did you get that?" Connor gasps.

Lachie looks from Aleks to the llama and back again. He's barely able to stand upright. "What, he's"—he hiccups loudly—"not yours?"

"No, I don't own a fucking llama!"

Lachie hiccups again. "Oops?"

"Where the hell have you been?" Easton asks.

"You and me both would like to know that." He scratches his head. "I can't promise this is the last of the"—hiccup—"wildlife." The llama looks around the group with its huge, creepy eyes as Lachie wraps his arm around his neck. "Can I keep it?"

"And how are you getting it back to St Louis, genius?" Easton asks.

"I dunno." He and the llama look at each other. "I'll ride him?"

"I think it's a her," Dex says.

"How do you know?" I ask.

"Easy. Tripp has big balls. The llama doesn't."

"We don't need to know about your husband's balls," Asher groans.

"He means dog Tripp," Tripp hurries to explain. "It's the dog he's talking about. Though that's not even true anymore since he got the snip. But he is not talking about me. *Not me*. My balls are perfectly normal size. Not too big or too small. Like Goldilocks. The Goldilocks of balls."

"I dunno …" Dex squints up his eyes. "The left one is kinda big …"

Asher scowls. "Enough. About. His. Balls."

"Can we *please* get the llama out of here?" Ezra begs, covering his eyes.

Anton moves from blocking his husband and drunkenly approaches the animal. "I dunno. It's kinda cute." He takes off his cap and puts it on the llama's head instead. "If you can ride it to St. Louis, I could ride it to Boston."

"But there's one of me," Lachie points out. "And two of you."

"Sure, that's the only issue with this plan." Connor sounds close to fainting. "Can you put it back wherever the hell it came from?"

"Fine …" Lachie turns and walks back inside.

"He didn't mean go through my house!"

"Maybe someone should go with him," Connor says.

"On it!" Quinn leaves too, and he's probably maybe the least drunk of the rest of us.

Lachie's back a second later though, and this time, it's not a llama he's got his arm around. It's a giant, good-looking man in a fireman uniform.

"That speed dial is speedy," I mutter as Ezra says, "How did you turn the llama into Gabe?"

"Ah, babe?" the fireman says to Aleks. "Why is there a llama in our house?"

"We're taking care of it."

"The stripp-ahs are heeere!" Oskar shouts, hands around his mouth like he's calling a boxing fight.

"For the last time," Aleks whines, "Gabe is *not* a stripper."

Gabe's huge dimples show as his face lights up, and another fireman walks in behind him. "We heard there was a noise complaint?"

The second fireman picks up a remote that must control the music, turns it off, and hits Play on his phone. A base-heavy beat comes from it.

Then he says, "I can't believe you're making me do this," to Gabe, and they both start to undo their shirts.

"What's happening?" Aleks asks weakly.

Ezra climbs off the floor with his jaw hanging open. "Maybe the greatest thing known to man."

I've never seen a group of men converge on one area so fast. Oskar is waving a wad of cash in the air, Asher and West are pretending not to look, Lachie is whooping and cheering them on, and when Colby drops down next to me, he's laughing.

"You should see your face."

"The pretty public servant is taking his clothes off."

He smiles at me. "You sound very Russian right now."

"I am very Russian always."

Behind Gabe and his friend, the llama walks back out again, still wearing Anton's hat.

"Oh no," Ezra slurs from beside me. "Now Anton has turned into the llama."

"That's not—"

Colby covers my mouth. "Oh really?" he asks Ezra.

"My baby … does that mean I'm married to a llama now?"

"Ah … sure."

The firemen are out of their shirts, huge muscular bodies rippling in the party lights.

Dex and Tripp are still arguing about balls.

Ezra is screaming something about bestiality.

Lachie has stopped cheering and has joined the strippers, swinging his shirt in the air. It's not until he loses his balance and almost face-plants like Ezra did earlier that Easton and Connor step in.

"Bedtime for you," Connor says.

"You're not my dad."

"You're drunk," Easton grits out, narrowly avoiding a flailing arm.

Then the brothers are somehow in a three-way brawl and argument that it's too hard to keep track of which Kiki says what.

"Am not—"

"Are too—"

"You're just like Connor—"

"Hey! I'm so much better now—"

"You take that back!"

"Never!"

"My feelings are getting hurt here, guys—"

Lachie tackles Easton, and the two of them wrestle on the ground as Connor tries to break them up.

"Fuck it." Ezra stands suddenly. "No one can say that Ezra Palashhhhhtook won't do anything for his man! I'm coming for you, baby!"

He runs at the llama, and the sudden movement startles it. The animal takes off, Ezra chasing, and the crashing around inside the house makes Gabe pause.

"Ahh …"

Aleks sighs and sits his ass on the outdoor coffee table. Then he turns up the music to drown out the noise inside. He plucks out one of Oskar's twenty-dollar bills. "Take it off! Take it off!"

That's all Gabe needs to encourage him.

We all watch the show, pretending to ignore Ezra's shouts.

"Anton, wait! One kiss should break the curse and turn you back into a man! Just hold still!"

I lean over to Anton, who is sitting right next to where Ezra was. "Should you put stop to that?"

"Hmm … maybe."

"Are you going to?"

"I'm curious to see if he'll do it, honestly. It's like a love declaration."

"Isn't that what getting married was?" Colby asks.

"You know," I tell Colby, "in Russia, we must battle a cow as part of proposal."

He stares at me for a long moment. "You're fucking with me."

"You will find out when you propose. But if there is no cow, do not blame me when I say no."

"Who says I'm proposing to you?"

"Because I am not allowed grand gesture without telling first. Then it will not be surprise."

He thinks for a second. "Fine. You don't have to talk to me about the proposal."

"*Ty vyydesh' za menya zamuzh.*" *Will you marry me?*

"I don't know enough Russian to know what the hell you said."

That was the point. "When you figure out, you let me know."

He tries to copy what I said under his breath.

Ezra falls back against the couch, panting hard. "It's done."

I don't think I want to know what *it* is.

Colby turns to him. "What does *ty vyydesh' za menya zamuzh* mean?"

Ezra gapes at him. "Are you hitting on me? I am a *married* man."

"Yeah he is," Anton says, wrapping an arm around him.

"You're alive!" Ezra goes for a kiss that Anton narrowly avoids.

"Why do you have llama breath?"

"It's your fault."

Anton shushes him. "You're distracting me from the strippers."

"There are *strippers*?"

Colby cuddles up to me. "Would you kiss a llama for me?"

"I would do anything for you."

"Oh yeah?" He turns an evil grin on me. "Even strip?"

I stand up immediately. "I will show these little boys how it is done!"

The others are cheering before I even get my shirt off. I toss it Colby's way and join the two men in their thongs.

It doesn't take long for Oskar to be beside me, and then Lachie scrambles out from under where Easton has him pinned and joins too.

When I get down to my underwear, Lachie and Oskar spank my butt as I twerk, but I do not blame them because it is a glorious ass.

Colby is laughing, Ezra and Anton are making out, because I am so hot, obviously, and Quinn's face is bright red as he watches us between his hands. Aleks and his boyfriend are dirty dancing, and Dex fist pumps awkwardly as Tripp drinks straight from a pitcher. Connor has given up on his brother, Lane's eyes are locked on Oskar, and West and Asher are both talking into the phone between them, watching like they can't believe their eyes.

But oh yes, boys. Radimir Novicov has moves on *and* off the ice.

No matter how many of our friends are here though, I only have eyes for one man. The man currently waving Oskar's discarded cash my way.

The one with hearts in his eyes.

Who puts love in my heart.

It took us a very long time to get here, so I appreciate every moment with him more than ever. Even when we are with the Collective. And a llama.

He is my whole world.

A loud *bleat* comes from behind me, and his attention immediately redirects.

Aleks freezes. "I don't want to turn around, do I?"

"Nope."

Connor scrubs a hand through his hair. "Seriously, Lachie? Where the fuck were you?"

He looks just as surprised as us to see more animals. "Umm … just a guess, but I think there might have been a farm involved."

That's my cue to leave. I slip past the others, grab my clothes, and then pull Colby back through the house.

"I am sure they have a free bedroom here somewhere," I tell him.

"I didn't know we're staying the night."

"We are not." I wink at him. "But I can think of far better things to do to you while they deal with the animals."

Colby's grip on my hand tightens as I lead him upstairs. "Not our monkeys, not our circus."

I pull him to a stop on the landing. "There are monkeys here? I take it back. Collective parties need firemen on speed dial."

"No, it's a saying. Like a phra—" Colby stops himself and narrows his gaze at me. "But you know that, don't you?"

"*Da.*"

"You're lucky I love you."

"Pffft. You are lucky to love me."

Colby rolls his eyes with all the love in his heart, and I wrap my arm around his back and pull him against me.

"To be serious—"

"Is that even possible with you?"

"Ignoring that. No jokes. I am lucky that you love me. I am privileged to even have the chance for you to love me. And I don't want to mess this up. The world might love Novi, hockey extraordinaire, but only you get to love Radimir Novicov, the real me. The scared boy who grew up to be a scared man."

He cocks his head. "But you're not scared now, right?"

"The only thing scary in my life is the possibility of ever losing you."

Colby's lips curve at the edge. "Then I guess we better make sure that never happens."

I kiss him in agreement. "Never."